*Broken Glass*

—The Maggie Barnes Trilogy—

# *Broken Glass*

MARY VANDERGOOT

RESOURCE *Publications* • Eugene, Oregon

BROKEN GLASS
The Maggie Barnes Trilogy

Copyright © 2019 Mary VanderGoot. All rights reserved. Except for brief quotations in critical publications or reviews, no part of this book may be reproduced in any manner without prior written permission from the publisher. Write: Permissions, Wipf and Stock Publishers, 199 W. 8th Ave., Suite 3, Eugene, OR 97401.

Resource Publications
An Imprint of Wipf and Stock Publishers
199 W. 8th Ave., Suite 3
Eugene, OR 97401

www.wipfandstock.com

PAPERBACK ISBN: 978-1-7252-5137-3
HARDCOVER ISBN: 978-1-7252-5138-0
EBOOK ISBN: 978-1-7252-5139-7

Manufactured in the U.S.A.                                    10/24/19

*Broken Glass* and *The Maggie Barnes Trilogy* are works of fiction. Names, places, characters, events, and institutions that appear in these stories are products of the author's invention. Used as they are in a fictional narrative, they are not to be taken as either real or referring to real persons, places, or events. Any resemblances are coincidental.

Scripture taken from the HOLY BIBLE, NEW INTERNATIONAL VERSION ®, Copyright © 1973, 1978, 1984 by International Bible Society. Used by permission of Zondervan. All rights reserved.

For Andrew, Peter, and Anna

There is a time for everything,
and a season for every activity under heaven:

a time to be born and a time to die...
a time to weep and a time to laugh...
a time to mourn and a time to dance...
a time to embrace and a time to refrain...
a time to search and a time to give up...
a time to be silent and a time to speak....

Whatever is has already been,
and what will be has been before.

Ecclesiastes 3

# PART I

Chapter 1

# BROKEN GLASS

The sound of glass breaking in the kitchen terrified me. We were in the basement playroom and my children were sleeping on the second floor. My three toddlers were lying in their beds like angels, and I wasn't there to protect them.

Before I could ask, "What is that?" he was already pulling on his jeans and leaping up the steps two at a time. I heard the struggle on the floor above. Heavy uneven footsteps, and the thud of someone falling against the wall in the entryway. I heard him yell, "Get out." And then even louder, "Out! Get outta here! I mean it!" It was followed by a voice I didn't recognize. A young voice protesting "Let go of me." The familiar voice again, "Stop! Don't! Give me that!" And then something falling to the floor.

I was grasping for any sound that made sense, something other than the struggle. I heard the back door bang hard against the doorstop. The same sound when the wind slammed the door, but this time it was harder. Then I heard the creaking of the screen door and the familiar slap of it closing, pulled shut by the spring. The sound of the dead bolt clunking into place was ominous. I couldn't tell if danger was being locked out or if now it was locked inside with us. I was frozen in place, staring at the dark stairway. Waiting.

Footsteps were coming down. His bare feet appeared on the linoleum steps. Then the rest of him dropped down toward me one step at a time in the dim light. There was blood on his hands, a gash on the side of his chest, and a cut, a small one, on his right forearm.

"Thomas. You're bleeding."

"Help me! I need to wrap this up."

"In the laundry room," I said, pulling him toward the machines and the tub. He slumped down against the washer. Blood glistened against his ribs and ran in a thick line down his side. His jeans were buttoned, but the zipper was open, and the waistband was blood-soaked. I grabbed a terry-cloth beach wrap from the laundry room floor. It was the cover-up I'd worn in the afternoon when I was out in the yard watching the kids play in the kiddy pool. The wrap was damp and had grape juice stains and peanut butter smudges from our lunch. It wasn't clean, but it was within reach.

I knelt beside him and laid the wrap against the wound on his side, flattened out my hand against his ribs, and pressed the cloth hard to stop the bleeding. My face was against him. I could smell him, the musky smell of fear mixed with the more familiar smell of his warm skin.

"I'll call an ambulance."

"No, don't! I'll be okay."

"You're bleeding a lot."

"We can stop it. Razor cuts. They're not deep."

It was a mess. Drips of blood everywhere. On the steps, in the playroom, and on the laundry room floor. A small puddle of blood pooled on the uneven concrete of the floor where it dripped from his arm. I grabbed an old dust cloth from the shelf above the washer. "Wrap this around your arm" I said and pressed one end against the cut on his forearm, as I wrapped it around tight, and tucked the last end in. There were deep scratches like claw marks down the center of his chest beginning just below his neck. They were red and raw, but not bleeding.

"I'm going to get bandages. Put your hand here. Hold this. Press hard! I'll be right back." While he held the cloth tight against his own chest, I rushed upstairs to the second floor to get bandages from the random collection of tapes and dressings leftover from past wounds and injuries. In a box in the hallway closet were the gauze pads and the roll of tape we had taken home with us from the hospital when little Will had his appendix removed, but the yellow tape with happy faces didn't seem fitting. Instead I took the non-descript white gauze dressings and the plain tape. They were still there from when Ross slashed his finger on a fillet knife while cleaning fish and had to have stitches.

Before going down I glanced quickly at the children in their beds, deep in sleep. On the stairs my knees were weak. I climbed these same stairs effortlessly every day with a child in my arms, and sometimes two of them at once, but now going down I was unsteady. I shivered, the shudder that follows a surge of adrenalin.

When I got back down to the basement I spoke to Thomas in a calm voice as if my being unafraid would soothe him. "I'm going to lay this pad against your cut, and then I'll wrap the gauze around you to put pressure on your wound and hold the pads in place. Does that feel okay? It's not too tight?" Like a counterfeit Florence Nightingale I dressed his battle wounds. Working slowly, I wrapped the gauze as evenly as I could, but the cut on his side oozed through the dressing several times before the bleeding was stanched.

At first Thomas was silent. Then he spoke in short sentences with silence in between as he pieced together scraps of a fragmented story. He was trying to make sense for me of what had happened. "Young guy . . . cut the screen with a box cutter . . . I surprised him . . . he slashed me." Thomas was breathing hard between words. He paused to catch his breath. "He had your purse . . . dropped it when he saw me . . . don't know if he got your wallet?" I didn't respond and stayed focused on bandaging. Thomas paused and then continued. "I think he knocked your wine glass off the counter . . . that was the noise . . . be careful . . . there's glass on the tile in the kitchen."

Thomas didn't look like he was going to pass out. He was alert, and I was relieved that he was talking and made sense. It felt good to be near him; there is tenderness in touching the wounded. It's not the searching touch of a lover or the soft soothing touch of a child. It's something different entirely, but the feelings it stirs are deep.

When I was done pretending to be a nurse, I leaned over him and pressed my face into his hair, resting it there for a few deep breaths. I wanted to stay there near him. Draw in the scent of him. Instead I said, "I'll clean up the rest now." I stood up, and he slowly got to his feet too. For a moment more we held each other, my face in his neck and my fingers woven into his curly hair to keep him close. He wrapped his arms around me, and I felt the warmth of him, felt him breathing. But I couldn't hold on. I had to let him go because there were other things I had to do.

I went up the stairs with him, saw him leave through the side door, and through the small window in the door I watched him go out into the night. I went quickly then to the front windows in the living room and saw his green VW drive away down Whitney Avenue and around the corner. Then I went back down the stairs to clean up.

Blood leaves bold traces. Evenly spaced drips in the upper hall and down the stairs. Footprints, either mine or his where we had stepped in it. A broad smudge down the front of the wash machine. Bloody towels. A bloody scissors. Stained gauze. There were streaks of his blood on my arms, and my knee was dark where I had knelt in his blood when I was bandaging him.

With a bucket of sudsy water and old cleaning cloths I followed the drips and wiped them up. One after the other I retraced his steps. I cleaned the broken glass on the kitchen floor, carefully, thinking of little feet that would walk there in the morning. What is it about broken glass that you can't see it on the floor until you look at it sideways so it catches the light?

I was determined my children would not see evidence of this struggle. There must be nothing for them to notice, and nothing for them to ask about. It must not cut into their precious little feet. When I thought I had removed all the traces of glass, I gathered up the bloody rags and the terry-cloth beach robe, stuffing them into the wash machine. Then I stripped off his t-shirt, the one I grabbed from the floor and pulled on to cover myself when we heard the glass break. The stained white cotton looked like it had been worn on a battlefield. I put everything in the washer with bleach, wanting all the stains to disappear. When I heard the filling stop and the washer begin to churn, I crept silently upstairs to the second floor.

My children were sleeping as if nothing had happened. I went into the bathroom to wash my hands once more. Standing naked in front of the mirror, I saw a smudge of blood across my cheek, and on my breast a large patch of his blood that had printed on me when I held him close.

A dazed woman stared back at me. *Is this me?* It was that hollow look we all know when we catch our own image in a mirror and see a stranger. When I was hospitalized for pneumonia, it was my own bedraggled face I could barely recognize in the mirror. There was that time after I'd had a miscarriage when I caught sight of myself in the plate glass window of the drug store and didn't recognize myself. We look strange to ourselves when we know something has changed, and we will not be the same again. We are no longer the old familiar person we meet in the mirror day after day when we brush our teeth.

I couldn't sleep. I kept going over the evening. We had laughed a lot, but now the memory of that laughter was a ghostly echo. What had we laughed about? Nothing really. We had laughed in the pleasure of being together. Over and over I went back and started the evening again from the point when I opened the door, and he came through it to embrace me. Again and again I tried to stay with the memory of his warm lips against mine and the eagerness of his hands finding me. Each time the memory shattered in the sound of breaking glass.

Toward early morning when it was still dark, Row came to the side of my bed. "I have to go potty, Mommy." I got up and went through the hallway to the bathroom with him. When I brought him back to his bed and fluffed his pillow, I found toys tucked under it. "I couldn't sleep, Mommy, but I didn't make noise." I saw then that Jumper was on the windowsill where Row liked to stand with his stuffed kangaroo. He would say that he was counting the stars, even though both he and I knew he was delaying bedtime.

Every night when I tucked Row in, he acted as if I were wrenching myself away from him. I blamed it on the fact that he was missing his Daddy, and that Ross's long assignment in Switzerland was hard on our family. Until this night I'd reassured myself that Row's difficulty sleeping would straighten out when his Daddy came home again and our household returned to normal. Night after night in Row's little bedroom the routine repeated itself. "Please don't go away Mommy," he would say.

Sometimes to calm Row I stayed at the window to count the stars. He would go as high as he could count and then say, "Let's count again. I missed one." One evening when there was a full moon he asked me if Daddy could see the moon. "He's far away, isn't he Mommy? But he can see the moon, right?" And I assured him that Daddy could see the same moon we could see. I actually told him there is only one moon, and it also shines where Daddy is staying. Did I think a three year-old needed an astronomy lesson? This night though, I didn't think about the moon or the stars. Instead I wondered how long Row had been at the window. I wondered what beside the stars he had seen. I tucked him in again with the kangaroo beside him, and when he shifted to his side, I softly stroked his back until I heard his breathing change and knew he was sleeping.

In the morning I got up before the children were awake, and when I looked in on them, I was more grateful than ever to see them sleeping peacefully. I went down to the kitchen to make coffee. In the back entryway along the wall was a box cutter with a smear of dark blood. On the door knob and the dead bolt were smudges that someone else might not have noticed, but I knew what they were.

In the afternoon my little Laura found a money clip with several bills and a driver's license under the sofa in the playroom. "Mommy, who is this?" she asked.

With a forced calm I replied, "Oh thank you, honey, give it to me and I'll take care of it." As the words were coming from my mouth I was thinking how to make it disappear. To not draw attention to it. I couldn't help wondering, "What have I done, and what am I going to do?"

I hardly ever spoke again of the night the intruder broke into my house. Thomas and I reviewed it enough to be confident we had taken care of everything. When I returned his license and money clip to him I assured him that I had cleaned up all the telltale signs in the house. We agreed there would be no purpose served by calling the police, because making the break-in public would only cause problems.

A few times afterward I looked at the wound on his side when his shirt was off. I wanted to be sure it was healing. It faded gradually until it was a thin bowed line etched into his skin. Once I said to him it looked like one side of a parenthesis, and he replied, "Where is the other side?"

I never told my children about that night. They were present, but I want to believe if they had memories left from that night it was only those gathered from their own sweet dreams. When Ross returned from his work in Geneva, I didn't tell him what had happened. We picked up where we had left off before he went; the children were delighted to have their daddy back again, and we went on with ordinary family life. For years I kept the memory of that season with Thomas hidden away. It was carried in my memory like a picture in a locket. I only opened it when no one else was around.

Decades later I mentioned to my nurse the evening an intruder broke into my house. I only told her half the story; recounting how an intruder cut through the screen and came into our kitchen during the night when I was home alone and the children were sleeping. I told her of being startled by the sound of breaking glass and that the intruder fled when he realized that he could not steal in and out of the house silently. The evening I told my nurse the story was the same one on which she told me of her own lingering fear of a stranger who accosted her late one night as she walked home to her apartment. We swapped stories in shared empathy, the way women do when they are getting to know each other. We found comfort in confessing our vulnerability.

My nurse was a keen listener. Not judging, but attentive. She never forgot past conversations the way some people do who listen politely while thinking of other things. She was not a pretender, and that is why I liked her. So why did I tell her a half story? Telling half of a story isn't really half honest. It's half dishonest. It's a stroll through a field of landmines while pretending it's a grassy meadow. In the end my nurse understood that, but it took a long time before I dared to tell her the rest of the story. She forgave me easily for telling her a half story. She assured me that she understood. The full story? She told me it was not hers to judge.

Chapter 2

# THE NURSE

My nurse was the first in her family to go to college. She needed to support herself by working part time, and she had the good sense to take a class to become a nurse assistant so she could work while going to school. Her part-time work was our connection. A friendly nurse assistant for ten hours a week was what my adult children thought their mother needed. I've wondered since whether it was what I needed or if it was what my children needed, but that's another story.

The accident that opened this chapter of my life was unremarkable. I broke my wrist. It might have created a more interesting story if I had broken a leg doing something glamorous like downhill skiing or skydiving. In fact I broke my wrist stumbling on a step in my own apartment. Most of my living space is on one floor, but there is a partial second floor. A loft. When my children or grandchildren visit they sleep there. It's a pleasant space with a small sitting area, a very small bath, and a room large enough to hold a set of twin beds. It also has a storage closet. I seldom go up to the loft because I've no need to. Everything I need is on the main floor.

The day I broke my wrist I'd gone up to retrieve a decoration I wanted to put on my apartment door during the holidays. It's stored for the rest of the year in the closet in the bedroom upstairs. I got it down quite handily, and had no difficulty maneuvering the steps with my hands full. On the very last tread when I thought I'd reached the bottom, I stepped out with the confidence of a mission accomplished, but there was one more step. In that instant my life changed, not because of a dreadful accident but because of a tiny swerve in the usual course of things.

When I fell forward, I broke my wrist. It was a small break, not one of those awful falls that leaves a victim lying helpless for hours or days, waiting to be discovered. I was not like the woman in the TV ad who is calling for help because she can't get up. I managed to get up on my feet and onto a chair from which I called my friend, Alethea, who lives here in the same building. She drove me to the med center. I have wondered since how different my life might have been if I had gotten down the stairs with the decoration and hung it on the door of my condo exactly as I had planned. I would not have needed a nurse. I would not have met Tee.

Because my arm was in a cast my children decided I needed help. This broken wrist was like catching a cream pie smack in the face. It wasn't that it hurt so much; it was the insult of feeling old and helpless that bothered me. My pride and self-sufficiency were as injured as my wrist.

The hardest part of having a broken wrist was how isolated I felt. I gave up my volunteer hours at the senior center on Wednesdays because it's hard to push a wheel chair with one hand. I gave up playing bridge on Mondays because there's no deft way to shuffle, deal, and play without two hands. My usual routine of walking to the teashop for a daily indulgence of a latte and a newspaper was no longer a treat. I didn't like walking in the neighborhood with my arm in a cast because, until this happened, I prided myself on being one of those vigorous, active, older women.

My children thought I was depressed. Maybe they were right, although I prefer to say I was bored. I don't like being called depressed; it sounds like a failure of character. I admit I felt negative about lots of things, including my children. There was no point in clarifying for them that I was feeling old, and that aging is disappointing. I knew how they would respond. They would sweep it aside and remind me "you are only as old as you feel." That comment about being only as old as you feel is inconsiderate. A seventy-something woman who feels sixteen is probably demented, and that's one of the things we fear most as we add on years. For the rest of us, old is just plain old, and if counting the years isn't enough to remind us, the way our bodies work certainly will.

Young people have no idea that lurking deep in the psyche of every person who sees the years taking their toll is the fear of being put out to pasture. Before it happens to us we see it happening to others. Those of us who visit nursing homes see it starkly. Lives done before they're over. The good parts of life shrinking away. Families reviewing end of life planning with old people, and if they are mentally competent encouraging them to sign documents outlining the interventions for which they give permission and those they wish to refuse. The agreements include words like "do not resuscitate."

I've done end of life planning myself. I knew it was due when my doctor asked me for the second time if I had discussed advance directives with my children. After my minister saw me in church with a cast on my arm, she stopped by for a friendly visit, and while we chatted about other things she slipped in the suggestion that it is helpful for families to do some planning ahead of time. She had experience with families that got into nasty quarrels when adult children were forced to decide what their parents hadn't wanted to face. So I did the right thing. But no one other than my closest friends, who are my age, understand how daunting it is to think ahead to empty days spent in a nursing home between the time when life is "done" and when it is finally "over."

My children avoid facing aging themselves by eating organic, coloring their hair, and slathering their skin with expensive creams at night. Thinking about aging too early is hazardous for them, because they still have a hard time even calling themselves middle-aged. If they stepped into the reality of what inevitably lies ahead, it would knock the stuffing out of them. I was their age once upon a time. At the time I found life challenging enough as it was, and I didn't give any thought to aging and death except to avoid it. Why would I expect it would be any different for my children?

Forgive the aside. Back to what happened after I broke my wrist. Friends sent books my way that were supposed to be comic views of old folks. One was about a group of oldsters raising the dickens in a nursing home. Another was about an old guy who wants to end it all but is repeatedly interrupted by his neighbors, or has to delay his plan to do himself in because things keep popping up on his schedule. Young readers find this charming or even comic because they don't really understand. I didn't finish reading the book because, apart from the fact that I didn't find it entertaining, I realized it was feeding my pessimism.

All of these things played into my children's decision that I should have a nurse to help me. They were considerate and never said that the nurse was there to take care of me, as if I were helpless or incompetent. They said she was there to assist me, suggesting that I was in charge. They referred to her as "the nurse," and at first that's what I called her too when I spoke to them about her, although when I was with her I soon began calling her by her nickname, Tee. She was the only "Tee" I'd ever known. Not a usual name, but it was more comfortable to think of her as "Tee" than to think of her as "my nurse."

For the first few days Tee came to assist me, she called me Mrs. Barone, my family's name. I didn't correct her and tell her that I'd kept my maiden name when I married, that my name is Maggie Barnes. I didn't have to correct her because soon I noticed that she didn't call me anything at all. You can work around a name if you have to. I did that with my mother-in-law because I was uncomfortable calling her by her first name and couldn't make the leap to calling her "Mom." Eventually, along with my children, I called her "Gramma Jeanne," and that solved the problem.

Even after Tee came to help me, my friends continued to stop by to see if I needed anything when they were out to do their own errands. My neighbor Alethea referred to me as "Maggie" when Tee answered the phone or the door, and that made it oddly formal for Tee to call me Mrs. Barone or Ms. Barnes. Really, I'm not the dowager of Downton Abbey. After one of those awkward exchanges I said, "Tee, just call me Maggie. It's easier." She smiled and said, "You noticed, huh?" And that was that.

My broken arm healed, but my children decided that I should keep the nurse. They hinted that Tee could drive me places and check that my refrigerator was neither empty nor harboring moldy leftovers. I don't know if my children realized that after my wrist healed enough for me to handle a steering wheel, I drove myself, and I was perfectly able to mind my own refrigerator.

My children have lives of their own. Good ones. When I suggest that it was they who needed me to have a nurse, I'm not implying they neglected me. As a matter of fact, working together like a committee, they managed to track me fairly well. Like many middle-aged children of older parents, their love language is tracking and managing. They do that for their own children, and they do that for me. If I had a dollar for every time one of my children asked, "What did you do today, Mom?" or "Got anything interesting planned for tomorrow?" I'd be a millionaire.

What my children probably feared most, but never said, is that I would become one of those old women whose clothes become stale from being worn and returned to the closet too many times. The one whose hair is flat in the back and pushed up on the crown from morning and afternoon naps in the easy chair. The old woman whose nails don't get clipped, whose feet don't get washed, and whose pantyhose sag. They would be embarrassed if I became the bent over crone whose bifocals are smudged so she can no longer see well enough to pluck the hairs on her chin. An unkempt mother would be a reflection on them.

Until I tripped on that step I was a frisky old woman. Furthermore a broken wrist did not make me doddering and helpless. Here's the problem in a nutshell. I resisted being dependent on my children. I don't like to imagine one of my children breaking off another perfectly good or enjoyable activity with the excuse, "Well I've to get going now because I have to check up on Mother." I can imagine the tone of voice like the one in the movies when young people stop by to visit their mothers. They don't stop by for a good time. They complain about those visits as if they are on their way to a colonoscopy. The long and short of it is that I did not want to be someone who needed to be taken care of.

I don't know which of the children first had this idea of finding a nurse for me. I suspect it was Will who checked it out with Jenna by phone because, although he lives a half-continent away, he thinks of himself as the one who is responsible for Mother. Jenna, who lives nearest of all my children, is his foot soldier. Or it might have been Laura who brought it up with Row during one of their business-like cross-country phone calls to check up on Mom who lives at least five states away from either one of them.

Laura has the executive style of a first-born child, while Will has the executive style of an alpha male. How they balance this out between them, I don't know, although I'm not aware they have conflicts. When it came to working out how to care for me, I suspect that Laura knew when to use tact to reduce tension, and Will knew how to use money to do the same. Let me say in my own defense that the paychecks for the nurse came from my account, even though the nurse was their idea.

It was a Tuesday in November that Tee first arrived at my door. She rang the buzzer at the street level, and I answered the intercom and told her to come up. It was a minute or so until she tapped softly on the door of 4-C.

I had already put my guard in place, telling myself this was an initial interview, and I did not have to like her because Will and Laura got a good impression when they spoke with her by phone. I promised myself that if I didn't feel comfortable, I wouldn't invite her back. Frankly, what worried me most was that a young woman in her twenties would be bored spending time with an old woman like me. How would she understand me? Would I feel comfortable with her? Our worlds were separated by half a century.

When I opened the door she stood there quietly and said, "Hi." She did not say, "Hello, I'm Tee" or "Hello, I'm the nurse assistant your children spoke with by phone" or "Hello, Mrs. Barone, it's a pleasure to meet you."

And I did not say, "Hello, I'm Laura and Will's mother," or Hello, I'm Maggie." I just said "Hi" back and turned to walk into the apartment, knowing that she would follow me. She had a light step; I noticed that. I went to my chair in the living room, and she followed. I sat down, but she did not.

Instead she said, "Would it be good to start with tea?"

"I don't usually drink tea. I prefer coffee."

"Coffee then?" she said. "But you will have to show me how to make coffee in your kitchen."

She walked over to me as if to help me from my chair, but I got up easily on my own. After all it was a broken wrist I had, not a broken hip. She turned and walked toward the kitchen, and I followed. I showed her the French press and the coffee, and I told her I like the coffee strong with a generous splash of half and half but no sugar or sweetener.

"Do you drink coffee?" I asked.

"Only if it's really good," she replied with a grin.

While Tee made the coffee I sat down at the small table in the eating area, and when the coffee was ready Tee joined me there, placing the two mugs on the table between us like an invitation to conversation. I told her about my children, the other children because she had already spoken with Will and Laura. She told me about school.

"I especially like the required course in World Literature," she said. "It doesn't have much to do with nursing, but it's way more interesting than chemistry."

I asked her if there are some selections she especially likes, and she told me she prefers poetry that rhymes. She didn't like the poem by Marianne Moore they had studied in the last class, because she didn't think that the poem made sense, even though her professor said Moore is one of America's greatest poets. "Could be," Tee explained, "but that didn't help me understand a poem that goes on and on about apples and hazelnuts and hedgehogs."

Tee asked her professor why someone would write a poem about such trivial things, and was told to check out the last verse because it explains that the poem is about fortitude. To this Tee's commentary was, "Why not just write about fortitude then?"

I tried to remember if this was the poem in which there is the line to the effect that we do not admire what we do not understand. It may have been in another poem or even another poet, but I voted with Tee on this one. I never liked Marianne Moore's poetry very much either, and it was decades since I'd been made to force my way through it under the whip of an English teacher.

I wanted to hear about a poem Tee liked. I thought maybe it was a Shakespeare sonnet. Who doesn't know about "How shall I compare thee to a summer's day?" Or this other sonnet, the one with the line that says, "To love that well that thou must leave ere long." I need to look that one up again.

It wasn't Shakespeare that hooked Tee's attention. It was "a guy named Gerard Manley Hopkins. That's even a kind of poetic name, isn't it," she began, "I mean, couldn't you guess that someone with a name like that could be a poet?" The students each had to pick a poem to present in class, and Tee picked "Spring and Fall," the poem Hopkins had dedicated to a young child, although Tee was quick to add that she thought he had written it for someone about her age. "It's especially beautiful if you read it out loud," she added. "You can feel it."

We talked more about books. I told her I was reading a novel about war and a young blind girl. She seemed genuinely interested and typed the title into her phone. Tee stayed for about an hour. Both she and I knew it was a "get acquainted visit." Once we finished our coffee she put the mugs in the dishwasher and cleaned the French press, and then she asked, "Is there anything I could do for you today?" I told her that I was okay for today, but that tomorrow I had an appointment and was hoping she would drive me.

We agreed on the time. I walked her to the door. At the door she paused. "Mrs. Barone, a little bit ago when I first arrived . . . were you surprised when you opened the door?"

I didn't want to answer, but it would have been awkward to ignore her question. "Yes . . . a little, I guess." The admission on my part felt awkward. I wanted to level the playing field. "Were you surprised?" I asked her.

"Of course not," she said. "That's the difference between you and me, but you must know that. Do you know why I asked the question?"

"I'm not sure," I told her. "I guess I don't really know why you asked."

"I wanted to see if you're honest." She didn't say anything more. I didn't pursue it either, and was relieved when she said, "I'll see you tomorrow."

"Okay. I'll count on it."

When the door closed, I realized that we had not spoken of my broken wrist, or how it happened, or exactly what I needed from her every day, or even about a schedule. Our visit wasn't at all what I'd imagined it would be. I thought she would arrive, and we would exchange the information she needed in order to do the job. I would walk her through my apartment to show her where things are. I had put out a sticky note with the name of the medication I take each morning, and I'd imagined that when I gave it to her I would brag a little about taking no other medications except occasionally a Tylenol PM on nights when I feel sore and can't sleep.

The other sticky note that I left in the kitchen said "driver's license" on one line and then "class schedule" on another line. I suppose Will or Laura had already asked her if she had a driver's license and could drive my car. She had agreed to drive me to my appointment. Apparently she had a license, and it fit her schedule.

I was touched that Tee had thought to ask me what I needed today. At least for now I did have what I needed from her, which was to know that I felt at ease with her. In the quiet after Tee left I had a strange lonely feeling. It isn't easy growing old or living alone. No matter how skilled I become at filling time with interesting things, the absence of others never becomes ordinary and there are always hollow hours.

So I daydreamed on. I imagined Tee going home to an apartment where she lives with her family. Lacking anything more specific to work with, I imagined a layout similar to one of the other apartments in this building. In that apartment I imagined Tee in the kitchen, talking to a woman who looked vaguely like her but older. She was telling her mother that today she met a woman with a broken wrist and tomorrow would drive her to an appointment. Then I realized how little I knew about this young woman with whom I'd shared a cup of coffee and a conversation here in my own familiar space. A young woman with whom in an hour's time I'd already talked about beauty and death. This I do know: I didn't feel on guard with Tee.

Sitting in my chair sorting through the day, I felt I could trust my first impression of Tee. It was not my imagination. I had noticed something about Tee's face. She didn't smile much, but she had eyes that looked out frankly, and it was easy to look into them. At moments in our conversation when a less genuine person might have broken into a charming smile, she only softened around the eyes.

I would not have held it against her if she were a smiler. People do that when they are slightly ill at ease and want to leave a good impression. I do that sometimes myself in order to convey that I'm a friendly older woman and not a cranky one. But smiling isn't what I remember of Tee. Instead I picture her now with a pleasant face and a soft gaze.

There in my favorite chair I let my thoughts float for a while longer. One of the gifts of growing older is that there is time for wandering around in the garden of random thoughts. I noticed that the afternoon was beginning to draw shadows. It was the time of day when it is not dark, just dull. When the shadows get long, but there is still light in the sky. I started to feel tired of my own thoughts, so I turned on my reading light and picked up my book. And for a reason I cannot explain, the book felt lighter in my hands.

# Chapter 3

# WILLARD AND ROWLAND

Although my children counted on Tee to assist me with day-to-day matters, they also checked up on her regularly. Will called most often. He asked if I was satisfied with the nurse. I assured him she was very nice, and the things she was doing were making my days easier. He instructed me to be direct with her and tell her exactly what I needed her to do. Coaching me about how to be a good manager, he said I should call him if I needed any help handling the nurse's hours and her pay. I thanked him and told him I was managing it just fine. "Okay, then," he said. And that was that. Sometimes he could be all business.

My children, their partners, and my grandchildren are a large group. When Tee began spending hours with me it was natural to tell her about them. Sometimes when she was cooking dinner for the two of us, I'd sit at the small table in the kitchen. "Tell me about your kids," she'd say, as if she were suggesting a neutral topic. It was easiest to begin with stories about the children when they were young, and I enjoyed having someone with whom to review those times. I'd talk and she'd work. Sometimes Tee filled in small details about herself, but on balance I did more of the talking. Telling her my stories sometimes reminded me of assembling a puzzle in which a piece, one I'd passed over before, finally fit in place.

One day while I was out in the afternoon and Tee was in my kitchen beginning dinner, Will called to check in on me. I assume Tee chatted with him for a few minutes, and when I returned she filled me in on the conversation. "Is Will your oldest?" she asked. "He talks like an oldest child. Very confident and in charge."

Will is a twin born after his brother Row. He is not my firstborn, but sometimes I nearly forget that myself because he's assumed the role of head of the family since his father passed away, and no one seems to question it. The birth certificates of the two boys state that they made their appearances thirteen minutes apart. I've wondered sometimes if the nurses, who took them quickly and wrapped them in receiving blankets, switched them. Not intentionally, but because there was a lot of busywork going on in the room as the nurses counted fingers, weighed the boys, and stuck stethoscopes on their chests. Maybe it was Will who was born first. Certainly for the rest of his life he acted as if he were. In the final analysis how much difference can a head start of thirteen minutes make?

The day Ross and I brought our twin sons home from the hospital to our little starter house on Whitney Avenue we had set up two bassinets in the smallest bedroom, and they were so little the room didn't even seem crowded. Laura was moved into another room. She was only two years old, and could not appreciate what a luxury it is to have a room of your own. It did not take long for us to realize that three children can fill a house with noise and toys. By the time Laura was four and the boys were two we were already looking for something bigger. But for their first years our little house on Whitney Avenue was our nest.

Will was an active child. Images of him stay with me like little videos. When he first learned to ride his two-wheeler, Will put playing cards in the spokes because he liked the sound they made when he rode fast. He called it his helicopter. At night, still dreaming of his helicopter, he lay in bed talking to himself, and I could hear his voice barking directions and recounting what he saw as he floated over the trees and between buildings.

He couldn't have been much more than seven or eight when the space under the deck of our second house on Woodward Street became his cave. My complaints about cobwebs in his hair, filthy clothes, and even threats of mouse droppings and spider bites made no difference. What gave him exclusive claim to the space under the deck was not obvious, but his brothers and sisters did not disturb him there. Later when a deck forty inches off the ground resulted in too many bumps on the head, he moved from under the deck to his tree house.

Will took the idea for the tree house from a handyman's magazine and persuaded his dad to help him with it. He was proud that he had constructed it with a level, the one that had gathered dust above the workbench in the garage, although from that time on Will claimed the level as his own and kept it up in the tree house. It was his little kingdom, a place over which he ruled with clear authority, and a secure hideaway where he stowed his treasures.

From time to time for his dwelling in the tree Will appropriated "borrowed" objects. It caused a stir when his father discovered that the filleting knife, so carefully cleaned and stored in the tackle box after each season of fishing, had been repurposed as a wood carving knife for the tree house. The broken tip of the knife may still be embedded in the large maple that shaded the yard of our old Tudor house on Woodward Street, that is if the tree is still standing.

When Will was a teenager he took the small storage room off the airing deck at the back of the house as his bedroom. It was not large enough to hold a bed, so he had a sleeping bag on the floor. The walls he painted entirely black. The light yellow curtains came down, and he lived with bare windows until he came up with the idea of buying a closeout bolt of black cotton from the fabric store and tacking it across the window frames. I wonder if the tack holes are still in the window frames of the little back room in the house on Woodward, or if by now successive coats of paint have filled them in.

We named Willard Francis after his grandfather, his paternal grandfather. I wasn't particularly fond of the name or the man, but it seemed important to Ross to honor his father in this way, and I didn't object. "The old man" as his own children called Grandpa Willard, was delighted. I was the one who first started calling our baby "Will." I wanted to be clear that our little Will was not a clone of big Willard.

Will got in a fight when he was in high school. There were boys who bullied Row, and Will would not stand for anyone mistreating his twin brother. After football practice one afternoon when these boys made insulting comments to Will about his skinny brother, he took off after them. He grabbed one boy by the arm and twisted it behind his back so hard that he dislocated the kid's shoulder.

When a second boy stepped in to defend his friend, Will got a fist in the mouth. By the time the coach came out to break up the fight, Will was bleeding profusely from his nose and holding a bloodied tooth in his fist on which the knuckles were ripped open. Fortunately the coach had the good sense to wrap the tooth in a clean tissue and take both Will and his tooth to a dentist who had done repairs for the football team on numerous other occasions.

Ross picked Will up from the dentist, and by the time they reached home the pain medication had taken effect. Will went directly to his cave, ignoring my suggestion that he should not sleep on the drafty floor in his sleeping bag. Several times in the night I went in to check on him. His sleep was noisy. His face looked terrible, swollen and lop-sided. Once I knelt beside him and kissed him lightly on his forehead. I could not see my little boy in this big bruised man on the floor, but when I tasted the saltiness of his skin and felt the texture of his hair, I knew it was my Will. I think this was the last time I kissed him while he was a boy.

Will wouldn't talk about the fight. He wouldn't tell us what the boys had said about Row. Even more puzzling was the fact that the school did nothing. Both the coach and the principal were nonchalant about it. "Boys will be boys," was all they had to say. Their father had the same reaction, but I always wondered if there was something Ross wasn't telling me. Did he know what had triggered Will's fury? I asked a few times, but the last time I asked, his voice had a harsh edge when he responded, "For heavens sakes, Maggie, do you ever just let sleeping dogs lie?"

Will endured the remainder of high school, but he refused to play football again. When it was time to plan for college he was uninterested. His twin brother Row was making a project of picking the right college, but Will refused to visit campuses and did not complete applications. Just before the fall semester began he hastily submitted an application for the local community college, and he was accepted.

I don't remember much about that year when my twin sons went to college. I have one image of Will that I hold in memory like a photo. He was working in our yard, pulling out overgrown shrubs. It was a warm day, and he had taken his shirt off. From the kitchen window I saw him. What a strong man he had become. A beautiful man. The muscles across his shoulder rippled as he worked the shovel. He paused a few times to wipe the sweat off his brow with his forearm. I could see the sculpting of his arm, his solid neck, and the damp golden hair in his armpit. I caught myself gazing at him.

Captured by his beauty. Lingering, but then wondering if a mother ought to relish the beauty of her own son this way.

I turned away from the window, but I felt tearful. Was I only allowed to delight in the physical beauty of my sons while they were little boys? The symmetry of their eyelashes, the texture of their skin, the exquisite fit of the flesh clothing their bones, their perfectly sculpted feet, the honest scuffs on their strong hands, their narrow hips and firm thighs made for running? I had seen it with my own eyes; I had delighted in it. Did I have to tear myself away from that now and train myself not to notice, because my sons had become grown men? I cannot explain the feeling, except to say it was both treasure and loss. It is a conflicted feeling I have never forgotten.

The summer after his first year of college Will rode his motorcycle all the way to the Pacific. He left without a plan except for the destination "to keep going west 'til I can't go anymore." How he paid his way, where he stayed, and how long it took him to get there remained a mystery for a long time. In mid August there was a call from a phone booth somewhere in California and the announcement that he'd "hit the Pacific" and that's where he was going to stay.

To us it was not as simple as that. There were obvious questions. "What about school? What about the stuff in the apartment you leased for next year? How are you going to support yourself?" Each concern was met with a variation on the same retort. "Got that handled. No problem. Don't you sweat it; I'll figure it out."

Will had made up his mind. We never knew how he did it, but he managed somehow. He worked for a while, and then some time later finished college. This latter accomplishment, I think, was to prove himself to his family and most of all to his dad, although he probably didn't need that diploma after he started his construction company during the California housing boom.

As Will became more successful he reestablished some contact with us, and his calls followed a pattern. First in a deep voice that sometimes was more like a rumble than words when he spoke too softly to me on the phone, he asked about the family. Polite but disinterested questions. I could imagine he was doing busywork at his desk while he went through this perfunctory conversation with me. Maybe he was sorting old receipts or cleaning out the pencil drawer. Then there would be a pause in the conversation that indicated he'd finished talking with me, and Will would say, "Is Dad there? Put him on."

Will talked with his dad about the stock market and some of his recent California business ventures. I only heard one side of the conversation, but the topics were obvious. Ross would toss around the names of stocks he was watching and give Will his appraisal of what was happening on the bond market. They talked about bank loans and interest rates. Clearly Will understood the benefits of having a banker in the family. Of all the children, Will was the one who could keep his Dad longest on the phone. Often when the call was finished Ross would say with some evident pride, "I think that lad is doing fine."

I don't know what Ross expected of a grown son. Maybe the contact he had with Will was enough. Safe. Distant. Manly. Maybe they were satisfied that they had found common ground on which they could admire each other. But that was not enough for me. I gave birth to Will, nursed him, rocked him during restless nights, soothed the toddler who fell and scraped his knee, protected him from a dangerous world that was too big for him, fed him ten thousand meals, and drove him thousands of miles in our old station wagon. Did he not know that those things were forms of love? When he was grown and didn't need me anymore, was I disposable? Like the container for a sandwich from the fast food mart?

Sometimes when Ross would say in his self-satisfied voice that he thought the lad was doing fine, I felt angry with both of them. But what could I say? They wouldn't have heard it. So I kept silent and got caught up again in the vicious cycle of missing Will and sorting through the same painful tangle of clues, trying to figure out why it had to be this way, why had he chosen this distance?

I seldom if ever discussed the pain of Will's estrangement with other family members, and later when Tee was staying with me she sometimes spoke with him by phone and commented that he was nice in that guy sort of way. Not too many words, but no trouble either. Nonetheless, the day I told her my own story of Will, I found myself shaken at certain points. The years had not erased that old sense of loss. Tears trickled down my cheeks. I felt both a soft love for him, and a deep ache from the estrangement that had robbed us of so many years.

Tee listened without interrupting, but when I finished she continued with her cooking, and without looking in my direction she said, "It's a waste, isn't it, to let time go by like that? I'd do anything to be able to see my Mom again, or even have a conversation with her on the phone." That was the first inkling I had that Tee's mother was no longer living.

The way we distributed the names of the two grandfathers to two squirming little boys, each in his plastic nursery tub, in that row of a dozen or so infants who just happened to be born at the same hospital on the same day, was somewhat accidental. It was not exactly a flip of the coin, but neither was it more thought through than that.

They each needed a name, and if one grandfather was going to be honored it only seemed right to honor the other as well. And so Rowland Barnes, named in full after my father, became Rowland Barnes Barone. And soon he was "Row" for short. It is interesting that Row was born first, but his brother, born second, was the namesake of his paternal grandfather and always assumed the role of the eldest son. Very early Row resigned himself to standing in Will's shadow.

As I think back to the time of their birth I have an image of Ross standing at the foot of two bassinets in the hospital nursery and saying, "Well okay then, let's name this one Willard and this one Rowland." And I have the image of the nurse glancing over with a look that said, "How can you put two such heavy names on two such tiny boys? Do you realize that they will be carrying those names around for a lifetime?"

As I pause to think about this now I realize I must be imagining how it went, because I'm sure neither their father nor I ever stepped inside the hospital nursery. It wouldn't have been allowed. The boys were brought to my room so I could become acquainted with them and introduce feedings.

The nurses always brought two bottles of formula and repeated their reassurances that formula was so well researched I could be confident all the nutrition my babies needed could be gotten from the bottle. And each time I argued back that I was going to nurse my babies just the way women have fed their newborns from time immemorial. If it was good enough for all the mothers before me, it was good enough for me. Mostly the nurses responded with a condescending smile and a patient offer. "Whenever you're ready to start the bottle just let us know."

One nurse, a course woman with a megaphone voice, cautioned me that nursing twins would leave me with breasts sagging down to my knees like hound's ears. I snapped back at her, "I guess that's my business." From the hallway I heard her warn the other nurses that I was irritable and they should keep an eye on me when I had the babies with me in the room.

After the feedings the boys were picked up again and delivered back to the nursery so I would have time to rest. That's the way it was done in maternity units at the time they were born. The nurses owned the babies until the day I was sent home. The responsibility for registering their birth certificates with the little inked footprints was turned over entirely to Ross. The truth is, I don't remember how it happened that Willard got the one name and Rowland got the other.

When Row was about three years old, he discovered that there was a song written about him, and then within an hour the honor was stripped away, and he learned that the song was not about him at all because it was about a boat. He was singing "Row row row your boat, gently down the stream." Our first little house on Whitney Avenue had two doorways into the kitchen, one from the front door through the back entryway and one from the dining room. This meant that Row had a continuous loop from kitchen to dining room to living room and then through the entryway back to the kitchen again. In precise little steps Row marched the circle swaying from side to side in perfect time, as if he really were in a boat floating down a river and headed out to sea.

I understand that Row thought it was a song to honor him because we often called him Row-Row when he was little. He believed this was his song until his sister Laura stepped in and corrected him with the self-confidence of a child just a little older and a few inches taller. "That's not the way it goes, Row." And then with the raise of a shoulder and the tip of her head that are the true marks of absolute conviction, she set him straight. "It's a song about a boat . . . you know rowing . . . like with oars . . . like at Grandpa's cottage? It's not about you, silly goose." Little Row listened as if to register the correction, and did not argue back.

As it remains with me now in memory it is one of those moments when a mother sees in her small child that life is cruel, and the cruelty begins early. It gives and takes away. In this case the fall from delight was sudden and without warning. I can't explain why that moment spoke so clearly to me. Perhaps it was because of Row's innocence, or it was because I knew in that instant that no matter how much I loved him, I could not replace what life would tear from him. This deep feeling of Row's wounding is the same stab of pain I felt when Laura was sitting on her Daddy's knee and Row asked, "Daddy can I sit on your lap too?"

Instead of making a place for him, Ross replied in a firm voice, "It's time for you to pick up your toys and put them in the toy box, Son."

Row swiveled around and looked toward me. "May I sit on your lap, Mommy?"

Before I could respond Ross broke in, "Don't contradict me, Maggie, and don't encourage him to be clingy."

Although normally we observed the rule of not contradicting each other in front of the children, this time I said, "He's only three, Ross." And then to Row I said, "Come sit on my lap for just a little bit, and then you can pick up your toys. I know you'll do a good job, won't you?" He stayed on my lap for only an instant, and then with a look in his father's direction he hopped down and picked up his toys, putting them all in the toy box. He didn't want to disappoint King Daddy. It hurt to watch it. It hurt to see Row be such a brave little boy, as if he hadn't been wounded when he discovered that his father was willing to show love for a daughter with a sweet familiarity that he was not willing to offer a son.

I suppose there is little reason to belabor these memories all these years later, unless of course you are an older woman sitting in a comfortable chair near the window on a Tuesday morning and have all the time in the world for musing. Those are the times when I would catch myself pondering whether, when parents choose the name by which their little one gets written into the book of life, they also are shaping a child's fate?

There was something of this same conundrum about names when in junior high Row discovered the story of Charlemagne and his twelve loyal Knights. He wanted me to clarify if he did or did not have the same name as Roland. I had to admit to him that his name was similar but not quite the same. That's the best I could do for him. And that was a running theme in his life. Always a hint of possibility, but never quite enough.

Why did I answer Row the way I did? That is so often how it is with children. How many thousands of times did I say "yes" instead of "no" or "no" instead of "yes?" Why did I decide to do this instead of that? Why did I say a stupid unlaundered thing at a moment of being clever or caught off guard only to realize that once it was out of my mouth it was impossible to collect the words and stuff them back into silence? I don't mean to make a big deal out of small details, as if they can determine the course of a life, but there is something about Row that now and then causes me to review those events that one would think should be long gone and forgotten.

When Row finished school and was teaching for the first time he came to stay with us at the lake house for a few weeks one summer. He and I often walked the shore early in the morning, and on one of these walks he said, "Mom, do you remember that once when I was a kid you told me I was co-pacetic?" He went on, "I never knew how to be in our family. If I should be a fighter like Will and Laura or if I should walk away when shit hit the fan." He admitted that he was still having that problem, that he was a doormat, and people could walk all over him.

Row was seeing Andrea, and they were planning to marry, but he had trouble standing up for himself in their relationship. She was beautiful, smart, and rich. That was the upside. The downside was that they seemed to fight often, and Row usually lost. During one of their arguments Andrea slapped Row. On another occasion she left his apartment in such a rage that she nicked the bumper of his car with hers as she pulled out of the parking space next to him in the lot. He wondered if she did it on purpose, but he didn't dare to ask her.

Row turned his criticisms of Andrea back on himself. He wondered if he was a coward and gave in so easily because he knew he couldn't win anyway. Sometimes he had doubts about whether Andrea was the right person for him, but then he second-guessed himself and concluded, "I'd probably have the same problem with any woman if it really comes down to the fact that I'm a wimp." And then Row summed up the reason he had brought this up with me. "I don't think you ever helped me with this," he said. "Didn't you see it? My shrink thinks the problem I have with women started in my childhood."

I didn't know what to say to Row. I wanted to come to his defense and warn him not to marry a woman who treated him badly. I admired him for being a harmonizer, even though he thought it was a flaw for which he wanted to blame me. He was irritated with me, and as we walked he accused me of not helping him sort this out. I had not paid attention to the problem. Not given him his due. That zinger made me angry.

I was annoyed with Row for bringing this up in this way. I wanted to defend myself and point out to him that holding on to a grievance about something so trivial for so long was small of him. It was on the tip of my tongue to say, "Be a man!" But I drew it back out of fear that later I might regret it.

Deeper, far deeper, there was something in me that also wanted to confess to Row that I knew he was right. That over and over in his life he was the one who never got his full allotment of time and attention. Never got the full portion of minutes and space that should have been offered for nurturing the intricacy of his little soul. It's true; he never got his due. There was seldom enough space for him in the din and drama of our busy family.

In the moment of feeling this, because of course I did not stand there mute and think all of this in detail, I just said, "Row, you're not a wimp, and you deserve better." In a tentative gesture he turned slightly toward me as we walked along the shore, and our eyes met for a long moment. And then we turned our gazes forward again, and walked along that edge where the water meets the sand, but you can never define exactly where it is.

I don't want to exaggerate the contrast between my two sons. Theirs was not a Cain and Abel story. Not a Jacob and Esau story. They are two good men, each with good qualities, but they are very different. That is most striking. I don't think anyone made them that way. I'm not sure that they even made themselves that way. It is just who they were, and who they are still.

On the day when they made their first appearance, two squirming infants in blue nursery blankets, I could never have guessed what this would mean. At that moment I was overwhelmed with thinking how I would carry two infants at the same time and also keep their toddling sister from running into the street.

# Chapter 4

# LOSING LAURA

Twin boys working out their fate in a shared life is a story in itself. In our family, however, the picture was complicated by an older sister, who had already constructed the space into which the stork dropped her little brothers.

When Laura was born I had my heart set on a girl because I felt confident I would know how to mother a girl, while mothering a boy would be guesswork. This baby was my first, and I wanted to do it right. We were meticulous about picking names in advance. I wanted a name that would fit a baby, but I also wanted a name that my daughter could carry with style into adulthood. A name that suited a woman. Something feminine but not fluffy. In a moment of inspiration the name "Laura" came to me, and I knew immediately that it was right.

Children change parents. There were crossover points at which I said something or did something, and I knew I'd been altered. One of those occurred when Laura was an infant, and we lived in Geneva where Ross had been assigned work in a Swiss bank for six months. For Laura's convenience and for ours, I decided to nurse her throughout our stay. We were sitting on the balcony of our apartment in Geneva one evening, and she was reclining against me in the sleep of a baby who has a tummy full of warm milk. Out of nowhere Ross asked, "Does it ever strike you as odd that she drinks a fluid your body produces?" It was such an odd thing for him to say that it caught me off guard.

"Would it be any different if she drank fluid from a cow's body or a goat's or maybe fluid produced in a factory owned by Nestle?" I replied.

"If she were eating meat produced by your body that would be cannibalism, right? So if she's drinking your milk is that half cannibalism?" I sensed he was jealous. That Laura was sometimes an intrusion on his claim to me.

I didn't know what had gotten into Ross, but I didn't like it. He was a smart man saying foolish things. I heard my own tone of voice shift to one specific to wives and mothers. It is the way a mother speaks to a boy who has just gone out with a brand new shirt and come back into the house a few minutes later with three buttons torn off. "Oh, Ross!!!"

I also spoke to Ross in this tone when he said something in the presence of others that was entertaining but inappropriate. Like the time he said, while we were visiting with the couple next door, that he liked it that I'd become buxom since nursing Laura, because he liked having a woman with grip. He definitely got the "maternal reprimand" for that one.

When I heard that certain tone in my own voice, I knew I had joined wives and mothers all across the ages, who rebuke their husbands and sons while cloaking the reprimand in an assurance that they only intend to retrain them, not reject them. And so with the addition of Laura to our family I began to speak that dialect called "mother."

It was also around this time that I began to address Ross as "Honey." I used it when I ordered him to do something for me but didn't want to seem bossy. "Honey, could you go upstairs and get Laura's sandals? I think I left them up there when I tucked her in for her nap." The "Honey" softened the order, but left no mistake that it was time for the other adult on the team to pitch in with a little help. Usually it worked. Ross would let me interrupt him even if he was working on his stamp collection or reading the newspaper. Even after we had children he carved out time for these things, because he was sure a man needs leisure to balance the stresses of work life.

Ross's role differed from mine. I didn't interrupt what I was doing to help with Laura. I was in charge of her all the time. When I handed her off to Ross for a little while, she always came back to me. Like so many fathers and mothers, Ross and I had different roles.

When Laura began to talk, Ross sometimes called me "Mommy" when he was speaking with her. "Let's go ask Mommy if we have time to go outdoors for a little while before dinner," he would say in a voice just a little higher than normal. It would have been odd if he spoke of me to Laura by my first name. I think if he'd said, "Let's go ask Maggie if we have time to go outdoors," I would have corrected him.

Once when Laura was napping Ross said to me, "Mom, do we have anything planned for Saturday night?" And before answering him about the calendar for Saturday I turned and said, "Ross, I think we have a decision to make. Do you really want to start calling me Mom?"

We laughed and kept laughing. Got silly. I said some things to him in a high baby voice, calling him "Daddy." And he said more things to me in the same baby voice calling me "Mommy." The more we spoke the sillier it seemed and the giddier we got. We were trying to get the mommy-daddy dialect out of our system to make sure it did not intrude completely into the space we wanted to keep for being a husband and wife. I think the laughter worked. He didn't call me Mommy again except when necessary in the presence of the children.

Reshaping mothers and fathers for parenthood is the work of firstborns. Laura did this for us. I wonder if the baby who's born with this responsibility already feels like a pioneer at an early age, bushwhacking the trail and giving shape to the path that others will follow after her. In any case Laura became the child CEO in our family. She was never hesitant about her own opinion, and always clear she deserved to have at least one vote and often more than one even in matters that were not primarily about her. Which of the twins should have the top and which the lower bunk? Should her little sister have pigtails or a ponytail? Or especially what each of them should be at Halloween.

Now and then Ross and I wondered about this strength of character in our firstborn. I would say, "Do you think being a firstborn did this to her?" And Ross would say, "No, Maggie, she was born that way."

When Laura was in fifth grade she went missing. It was a waking nightmare. I gave Laura permission to take the school bus home on Friday afternoon after school with her friend Jenny. Her mother, Kathy, and I agreed I would pick Laura up at 8:00 pm. Unbeknownst to me, plans at Jenny's house changed over the course of the day because Kathy was asked to work beyond the end of her shift, so she called the school and left a message for Jenny to let herself into their apartment with the key that was in the clip in Jenny's backpack. This was the emergency key that Jenny carried in case she arrived home before her mother. Jenny was an experienced latchkey kid, and Kathy was an overworked single mom who had to ask her daughter to adapt while she worked to make ends meet.

When Kathy arrived home at 5:30, the girls weren't there. When I arrived at 8:00 Kathy was hysterical, and there was a detective at their apartment. They hadn't been able to reach me at home because after school I took my other kids to the Y to swim and then out for pizza. Just before picking Laura up we stopped at the grocery store, and I only arrived at Kathy's apartment a few minutes before 8:00 as planned. The sight of me triggered Kathy's guilt, and between sobs she made excuses, "I've been doing the best I can. I can't be with Jenny every minute because I have bills to pay. Why couldn't the girls just do what I told them?"

I felt I had to do something, so I walked over to the wall where the phone was hanging and called Ross. He was still at work, meeting with clients over a working dinner at his office. His secretary was already gone, and Ross answered the phone himself, but seemed annoyed that I was interrupting his meeting. Echoing in my mind were the times he belittled the other men whose wives interrupted their work. "Most things can wait," he'd say. His first response when he heard my voice was, "I'm in the middle of a meeting, Maggie. Is this really important?"

"I'm at Jenny's and Laura's not here."

"What do you mean she's not there?"

"She went with Jenny after school, and when Jenny's mom got home the girls weren't there."

"Geez, Maggie, take charge. I'll deal with her when I get home."

I detected immediately that Ross thought I was calling to complain that Laura had misbehaved, and I felt too confused and close to tears to set him straight, so I said, "Okay, Bye," and hung up.

Other police arrived. They asked Kathy why she was late returning home and how often her daughter was alone by herself unsupervised. They questioned me about where else I'd been in the previous five hours. They asked about the girls' fathers, and I told them Ross was still at work. Kathy explained that she and George were divorced, and he had recently moved to Oregon but didn't have a new address or phone number yet. I didn't understand the point of all these questions. Why weren't they looking for the girls?

My four other children were waiting in the car. The officers told me to take them home and they would come to our house later to talk to us.

It must have been confusing for my children to see cruisers wheel up and police officers go inside. When I got outside, the two youngest were crying. Will was browsing the contents of the glove box, and Row was pale. The moment he saw me he blurted, "Mom, I thought someone killed you."

At home I shifted onto automatic pilot. Made snacks for the kids. Organized their baths. Emptied the backpacks that were still piled in the back hallway. Took the dog out, but stayed within shouting distance and told the kids to get me if anyone called. When finally I had them all settled down for the night, I stood beside Laura's empty bed. Instinctively I picked up her pillow and smelled it. I cried. I wondered if she would ever come back. If she was gone, and this was it, I wasn't sure I could survive it. At the moment I wasn't even sure I could keep my wits about me while waiting to know what had happened to her. If she were gone, gone for good, would I go mad, stark raving mad?

When Ross came home and realized that Laura was still missing, his response was predictable. "Why didn't you tell me that she was really missing? Really, Maggie, did you check these people out before you gave Laura permission to go over there?" Was he really suggesting that this was my fault? Along with my terror about where Laura could be, I was furious with Ross for showing up now, hours late. Angry that first he had to finish his meeting with his clients. Only then could he hear me say what I had said hours earlier, and he had the gall to hint that I was the neglectful parent?

"I did tell you. She's gone, Ross. She's gone and we don't know what's happened to her. The police are coming over to talk to us. What if we never get her back?" And then I started to sob. I cried so hard I could barely catch my breath. I drooled. I pounded my fist on the table. I had a taste of madness.

"Get it together," Ross said. "Crying isn't going to get her back. You'd better start thinking about where she could be." He went into the other room. I stopped crying and blew my nose. I wanted to run after him, to pound on him, to scream at him that he had no right to walk away and leave me in my misery.

The police took our fingerprints and told us this was standard procedure in the case of a missing child. The words "missing child" were like a razor slicing through my skin. They asked to see her room and wanted clothing she had worn that had not been laundered. They put her hairbrush in a clear plastic bag to take it with them. Detective Moore informed us he was assigned to the case and gave us his card. "Call for any reason," he said.

"Any detail that catches your attention I want to know about. I'll sort out if it's important. Let me make that judgment." He talked in a condescending voice that implied, "if you're stupid enough to lose a child, we aren't counting on you to know what's important. Leave that to me."

When Detective Moore left in his car and the guys who had been collecting evidence pulled away in their van, we were left in our house, alone, without Laura. Ross started up the stairs and at the landing turned and said, "I guess there's nothing to do except get some sleep and see what happens by morning." I wondered if he was still allowing himself to think his daughter had not come home on time, and he could figure out later how to reprimand her for being tardy. I also knew he was trying to escape from me.

I was having other thoughts, a mother's worst fears, and I was sick with worry. My eyes hurt from crying. My hands were clammy, and my voice was growing hoarse. I couldn't think of anything else to do except take a shower, hoping that in that warm moist space I could close out this horrid world for a few minutes. But I couldn't. Even there Laura's absence followed me. Even there I cried.

When I dried off and went into our bedroom, Ross was sleeping. That's not quite true. He wasn't breathing like a sleeping man, and his body was not soft and heavy. His breathing was deliberate, and the sheet was wrapped around him like a shroud around a man playing dead. I wanted to shake him to tell him he had no right to pretend sleep until we found Laura. More than that I wanted to punish him for being willing to sleep instead of waiting with me during these hellish night hours. I wanted to pour ice water over him or scream in his ear. I knew it was no use because Ross can't abide hysterical women, so I went to lie down on the sofa in the family room. That is where I was in the morning when the light came in through the gap between the drapes and the patter of the children's feet upstairs told me they were up.

Ross appeared, freshly shaved, in his jeans and sweatshirt, looking ready for an ordinary Saturday. "Until we know what else to do I'm going to take the boys to their soccer practice." And then as if indulging me he added, "If we get going right away I can take the kids for bagels on the way and you can forget about breakfast."

"Take the little ones with you too. They can watch the practice, but keep an eye on them." What I really wanted to say was, "Don't let any of them disappear. One is already more than I can bear."

As soon as I heard the car pull out of the drive, I went to the phone. I whispered the number to myself as my fingers sought out the familiar pattern on the phone. A cheery voice answered, "Parish Office."

I heard my own controlled voice say "This is Maggie Barnes, I have a serious family emergency, and I need to speak with Father Thomas as soon as possible."

The voice responded, "Let me take your number, and I'll have him call you."

Thomas did not call back. Instead he appeared at the side door. I heard the knock, thinking it might be police. When I opened the door Thomas stepped inside, and I began to weep. Not the silent trickling tears I had been holding back so that I would not upset our children or appear weak to Ross. I sobbed out my worst fears, the ugliest ones. I told him all the terrible images that were ravaging my mind. He held me.

Thomas was still there and Ross had not come back yet when Detective Moore stopped by. They greeted each other and shook hands. I wondered if they knew each other. They seemed to recognize each other. The detective informed us they had put out a missing person's alert, and he warned me that as information about the missing girls became public we might get phone calls or reporters coming to the door. "You don't have to be polite," he said. "Keep the other children inside and don't answer the door." With his coaching done Detective Moore left.

I made coffee for Thomas, and we went to the table in the kitchen. I sat at the end, and he sat near me along the side and held my hand. "Your hand's cold," he said.

"Please don't leave me," I said. "I am so terrified. I can't be alone right now."

"I'm here," he said.

"Do you think God knows where Laura is?" I asked him.

"Yes," he said. "The problem is that right now we don't know where she is, and that's frightening." A tear ran down my cheek, and he wiped it away gently. He stroked the top of my hand. I noticed he had new lines around his eyes. They were not laugh lines. And I wondered if he still had a bowed scar on the side of his chest. There wasn't much to say. But he was there.

When Ross returned with the children Thomas was still there. He explained to Ross that the parish office has a police radio, and when he heard that one of our children was missing he came over to see if there was anything he could do. He offered to recruit women from the parish to watch our other children if Ross and I needed to leave the house for anything. Ross thanked him and said it wasn't necessary. Then Thomas excused himself and left. At the door he paused once more to say, "If there's anything, please call." As he spoke he looked at Ross, but I knew his offer was to me.

I made spaghetti and meatballs for dinner because the children would eat that without complaining. I didn't bother with vegetables. After dinner the kids watched TV while I cleaned up the kitchen. Then I organized the bath routine and made sure they brushed their teeth. After baths Ross played chess with the big boys, and I took our two youngest up to tuck them in. I put lotion on Steven's elbows and knees to calm his eczema. Just before I said their prayers with them, Jenna asked about her big sister. "Mommy, where is Laura?" She put the emphasis on "is" as if she knew that no one was telling her about something very important.

"We don't know exactly," I said, "but we hope she'll come home soon."

The big boys didn't ask. They already understood something was dreadfully wrong and had figured out how to keep an eye on us while also staying out of our way. Little Steven didn't ask questions, but he sucked his thumb more than usual, and he wanted all the Little People from his Fisher Price School Bus in his bed.

I dreaded the night. My images of a little body in the woods, or two little girls blind-folded in a basement were torturing me. The stream of my imagination was brutal. I wondered if other parents who lose children fear insanity. Around 9:30 Detective Moore appeared again. He wanted to update us about the investigation. They had found Laura's backpack in a trashcan near the bus station. The detectives had sealed the backpack in a transparent bag, and they wanted us to identify it, but we couldn't touch it because it was evidence.

The detective left, and Ross went to bed. The thought that he might be sleeping enraged me. The thought that he might not be sleeping and was beginning to worry also frightened me. So I stayed away from him. Close to midnight I called Thomas. I told him that I wanted to update him about what was going on. He told me that a prayer guild from the parish was keeping a vigil. Someone was awake and praying continuously, reciting the rosary and offering prayers for those missing. I thanked him.

Instead of saying "good-bye" he said, "Maggie, would it help you to take a walk?"

When he arrived I was ready at the door and did not wake Ross. I assumed that if the phone next to my side of the bed rang long enough Ross would answer it. It occurred to me that he might not be sleeping and would question why Thomas had come again. But in an instant I knew that if he asked I would say, "I called him because you weren't there, and I couldn't stand to be alone with this terror." It felt good to walk, but it was hard to be away from the house. In the dark we circled the blocks close to home, passing our corner time after time. With each pass I peered down the street to check if a police car had pulled up at our house. We spoke little. I'm not sure how long we walked, but I was the one who finally said, "I think I should go back in now."

When we turned back into our street and stopped in front of the house, Thomas said, "Call if you need to. And, Maggie, I . . . " and then as if he could not find the word or did not dare to say it, he put his hand against his heart. "You know what I mean?"

"Yes," I said.

He watched me go into the house where everyone was sleeping, the house where there was an empty bed in the girls' room. I went to the front window and watched Thomas walking up the street. He had left his car around the corner in the parking lot at the school. I wanted to run after him and call him back. I wanted to beg him, "Please don't go! I can't be alone. Please stay!" But I knew that was impossible. In the stillness of the night I heart a car start, then fade away, and I collapsed onto the sofa.

I don't know how long I stared at the shadows on the ceiling, worrying about what we would do if another night passed and this went on until Monday, a third day. Would the children go to school? Would Ross go to work? Would I get groceries? Would I do laundry? It all seemed so unimportant now. Only Laura seemed important. What if this stretched out to ten days. A hundred days? What if Laura never came home again? Would we survive?

On Monday at 9:30 in the evening the phone rang and Detective Moore's voice announced in a very matter of fact way, "We've located the girls."

"Where are they?" I said. "We're on our way."

"No, that's not the procedure," he explained. "The girls need to be checked over by a doctor, and the investigators have to interview them."

"I need to see Laura for just a few minutes," I pleaded. "Please, I need to know she's okay."

"They're safe. We'll make sure they have everything they need."

Ross, who was listening from across the room, picked up that I was headed into a standoff with Detective Moore, so he walked toward me and took the phone from my hand. There were long silences as the detective filled Ross in. Mostly I heard, "uh-huh" and "yeah" and "okay." Finally Ross hung up, and as he walked toward the stairs, without looking back, he said, "Don't make things more complicated than they are, Maggie. This is enough for a day."

It wasn't all over when Laura returned. She was sheepish, like a kid who'd done something wrong. When I took her in my arms, in a high whining voice she said, "Mommy are you mad at me?"

"I'm not mad at you. Not at all. Oh, Laura, my precious Laura, all that matters to me is that you're safe and you're home with us again."

And then she said the oddest thing. "Well you knew, Mommy, that I would come home, didn't you? You should know I would never just go away and not come back. I'm your daughter." Even at that young age Laura could mobilize an air of confidence that said she knew exactly what she meant and that she was entirely right.

Detective Moore filled in the story. How the girls got off the bus on Friday, and Jenny's dad was there. He was surprised to see Laura, and told both girls to get in the car. They drove most of the way to Minneapolis before he picked up pizza and checked into a motel for the night. He promised them a special day on Saturday. In the morning they got their nails done and both had their hair cut in a Toni Tennille style, which worked well with Jenny's hair but not at all with Laura's curls. In the afternoon they went to the movies, and in the evening they went roller-skating.

On Sunday after breakfast George took the girls to the mall. He told them he had a job to do, but if they shopped and picked out what they liked, he'd buy it for them when he came back to pick them up. He gave them lunch money, and the girls wandered the mall. By evening they were still lingering, and mall security called the police.

It is harder than you might think to return a family to normal. It's not like TV when the drama resolves, the distress evaporates, and everyone lives happily ever after. Sometimes Laura would make an offhand comment about Jenny or George and all my fears of what might have happened to

Laura would come flooding back. She said one time that Jenny's dad had an icky mouth. Before I could stop myself I heard my own panicked voice asking her what he'd done to her. "Nothing, Mom," she said. "Not to me. He had these little packages he'd put in his mouth and sometimes he spit brown juice on the sidewalk. It was really gross. In the hotel he spit in the sink. He didn't give any of it to us, but I'd be really embarrassed if my Dad did that."

I prodded Laura sometimes to tell me about the hotel room. How many beds were there? Where did they sleep? She told me once, possibly because she wanted to give me something for the effort I was putting into interrogating her, that she saw "George's butt." That was the term she used. "What do you mean," I said. "Did he show it to you?"

"Not exactly," said Laura. "When he took a shower he told us that, no matter what, we shouldn't answer the door if someone knocked. I guess he wanted to listen to make sure we didn't because he left the door open a little. Just before he stepped into the shower I saw his butt. This is the embarrassing part, Mom, his butt what sort of hairy."

I tried to talk to Ross about my concerns, but he didn't want to hear it. "If you don't stop suggesting all the terrible things that you think happened to Laura, you're going to give her ideas, and before you know it she'll believe that those things happened. For heavens sakes, Maggie, let it go now. Let life go back to normal." I could tell Ross was angry. Maybe scared too, but his anger kept his fear locked up, and there was no way he was going to talk with me about it.

I called Thomas and talked to him about my anger toward Ross. He listened. He didn't blame Ross, and he didn't blame me. Finally he said what I suspect he'd been trained to say: "Keep the door open, Maggie. If Laura has something she needs to tell you she will. She knows that you care about her. For now maybe that's enough. Later if there's more she'll let you know." I didn't like his tone of voice. It was so professional. I think he cared about me, but I wondered if for him Laura was just another little girl in his parish, and at that moment I was just another fretting mother.

What Thomas said slowed down my pursuit of the truth by questioning Laura, but I was still angry with Ross. I can't say when life returned to normal again. It was not that all those disturbances that entered my life on the day Laura went missing went away again. I was more protective of my children, and more deeply moved by other people's losses. But I also got used to these changes in myself, the way one gets used to a scar. You know what it's from, and you try to ignore it, but now and then something bumps it, and you're reminded that, despite its thickness, it is more tender than undamaged skin.

Twice Thomas came over and spent an afternoon with me while Ross was away and the children were at school. Our time together was tender, but so much had changed. His presence surfaced my fear and my troubled memories. He was kind and loving, but he was also reserved. And he was clear that we could not create a secret relationship that threatened my marriage. I tried to argue with him that Ross's coldness threatened out marriage. "That may be true," he said, "but if I step in and try to make up for that chill I will be violating your vow. I'm sorry, Maggie, I can't do it."

We created distance. It wasn't distance I wanted, and I don't know if he wanted it or not. The distance became a fact. Sometimes when I walked the dog, I retraced the silent walk with Thomas through the neighborhood, and I tried to bring back the feeling that with him next to me I felt cared for. I tried to comfort myself by remembering the feeling of my hand in his. From time to time I had the urge to dial his number and hear his voice. On a particularly troubled day the thought flashed through my mind that sometime the number might be changed and this sequence of seven digits I was hanging onto for dear life might mean nothing. What if I was putting my faith in something that didn't exist? What if Thomas wasn't really there for me because there was no room for him, and I was drawing comfort from a fiction?

This was another half story I shared with Tee. I told her about those nightmarish days when Laura went missing. Even in the telling of it I could feel the panic again. Telling about the sight of Laura coming up the walk with Detective Moore when she returned home, was enough to stir up in me all over again those deep feelings of love for Laura that began when she was an infant, and I sat with her on the balcony in Geneva. These were the things I could tell Tee, but I could not tell Tee about Thomas, and I was very selective in talking to Tee about Ross.

Chapter 5

# TEE AND THE CAT MAN

Within weeks of the time Tee came to help me, we settled into a pattern that was different than first planned. My wrist healed, and I didn't need a nurse anymore. Instead Tee prepared meals. Sometimes I went with her to the farmer's market, and we browsed the stalls together. I could have done all of this for myself, but I was tired of food. I was tired from all the years of being the family shopper and the family chef. What Ross had called "chief cook and bottle-washer."

I looked forward to Tuesdays when Tee made quiche or spinach pie. It delighted me that before we sat down to the soup she prepared on Friday, the fragrance of the corn bread she made to go with it already filled the house. I liked being cooked for, and I enjoyed having someone with whom to eat dinner.

On Mondays, when I began meeting with my regular bridge group again, Tee got groceries and let herself in early to cook so that when I came home the condo was fragrant with pot roast or meat loaf. There was always enough so Tee could bring some upstairs to Alethea, my very dear friend, and she could take it along to the nursing home when she visited her husband, Mark. That way the two of them could have a home-cooked meal together.

Often while Tee cooked, I sat at the table in the kitchen and chatted with her. It was on one of those evenings that I told her about the time Laura went missing. Tee understood that things don't settle down immediately after something disturbing happens. Her own life had miserable times. She knew what it's like when adults pretend everything's okay even when it isn't, because they think they can spare children. In her own life she had been the child spectator to adult misery.

Tee asked if charges were brought against Jenny's dad, and I explained that it never came to that because within a few days after the girls returned, police in Kansas found George in a hotel room where he left a suicide note and ended his life. We told Laura that Jenny's dad died, but we didn't tell her how he died. We also didn't tell her about his note that said he could not live without his daughter, and he hoped she would always remember the good time they had together the last time she saw him.

Tee was puzzled by this turn of events. "Obviously he didn't understand, did he? Maggie, do you think some parents believe kids are that simple-minded?"

"Lots of adults under-estimate children, even though we've all been kids ourselves once upon a time," I replied. It occurred to me that Tee was probably one of those children who had never been simple-minded.

"That's it you think?" Tee asked. "He just made a bad guess? Doesn't get kids?"

"George was probably frantic about losing his daughter," I told her. There was something in me that needed to defend him. "I understand how hard it is to think straight when you're anguished over the loss of a child. I've been through that part of it myself. George wanted Jenny to remember him as a good dad, and he didn't have many options. When Laura showed up unexpectedly his plan went out of control, and then so did he."

"Couldn't he have come up with a better plan? After all he kidnapped Laura. You suffered a lot. He must have known that he was doing something risky. If he'd been thinking straight he would have known he would go to prison for what he did. Unless he knew right from the start that he would end his life." Tee paused a moment to think. "Besides, couldn't he have called home rather than drop two young girls off at a mall far from where they lived?"

"That's all true," I told Tee, "but I'm not persuaded that he meant to harm them."

"If he hadn't died would you have pressed charges?"

"I don't know what we would have done. I'm glad we never had to face that. Honestly, I feel sort of sorry for him."

"You're cutting him a lot more slack than I would," said Tee. "Shouldn't you step up and say that what he did was unforgiveable? I don't know how you got through it. Didn't you feel like you were going crazy while she was gone?"

"I did feel crazy," I told Tee. But I couldn't tell her how I got through it. I couldn't tell her about Thomas. Even after all the years that had passed, memories of Thomas surfaced with a little jolt of alarm or a slight shortness of breath. It takes a clever feint to direct attention away from the piece that doesn't fit the puzzle.

One night late Tee used my key to let herself into my apartment. It was after midnight, and when I heard the key in the lock it startled me. Through the dark of the entryway I saw her silently tiptoeing across to the kitchen, and I called out to her.

"Tee? Tee is that you?"

"I'm sorry. I didn't want to wake you up. Maggie, really, I'm so sorry."

I got up. Put on my robe and slippers, found my glasses and went out to the kitchen. But she was not in the kitchen. She had gone to the living room where she was sitting tight in the corner of the sofa. One hand on the arm of the sofa and one resting just above her knee, as if she were in the back seat of a car with a reckless driver, and she was holding on for dear life.

Before I could speak she was apologizing again. At first I thought she was afraid I'd be angry with her for waking me up at this hour. Or maybe she thought I'd not trust why she was using my keys to come into my apartment in the night. I tried to assure her that I wasn't upset, but when I got close enough to see her face, I could tell that she was terribly frightened. It wasn't embarrassment, and it wasn't fear of me. It was something else. She was shaken.

Tee explained she'd been at the bar with her friend Cicely. She goes to that bar sometimes because it's near campus. Almost any evening, even if she arrives by herself, there are people she knows and she joins them at their table, so she's never alone at the bar. She spent the evening playing cards at a table in the corner, and after Cicely left with her boyfriend, Tee stayed a little longer. The problem was that she had to walk home alone, and that made her uneasy.

Tee thought it out carefully, mapping the way she would walk, even though it wasn't the shortest way or the way she would've walked during the day. First she walked down the street from the bar to the campus. There she cut across the campus quad, intending to exit onto Prospect Street, and from there it was just a few blocks to her apartment.

As Tee spoke I could see her retracing the course in her mind, nodding her head slightly where she indicated she would turn the corner, leaning forward a bit as she described walking across the campus. On the other side of the campus she planned to walk down Prospect Street because it was along the row of fraternity and sorority houses. There was almost always activity there, even late at night, and when the weather was good the students hung out on the porches.

Her plan didn't work. Just before walking out of the gates on the other side of the campus a man stepped out of the shadows. "Headed home?" he asked. She recognized him immediately. He was known around campus as the Cat Man, and women were afraid of him. So instead of walking out of the gates and off the campus, Tee turned and walked back into the campus, hoping to see one of the security guards who walk the campus at night, or if all else failed using one of the blue emergency phones.

Tee knew she was in trouble when footsteps told her that the Cat Man was following her. She walked more quickly, and broke into a jog. He did too, and then he was beside her. When he said, "Where are you going," Tee replied, "Get lost," but he didn't. He stayed at her side and then put a hand on her arm above her elbow, gripping firmly. He was holding her far more firmly than was comfortable.

"I'm going with you," he said. He smelled of booze and bumped against her as they walked. She said nothing, but he made comments to the effect that he thought she was attractive. And then as if he thought she wasn't understanding his intent, his language became more explicit, more obscene.

Tee seemed embarrassed as she recounted this. "He said he thought I'm hot and what he'd like to do to me. I can't repeat that to you, Maggie," she said

As they walked farther into the campus Tee watched for a way to escape him. She was afraid of what would happen if she reached the gates on the other side of the quad and headed out into the street with him. Near the library she saw her chance. One of the guys, who students call "the uniforms," was coming out of the side door of the library. He had an oversized flashlight in his hand and a walkie-talkie on his belt. Tee turned quickly, wrenched her arm free, and ran toward the security guard. As she did her stalker ran around the corner of the library and disappeared.

"Why do you call him the Cat Man?"

"Because he's a creep, and he hangs around like a Tom Cat. I don't know who started that, but that's what the girls in our apartment building call him." Tee had seen him numerous times before. When she moved into the apartment with Cicely, the girls in the unit upstairs were partiers. On at least one occasion that Tee could remember the Cat Man had been there. After everyone left a party he lingered, and when the girls hinted that it was getting really late, he got aggressive and said he wasn't leaving until he was ready. They were frightened and barricaded themselves in one of the bedrooms from which Juliette called her brother and asked him to come over with a few of his buddies. When they arrived the Cat Man was gone, but he had succeeded in intimidating the women living in both apartments.

Because the Cat Man knew where Tee lived, she came to my apartment instead of going home, and the security guard from campus walked her over. She didn't know if the Cat Man had been at the bar earlier in the evening because she was with friends and hadn't paid attention. Whether he'd seen her leave the bar alone or noticed her walking down the street alone was not clear. In any case, the moment she saw him she knew it didn't feel right, and she was afraid.

"You did the right thing," I told her. "It wouldn't make sense to go back to your apartment if you're not safe there." We talked a little longer and then I said, "Just stay here tonight. You can have the guest room. Take some sheets and towels up with you. They're in the closet in the hallway."

Tee made a telephone call before she went to sleep because I could hear her voice, but I couldn't hear what she was saying. In the morning she left to go to class. I assumed she'd be safe in daylight and on campus

When Tee returned on Friday I asked her if she was okay. She told me that she'd called Cicely to check if she'd be staying home instead of at her boyfriend's apartment, and Tee added to the story she'd told me a few nights before. Cicely used to live in the upstairs unit before she moved to the lower level to share that apartment with Tee. Part of the reason Cicely wanted to move was that she'd had enough of the parties. The girls who lived in the upper apartment had a reputation for attracting "bad boys." These guys would show up at the apartment with booze and drugs, and the girls, including Cicely, had a hard time saying "no."

When Cicely and Tee moved in together they agreed they did not want strangers hanging out at their apartment. No parties. No drugs. No guys hanging around in their living room watching TV at all hours. Then Cicely started dating a nice guy who had a place of his own where they spent most of their time together, and that meant Tee was home alone at their apartment more often.

A few weeks later Tee came to my apartment at around 10:30. This time she knocked at the door and did not let herself in. She explained that she didn't want me to think she took for granted that she could drop in whenever she wanted. Again something had happened, and again she didn't feel safe. When Tee returned to her apartment in the evening after her Tuesday class she could see that someone had been hanging out on the front porch and stayed long enough to smoke quite a few cigarettes. The ashes were still on the steps, and on the wood of the porch with the char of a cigarette butt someone had scrawled, "Bitch."

Now two days later when Tee was heading home again, she saw the Cat Man sitting on her front steps. Not knowing what else to do she went to the frat house at the end of the block where there were guys sitting on the porch. By the time she'd explained to them about the stalker on her own front porch, she saw him walk a few doors down the street, get in a car, and drive away. Tee did not dare to go home and came to my condo.

We talked about what Tee could do. I suggested that she speak with the campus police, but she didn't think they would do anything. The Cat Man had come to parties and hung out at their apartment on other occasions. He wasn't exactly a stranger, which would probably be a reason police would dismiss his aggression as a misunderstanding. These things happened around the campus.

" Stay here 'til things cool down," I said. "Give this time to go away."

" I feel bad about staying. What will your kids say?"

"I don't need my children's permission. This is my home. Besides, they'd understand."

That's how it happened that Cicely moved in with her boyfriend, and Tee moved in with me. I hadn't realized how terrorized Tee was until after she began to tell me more about it. She didn't feel she could move around freely anymore. On campus she noticed where the blue light phones were and felt as if she was walking from one to the next trying to keep herself safe. Off campus she was on constant alert. Once she noticed a car approaching from the other direction, and it was moving slowly. As it got closer she could feel her heart pounding, despite the fact that they were in broad daylight. The car passed, and she felt foolish because it was a couple and in the back seat was a child in a car seat.

There wasn't much I needed help with anymore, but I enjoyed having Tee in my home. Our lives were quite separate. She had school and her friends. I had my circle of dear old friends, the ones who were like sisters to me, and over time I returned to many of the activities I had enjoyed before. Tee cooked for me and occasionally did a few errands. She was the one who brought up the matter of my expectations for how long she could stay. "I don't want you to think I'm a squatter," she said. "I know I need to get a place of my own again." I assured her she was welcome to stay as long as she needed. It flashed through my mind that I might be the one to move out before she did. That's how older people think. We try not to make promises that overshoot our life expectancy

# Chapter 6

# JENNA

Tee first met my daughter Jenna at my apartment, when she stopped by to bring a loaf of seven-grain bread. She regularly baked bread for her family, and sometimes made a tiny loaf for me. This time Jenna arrived with the small loaf wrapped in a cotton kitchen towel, and she set the bread out on the counter because it was still warm. I appreciated the bread, but I also knew that the reason for Jenna's visit was to meet my new nurse.

Jenna sat at the table in the kitchen and chatted while Tee put away groceries. When I was young we called this kind of conversation "gabbing." It was mostly a cheery review of stories about Jenna's children. Philip had come to dinner the night before with a kitten in each pocket, and Jenna didn't even know there was a new batch of kittens in the barn until they heard something mewing under the dining table. Interspersed with her stories Jenna asked Tee questions; however, when Jenna asked about family, Tee turned the question aside with, "Oh, that's a long story."

For most people that would signal it was an awkward question, but Jenna was unembarrassed and wanted to know about Tee's family, so she suggested a rain check. "Well, I'd like to hear about your family another time maybe." Jenna was curious about people and could find ordinary things interesting. By the end of her conversation with Tee, she'd discovered that Tee had two cats during her childhood, each at different times. The one cat never had a name. They just called it "cat." The other cat they called "Mr. Simpson" after a neighbor who, like the cat, had whiskers that grew sideways from his nose. In addition to the cats Tee had a canary. Jenna didn't ask what happened to it.

This is the way Jenna filled in her picture of people, beginning with the ordinary details and moving on to more substantial matters, such as the fact that Tee did not have a boyfriend and was not busy on Saturday. The next obvious step after that was an invitation for Tee to come to the barn dance that Jenna and her husband, Jak, were planning for the weekend.

When Jenna socialized with someone outside our family, she was warm and engaging. People were naturally drawn to her. Inside our family, by contrast, she often seemed to disappear as she blended in with the others. The pack of our five children had within it two small clusters. The only time we were all together was at the dinner table or in the station wagon. For the rest we were usually in groups, and for those groups we had names. They were "the big kids" and "the little kids." I don't know who invented those names, but everyone in the family used them.

The little kids were Jenna and Steven, the ones born after a gap of more than five years when Ross and I decided there was room in our family for another child, and then later decided that adding one more would be nice for Jenna so she'd have a sibling close to her in age. Our children could also be sorted by their house of birth. Laura, Will, and Row were born in our first house, the little one on Whitney Avenue. Jenna and Steven were born after we bought the old Tudor house on Woodward Street when we needed room for our expanding family.

Groups of children walk in conga lines, one after the other. Somewhere in the past of the species there may have been good reason for it. Bigger ones know where they're going, and little ones at the back of the pack understand that all they have to do is keep up. In our row of children Jenna obediently followed after Laura, then Will, and then Row. She scrambled to get in line with them as soon as she could walk. When the line stretched out too much, Row slowed down just a little to let Jenna catch up, but not so much that he fell out of line with the others. Linked in this way Jenna never got lost.

Later when Steven was added to the line, Jenna did this for him in turn, but just as often Steven broke out of the line and went his own way. Not Jenna. Ross sometimes called her our "tag-along" because she was always with someone, never alone. Considering the age at which our children settled into their conga line, it hardly qualifies as loyalty. They bickered and fought like all kids do. I suspect what held the line together was something more like magnetism. On some primitive level there was an energy that held them together.

Even in our picture albums Jenna is always with someone. There are many pictures of Laura alone because we carefully documented the accomplishments of our firstborn. She was the pioneer, the trend-setter. Laura standing at the coffee table. Laura eating with a spoon. Laura's feet in her first pair of sandals. Laura at the nursery school entrance with her first backpack proudly in place. Of the others too there are pictures to document events. Not as many as of Laura, but there are some for each of the twins. Will with a soccer ball. Row riding a bike with training wheels. Will captured mid-air jumping off the diving board. The long smooth image of Row swimming under water.

In the same albums there are no pictures of Jenna alone. Someone else is always in the frame with her. On her first Halloween Jenna the lamb stands next to Laura the princess. On her third birthday she is sitting on Ross's lap eating birthday cake. There is one of Jenna with a huge smile, and she is wearing a Camp Fire uniform; Will with a smart-ass look on his face is behind her making a hand gesture that is a two-fingered "Loser" and definitely not a three fingered "I Love You." The only solo photos of Jenna are the generic yearly school portraits with the non-descript backdrop.

My favorite picture of Jenna was taken at church when she was in cherub choir. She is dressed in the same choir robe as all the other cherubs, a shapeless purple robe with an over-sized white color. It was the Sunday the choir sang about being a sunbeam for Jesus. Unlike the little boy who was not singing at all and straining to see his mother, unlike the little girl who was pulling up her robe and then letting it billow down, Jenna was completely on task. She knew the words because she'd been singing them all week at home, and she was not distracted by the adults who chuckled at the other children's antics. Jenna was singing from the bottom of her heart, and of all the little sunbeams that day, none shone quite as brightly as Jenna.

This is the story of Jenna, the little sister of the clan, until she was twenty and met Jak. His real name is Michael, but his nickname came from his last name, which is Jakubowski. The name Michael didn't fit him, but the name Jak definitely did. And what fit him even better was what his father called him: Jakski.

Within days of meeting Jak, Jenna shifted from keeping Row in sight so she'd know where she was going, to keeping Jak in sight to lead the way.

His friends became her friends. The things he liked to do defined their time together. She would sit on the shore and watch him waterski while his friends pulled him behind the boat. I don't know if she ever got up on skis herself. It didn't seem to matter to her, and it's possible she never tried. What was clear is that Jenna became Jak's sunshine. She made his life warm, and he made her life dramatic.

Jenna battled us for permission to go with Jak on spring break, but it was Jak who decided. Soon after Jenna walked down the aisle on Ross's arm where Jak was waiting for her at the front of the church. She was a radiant bride and the first of our children to marry. There was a debate with Jak about the wedding invitations. Would Jenna be marrying Michael Aleksander Jakubowski or Jak Jakubowski? He won. In his good humored style he didn't gloat, instead he assured us that at least the people attending the wedding would always get the spelling right for both his first and his last name. We all accepted that Jak was one of a kind.

Our resistance to Jenna marrying Jak was not that we didn't like him. We thought she was too young and that she should do some things for herself first. As Ross liked to say, "She needs a chance to try her own wings." But she wouldn't be lured out into the big world by the promise of adventure. She wanted to stay close to home, which by the time she was twenty meant close to Jak.

After Jak graduated from college and got his first job teaching and coaching, they had their first baby. From then on pictures of Jenna are with a baby on her hip. Or with one at her side and one in arms. Or with three smiling little faces framing hers. And then finally there were four. Jenna's warmth and sweetness was the orbit for her children. She baked bread and put in a garden with them. They picked cherries and canned applesauce. They made costumes at Halloween, gingerbread houses at Christmas, and invited neighbors for Easter egg hunts in the spring. Their birthday cakes, which were Jenna's inventions, were legend.

Jenna's housekeeping was casual because there were always more important things than keeping order. I still recall coming through the backdoor and being warned by Jenna "don't step on the knife." It was the largest kitchen knife left on the floor next to some odd-shaped bits of sponge after Philip used the knife to carve off the excess from a pair of his dad's flip-flops so that Philip could wear them himself. This easy-going style might suggest a hazardous household or neglected children, but it never went that far. In the relaxed chaos at Jenna's house the good and nourishing offerings were always primary, so it felt lived in. Everywhere you looked were traces left by real people, and theirs was a household with plenty of love. The children had everything a child could wish for as part of a happy family, unless you stoop to measuring happiness by matched socks or regular haircuts. But this didn't matter to their children, and it didn't matter to Jak and Jenna. They were well matched for each other.

I couldn't have been the kind of mother Jenna was because I needed at least some order and predictability, but I would have liked to be a kid in a household like hers. There was freedom and play, and never the looming expectation that every good time ended with clean up and a mother hovering over to make sure it was done right. Even at my age I felt light-hearted around Jenna's family.

Jak had his own style of creating a homestead for the family. He spent an entire weekend building a swing set for the children, and soon they were playing on it even though it wasn't finished. The slide never got installed and remained propped against the wall in the garage, but no one seemed to mind. The children didn't beg their dad to finish the slide because, by the time they began to lose interest in the swings, Jak was already hauling home the trampoline that he set up in the back yard. And after that there was the aboveground pool.

It was fitting that Jak and Jenna lived on a farm. They didn't grow crops or raise animals; they gardened and hosted critters. They needed the barn and the space around it to expand. At first the outbuildings collected tools and materials for unfinished projects. Overtime things like outgrown tricycles and odds and ends hauled home from garage sales were kept there too, because they might be useful some day. Next to the garage Jak parked an old car that had no tires, but was a marvelous prop for children's play. The clutter grew, and by the time the children hit their stride as masters of their own inventions, the barn was a treasure trove. Jenna and Jak's children were as creative as any I have ever known.

As Jenna matured she did not grow separate from Jak. People were her life, and she was skilled at assembling circles of people around her family with Jak as the hub. They had lots of parties, which is what they called the spontaneous gatherings of friends who for any reason could collect at their house. The work of the party was Jenna's. The life of the party was Jak. And she was the one who carried on the continuing diplomacy of maintaining friendships as Jak danced on.

The social team of Jak and Jenna created big events at their home. These were not the spontaneous ones, but rather the ones planned for months in advance. Being on their guest list was valued. Ask any kid in the school district. Adults too wanted to be invited, but if by chance someone's name was not on the guest list, the welcome mat was always out and anyone could be included. Jak and Jenna were fun.

Usually the party began with a variety of entertaining activities so that as soon as the cars pulled into the driveway and the doors opened, the children hit the ground running and were happily occupied with fun of their own, supervised by the young guys from Jak's soccer team. Meanwhile adults sauntered off to something that caught their interest. Some would go to the barn to play pool. Others would play croquet with an old set Jenna picked up at a garage sale.

Those who were better listeners than talkers would gather on the patio where Jak regaled a small group circled around him with stories. At one party Jak had only half a head of hair. The other half had been sheared off by the soccer team as a reward for winning the previous week's game. And within no time at all Jak had his guests voting on three options: should he shave his head completely, grow his hair back, or keep what he called "the half shorn look?"

Later, when everyone was well fed and at ease, the party would shift into a mood that could go long into the night around the fire pit. Jak would tell more stories or get out his guitar and sing a new song he had written. Usually it was a song that would make someone at the party either drop a few sentimental tears or blush with pride. A song for a new baby or for the neighbors whose boy had gone off to the army. Jak knew his audience, and the audience loved Jak.

When the group was right and the evening had been smoothed out with enough but not too many drinks, the guests would sing along with Jak. He knew how to warm them up with the theme songs from old TV shows. The Brady Bunch was a favorite. Then he might go on to old Beatles songs for which nearly everyone knew the words.

Sometimes I got caught up myself in the energy of Jak and Jenna's parties. I did karaoke and danced freely in the flickering light around their outdoor fires. At their Halloween parties I was not shy about my costumes.

My best was an angel; my worst was Marie Antoinette because I hadn't predicted how uncomfortable an over-sized wig could be. Perhaps most striking was my ability to ignore Ross on those occasions, because I didn't care if he thought I was getting a little out of hand. I liked getting a little out of hand, and I trusted that my children could accept it. It delighted me that they even encouraged it. Ross had his own way of enjoying the event, which was to find a comfortable chair from which to watch as he sipped his pre-defined ration of scotch. He was proud of Jenna and adored her free spirit, and I wondered sometimes if she was compensation for the loss he suffered because his own free spirit was locked away.

I wasn't surprised that the first time Jenna met Tee she invited her into their circle. By the time they finished detailing time and directions it was also clear that Tee would need a ride because she didn't have a car, and that she could catch a ride with Melissa who would be coming with her boyfriend to the barn dance at Jak and Jenna's farm. Melissa was the teacher aid in the classroom where Jenna was a parent volunteer one afternoon every other week.

On that day when Tee and Jenna first met, I listened from my chair in the living room. As far as far as they knew I was resting a little and reading. I admired how Jenna could begin with a complete stranger and within the space of an hour blend her into their life at the farm. Later when Tee mentioned to me that she was uncomfortable barging into my family, I assured her it wasn't a problem.

It was not the last party at Jenna's house to which Tee was invited, nor the last time she had dinner there. When Jak and Jenna went to away games with the soccer team Tee stayed overnight at the farm with the kids. She became part of what Jenna referred to as her "extended family." Soon for any occasion on which I was invited to the farm, Tee was also included.

## Chapter 7

# STEVEN'S GHOSTS

Once Tee met Jenna I knew it would not be long before she would know about Steven. My youngest. The son about whom I did not speak when sharing the news of the day or letting Tee know of up-coming family plans. Steven was the absent son.

There are shelves in the bookcase in the den where I keep family pictures. Some of the pictures are recent ones of the grandchildren. And among the older pictures, the black and whites with lacy edges, it's easy to distinguish Laura, Will, Row, and Jenna. Of course their faces changed as they grew up, but not so much that it is difficult to tell them apart. There are also pictures of another boy there. They are pictures of Steven. What distinguishes his pictures from the others is the point at which his pictures stop.

On one shelf there is a photo of my four adult children arranged around me, as families do when on a special occasion someone thinks it would be a good idea to take a group picture. We still do that from time to time when someone says, "We should get a picture while we're all here." But unlike in other families, we do not add the second sentence. We do not say, "There's no knowing when we'll all be together again." A statement like that would carry too much weight in our family. The picture on the shelf was taken on the day of Ross's funeral. Steven is not in it.

There is one other picture on the shelf. It is the most recent I have of Steven. He is sitting in a boat with a fishing pole balanced across his knees. He is wearing shorts, his knees are tanned, and the soft covering of hair on his legs is bleached summer gold. In the picture I can see the hands that loved to draw. His left forearm does not have the tattoo and needle marks that later branded it. His t-shirt is faded and the neckband is worn. As usual he's wearing a baseball cap, and I suspect the photo was taken by someone standing slightly above him on the dock because Steven is looking up, enough so that the sun shines full on his face. When I think of him now, this is how I try to remember him.

The day Tee looked at the picture on the shelf in the den she was direct. "I guess this is Steven then" she said.

I acknowledged that it was, and then tried to explain myself, tried to explain my silence about him. " I'm sure Jenna has told you about Steven."

"She has . . . some."

"Lots of people know the story. It isn't that we hide it."

"I know. I understand. Jenna showed me clippings from the paper . . . and well . . . I googled him and read online what happened to him."

I wanted to make excuses for my silence. It's not that I think I can keep secrets about Steven. It's something else. As soon as I start to talk about Steven there is an angry voice inside that contradicts me no matter what I say. That reprimanding voice inside says, "That's not it. What's wrong with you, Maggie? That's not Steven at all." My story of Steven is fractured, and I never know with which shard to begin. In my memory it feels as if Steven has been parceled into three different people. That's the way I said it to Tee. "I have three different Stevens, and they don't fit together."

The first Steven is the one to which I'm able to go back now and then and still smile. He's the baby born on Woodward Street, the little brother born to follow Jenna in the family queue, the baby brother with eczema on his elbows and knees. From the very beginning he was an infant who left no doubt about what kind of day he was having. Some were easy. After he was born I got out the Snugly, and because it was worn and faded, I decided to buy a new one. I needed a way to carry Steven without hands because by that time I was dealing with five children and was always several hands short.

There were days that Steven could bounce around the entire day in the Snugly. Sleeping there for a while, sometimes for hours at a time. Only coming out long enough to feed or have a diaper change. At one visit the pediatrician asked me about Steven and the Snugly, warning me to give him time to roll around on the floor or in his crib to develop his postural muscles. So I'd take Steven out of the Snugly and put him on the floor for what I felt was necessary time, but both he and I seemed most at ease when he was back in the Snugly again.

Then there were those other days. Ross and I referred to them as Steven's "red-faced" days. I dreaded them. Steven could not get comfortable. He tightened up in a squirm of protest. He'd cry until his face turned bright red, and even when he wasn't crying he was cranking out complaints. We didn't know what was troubling him, and we didn't know what to do to soothe him.

I tried to get help for Steven, but the pediatrician didn't see it as a serious problem. The key word the doctor used to distinguish a routine from a worrisome complaint was "intermittent." Because Steven's distress was intermittent, it wasn't of concern to anyone but us. It was not connected to feeding, fever, constipation, or any of the other things that to the pediatrician would have indicated something was wrong. The medicine Steven's doctor offered was time. "Give him time. He'll outgrow it."

Before Steven was born I still worked one day a week at the library just to keep my foot in the door. I needed adult company, some hours out of the house and away from kids. To handle Steven, I had to give that up entirely. No one else seemed to think of that as a sacrifice. Ross's income was sufficient, but I missed my days at the library. The most difficult times were those when Ross was gone, especially when he traveled to Geneva, and I had to figure out how to handle Steven and the other children alone.

By the time he was school age Steven outgrew his bouts of irritability, and what followed were a few golden years. He wasn't the family valedictorian. Reading came late and spelling was always a problem, or if not a problem then a source of humor. One evening tucked into his shoes he left a note that read, "Plus don mov me shos. I huv gym tomrow." What amazed us was the one word in the sentence he got right. I asked him how he knew how to spell "gym." He said he saw it on the door to the gym at school. It seemed obvious to him. He was an observer. A child with a keen eye.

The compensation for Steven's academic struggles was his love for drawing. As difficult as it was to read what he wrote in words, it was easy to identify what he had in mind when he drew. He noticed things that others failed to see. We tried to validate his talent by hanging his pictures on the refrigerator and the bulletin board near the back door. One of his best we framed and hung in the alcove of our living room.

Sometimes reviewing our children, the way most parents do, Ross and I would reassure each other that if Steven wasn't cut out for school he could become an artist. But when Steven reached adolescence he became sullen and withdrawn. At home he spent time alone in his room because there was too much noise and activity in our household, at least that's what he said. The times when he wasn't withdrawn weren't much better. Small things would set him off, and he'd be explosive. Once he got into a down spiral, it was hard to regroup and get back on track with him again.

Steven got sent home from school one day because he spit on his teacher. He wouldn't back off from his claim that she deserved it. There was conflict with a neighbor because Steven took a CD from their house, and when I asked him about it he lied. I found it in his room, but he insisted he had no idea how it got there. Steven didn't read the world the way other people do.

By the time Steven was in high school, we found marijuana in his room and suspected that he was using other drugs as well. This was over the line for Ross, and we did what worried parents do in these circumstances. We talked to the counselors at school, who referred us to the first of several private therapists. With the best intentions we followed treatment plans for managing Steven's behavior. We were not successful.

Even before Steven finished high school he would disappear for several days at a time, and when we asked where he was, he would tell us he owed us no answers because he was not a minor. He was just over eighteen. We discovered things missing from our house, such as cash from Ross's wallet and gold jewelry of mine. Still following the advice of professionals, we set limits for Steven and told him if he could not respect the rules of our household, he could not live in our house. We should have known it was too late for an ultimatum. Steven left for good.

Horrible years followed. Sometimes we didn't hear from Steven for months on end, and we would try to talk ourselves into "letting go of him." But of course we couldn't. I don't know who came up with the idea of letting go of children. I never stopped thinking about Steven, and I never got over missing him. The only way I have of describing that feeling is that it's homesickness in reverse.

Once it was nearly two years that we had not heard from Steven, and then he dropped by like a long lost acquaintance just passing through. He told us he was using drugs, but was going to get clean and change his life, and he wanted to live with us until he could "get some things figured out." Jak and Jenna didn't like the idea at all. Their only explanation was "You don't want to get mixed up with the stuff Steven is doing."

So we went back to where we had left off several years before, telling Steven he could live with us, but that our house had rules. He decided that we were unreasonable and controlling, and that his freedom was more important than having free room and board with parents who didn't understand him. He left, and we had little contact with him after that. At one point Jenna told us she'd heard he was in Mexico, and then later that he wasn't in Mexico anymore. Most of the time we didn't know where he was.

Our lives changed the night the police came to our house on Woodward Street and told us that Steven had been in a fight. He took a gun with him to someone's house to straighten out a disagreement, but before Steven could use his gun, someone else used a gun on him. When we arrived at the hospital Steven was in surgery.

After surgery Steven was in the ICU and looked terrible. The machines hooked up around him made moaning, puffing sounds, and the only sign that he was alive was that his chest went up and down. I couldn't merge this image of a pallid, motionless Steven with the bright-eyed boy working on drawings. I couldn't fit this shape of a wounded man into the one of the young man who loved to fish. It was as if someone had stolen our Steven and replaced him with someone we could barely recognize.

The doctor escorted us from Steven's bedside to a conference room in the hall, and there told us that the next step would be to assess if Steven had suffered brain death. He had lost a lot of blood. As doctors always do, this one proceeded in a calm way to outline the steps. He talked like an orthodontist discussing braces for Steven even though in fact he was ushering us toward the stark truth that Steven was dead. First the tests, then the determination, and then we were asked as next of kin if we wished for Steven to be an organ donor. Ross answered, "We do." I don't think I said anything.

We followed the coaching of the doctors, who tried to be as humane as possible, but they were also in a hurry to do what they needed to do. When we were given time to say good-bye, Ross and I went in together.

"I need to see the bullet holes," I told Ross.

"Oh, Honey, are you sure you want to do that?"

But I did, and I wanted to touch Steven. I wanted to look at his hands one more time. And his feet. I wanted to feel his hair and the shape of his head because I had only this last chance to make a few more memories. I felt the nautilus shapes of his ears. I touched his lips. Traced his eyebrows. Brushed my fingers across his eyelashes. Touched the scar from the time he broke open his chin when he fell on his bike. I placed my lips against his forehead and held them there until I had drawn everything I could out of the sensation of one last touch. I was desperate to gather in a little bit of Steven that death could not steal away. I regret now that I pressed the end of my finger into the bullet wound. Ever since I have imagined that it was the one that shattered his rib and entered his heart. I cherish the other memories I gleaned from his silent form, but I wish I didn't know the texture of a bullet wound, not the one in my dead son's chest.

When the doctors returned to the room I insisted that I be there for his last breath. They tried to explain to me that Steven was dead already and only machines were keeping him breathing, but I was not persuaded. I didn't care about their explanations, and I didn't care if they thought I was a hysterical mother who couldn't accept her son's death. I didn't leave the room until he stopped breathing. I had been there for his first breath; it only seemed right to be there for his last.

We had a funeral. People felt awkward expressing their sympathy to us for a son who had died in a gunfight. They showed up and did their best. My close circle of friends was there. The dear friends I call my sisters. They had patiently listened to my laments during the years when we were worrying that Steven was destroying himself, and their quiet presence was comforting because they knew that everything that could be said had been said already. They didn't need the right words. I could feel their warm loyalty in the room with me. The visitation was hard and the funeral was even harder. So many of the things that are normally said at a funeral seemed odd to say about Steven.

Will gave a eulogy for his little brother. I can't remember it exactly. I only wept. For a son who had turned to ashes, and for another son whose voice shook as he tried to assemble for his brother a memory that could be cherished. On the day of Steven's funeral none of us had an inkling of how long that would take.

The story did not end with Steven's funeral. The other part is more recent, and it is also the hardest to explain. Steven lives on in absence. The awkward incidents were to be expected. It happened once when we met the parents of someone Steven knew in high school before that family moved away to another state. They were at a reception that Ross and I attended, and they had no idea what had happened to Steven in the time since he left school. They were not around. So, eager to tell us how well their son was doing, they asked about Steven and reminded us that the boys went to high school together. And we had to tell them that Steven is dead.

The subtle absences are the harder ones. At Ross's funeral the pallbearers, his sons and his nephews, lined up on either side of the coffin. Young men in suits, cleaned up for a sacred occasion. Steven was absent. But I saw him there at the side of the casket; I saw him there as a ghost. As the pall passed close to me I turned my gaze away just in case he should turn toward me, and I should catch his glance. Since Steven's death I sometimes feel myself getting very close to the line between sanity and insanity. Or maybe it is the liminal zone between time and whatever that is that isn't time. I don't know exactly what to call it. It doesn't feel dangerous to wander into that zone, but in that space I feel very alone. I know better than to tell anyone else where I am when I whiff into that zone, and then when it begins to feel as if I have been gone too long, I whiff back out. I have wondered if the reason we need the presence of others to send off those we love is that the others help us contain our insanity. They have a hold on us that tells us not to go over the edge. In my loneliest moments I felt as if I were near the edge, teetering, wondering if I might go over. That I might lose the ability to sort the living from the ghosts.

At holiday dinners I know where Steven's place should be at the table, near Jenna along the side. His place in the row of our children. And he is there. In his absence. Just when I think that I'm getting used to Steven's absence there is another reminder. Often they're small, or at least would seem so to anyone else. I hear a song on the radio about lost time and not having loved enough when it was possible. The song is about two lovers, but I think it's about Steven. My friend Lorraine's newest grandson is being christened, and his name is Steven, after someone I do not know who lives somewhere else. What can I say? That the name is taken?

I told Tee these things, but I did not tell her that after Steven died I was walking to the campus library on a perfectly ordinary day, and coming toward me across the quadrangle I saw Thomas. Either one of us could have turned away and gone into a building, but we didn't. Instead we met in the middle, and our greeting was as ordinary as that very ordinary day. "Hi, how are you?" I asked him and then followed with a question about his work. His work was going well he told me. He had just come back from two years in Rome. He asked about my children. "Steven died," I said.

"I know," Thomas said. "You were in my thoughts. It must have been so hard for you. I'm sure it still is."

"You knew?" I asked him. "Really . . . you knew? It was terrible. I needed you. I was so desperate . . . so I guess you were in my thoughts too. I wanted you to be there. Why weren't you? You could have contacted me."

"I wished that too," he said with hesitation. "I wanted to be there, but at a time like that it wouldn't have been right."

"I was in pain so deep I wouldn't have cared what's right," I said and looked into his eyes to watch his reaction.

"I understand that too," he said, "but those are the times that someone else has to care about what's right for you." I felt a spark of anger. It was too easy. As if he knew what was right for me. But I also knew what he meant. He'd moved on, and he felt awkward about the past.

"How are the other children doing?" Thomas asked.

"They're fine," I told him. "Row and Laura have lovely children, and they're doing well. Will lives in California and is very busy. Jenna is divorced." I didn't say anything more about her. I didn't want to know if he cared.

"Well, it's good to see you again," he said as he turned to walk on.

"Yeah, Bye," I said. It was awkward. It was obvious that I hadn't said, "it's good to see you too." As he walked away I turned full around and watched until he disappeared around the corner of the classroom building. I could feel the anger filling in what used to be a hollow of longing.

On the day when Tee asked about Steven's picture, I told her about losing Steven, and as I told her my tears spilled out. She didn't ask questions or toss back well-worn phrases that are so often offered as attempts to comfort. She listened. When I finished she was still, and I was still too. Then after the quietness had settled in, she got up from her chair and before gathering up her coat and her backpack, she said," Is there anything I can help you with before I go?"

And I told her "No, there is nothing just now."

With her eyes soft she said, "Then I'll see you tomorrow, Maggie."

# PART II

If an offense come out of the truth,
better is it that the offense comes than that the truth be concealed.
—Thomas Hardy, *Tess of the d' Urbervilles*

Chapter 8

# ROSS'S ANNIVERSARY

The date of Ross's death is a day in the circuit of my year that used to be ordinary and now stands out so that I cannot pass it by without thinking of him. This year his birthday slipped by me. I didn't think of it until a week after when Laura asked if we'd missed it. It isn't surprising that we brush by his birthday, because we no longer do the things we once did on that date. There is no one to wish "happy birthday," no cake to bake, and no point to commenting, as Ross and I always did, about how quickly the year has passed since we last celebrated the day.

The anniversary of Ross's death is different. On the calendar of my days it's a mark, a point. It is one more of the before and after dates that define the chapters of my life. There are others. They are like the pencil lines on the doorframe by the upstairs bath on Woodward Street that recorded how tall the children were. There a line and a date were evidence that time does not stand still. Life keeps changing. Days that mark life's passing are not party days, and no one sends cards for them. They are pensive days.

I'm grateful that the memories of Ross that stay with me now are mostly good ones. Ross was not a fan of drama. I recall the time he came in with greasy hands after draining the gas from the lawnmower to prepare it for winter, and I asked why he didn't just leave the fuel in and store the mower in the warm part of the garage. "It would save you a lot of work," I said.

Ross grinned and answered, "Maggie, this isn't work, this is drama control." That was Ross, an expert on drama control. It's hard to argue with a man who's convinced that changing the batteries in the smoke alarm on the first day of daylight saving, even if the batteries haven't run dead, is better than having the house burn down.

Ross's death took us by surprise, but I can't say it was dramatic. One afternoon when he came in from taking a walk, I noticed a spot of blood on the back of his shirt just under his right shoulder. Of course he hadn't seen it himself, so doing what any good wife would do, I suggested that he change his shirt, and also I checked his back. There was a sore on his back that didn't look like a scratch or a bite. Just a sore. It was a reminder to me that Ross was due for a skin check, and I made a mental note to set up an appointment for him to see the dermatologist.

When Ross came back from the appointment he looked serious. The doctor had checked the sore on his back and judged that it was of no concern, but he'd also noticed that under Ross's arm there was a mole that had changed. Various other things about the mole were cause for concern, and the doctor decided it should be surgically removed. What started as an innocuous looking spot on Ross's shirt kept getting more serious. This thing we hadn't even noticed turned out to be a melanoma that had spread to lymph nodes, and there were already spots in Ross's lungs and liver. Before we knew it, we were in the doctor's conference room talking about end of life decisions.

The children were stunned by their father's diagnosis. Each one made time to spend with him. During these visits Ross was gentle, but also direct in preparing for his death. He journeyed on toward his grave the same way he had always lived. Deliberate. Controlling the drama. It reminded me of the old stories of the patriarchs who on their deathbeds called for their children to come to them so that their fading father could give them a blessing. I noticed these blessings from Ross were not simple gifts with no strings attached; each was a delegation of responsibility.

When Will came from California the two of them sat at the dining table with documents for our estate plan and finances spread out in front of them. Ross wanted Will to be thoroughly informed. I could hear their conversation from the other room, but I didn't join them at the table because I already knew the contents from the planning Ross and I had done together. From the time Ross first became an adult he had been planning his own future, and then eventually it was our future, because he had always thought it was his responsibility to plan mine as well.

Once the materials had been reviewed Ross called me to the table after all; he wanted to speak to Will and me together. He assured Will that for now I could take care of matters myself, but also wanted to be sure there was someone I could turn to if I needed a second opinion or a second pair of eyes to go over documents. Ross was frank about his concern that at some point I might have difficulty managing these affairs myself. He gave Will a mandate, "Your Mom may be sharp as a tack now, but that doesn't mean she'll always be. You'll know when the time is right to step up and take over." Then he turned to me and said, "Maggie, you'll know too when that time has come. Will's your man."

Ross had something else in mind for Row. Someone would have to plan a funeral, and he wanted Row to do it. "Work with your Mom on it. Traditional. Good music. No guitars," he said. "Hire a soloist or two if you think that would add to the service." He shared with Row that he had been to a funeral at which there was music with violin and cello and he thought it "very fitting." Ross's advice for the eulogy was based on his own experiences. "Jokes at funerals aren't a good idea because usually they don't work." We could both remember the eulogy by a son who reminded everyone that his father cheated at cards and had been known to nudge the golf ball with his toe in order to get it out from behind a tree so he could line up a better shot. "Save the jokes for a party later," he advised Row. "The funeral isn't the right place for them."

Row was honored by the responsibility his dad delegated to him. "Would you like me to put something together and go over it with you and Mom? Pick out some music, readings, that sort of thing?"

"No," Ross said, "I'll count on you. Do it right. Be sure it means something."

The party after the funeral Ross delegated to Jenna. He assumed it would be at the farm. The two of them had a lot of time to talk about it during his remaining months because Jenna came almost daily to visit him. When they talked about the party they laughed as if they were enjoying it already. "Make it big. Fun. Invite some of my old friends, and make sure there's good scotch. Don't be cheap, and don't serve it in plastic."

Jenna assured Ross this would be a party to remember, and she added, "Dad, promise me you'll be there."

I've always had a feeling that Jenna was Ross's favorite. Not favorite in the sense that he treated the others unfairly for her sake; rather he seemed especially comfortable with her. They didn't get tangled up in the things others found hard. Of all of us, Jenna seemed least afraid that Ross was dying, and most able to set that inevitable event aside and waste nothing of the moment. There were many who commended her for all the time she spent with her Dad in his last months, and she would always say, "I loved being there with him." She referred to their time together as "our sweet days." For many that would be the gracious comment of someone fulfilling a duty, but spoken by Jenna it was simple truth. She kept enjoying Ross right to the very end. She was his sunshine.

The most unusual request was the one Ross made of Laura. "Promise me you'll keep up the tradition of the family Thanksgiving," he asked her. He knew we might not always have the house on Woodward Street, and he understood from the lives of his own children that people move away and spread out around the country. "Put it on Mom's credit card. Get the kids tickets to fly home. Rent a place if you need to, and don't worry about the cost. Just make it happen." Ross was talking to Laura who'd always been the most responsible of all the children about managing money and finding good deals. "Did you ever see the ads for the credit card that says some things are priceless?" Ross asked. "That's us." Ross was a practical man who understood that he couldn't take his money with him, but he also thought through into whose hands he wanted to put it.

It wasn't just the children with whom Ross made sure he was leaving his life in good order. He did that with me too. We talked about his decision to forego further treatment for his cancer because he was content that he'd lived a full life and didn't want to consign his remaining months to medical interventions. He was clear about the fact that he wanted to die at home and picked the room where he would be able to see into the garden. He wanted to watch the trees turn color one more time if possible. We had some beautiful moments remembering other times in our life, and he was full of gratitude.

There were things we could have talked about but didn't. Sometimes, at least in my thoughts, they were just beneath the surface. For many years I had felt that we had unfinished business from one of the ugliest confrontations of our marriage. I had always felt hurt by Ross's resistance to confide in me about his brother Lennie.

Years ago when I was dating Ross, a girl, who lived in the dormitory where I lived, asked me if "the thing about Ross's brother" bothered me. What bothered me immediately was that I had no idea what she was talking about.

When I asked Ross to explain the remark he said, "It's gossip, Maggie. Ignore it. There are always people around who like to make trouble about things that are none of their business. Don't give them the satisfaction."

That didn't put it to rest for me. I went back to the dorm and asked the girl what she meant by her remark. She was more than pleased to fill me in once she realized that she knew something about my boyfriend that I didn't know.

Ross had two brothers. The youngest was Leonard. During the Vietnam War, Lennie served hard duty in the Mekong Delta, and he left behind at home a woman he had dated before he was deployed. It was a casual relationship, but over the time he was absent Lennie had been building it up in his mind and was sure that when he returned she would marry him. He came back from war a changed man. Time also had not stood still for the woman Lennie had dated. She was nice to Lennie and went out with him a few times after his return, but she had discovered there were other men who were interested in her, and she wanted the freedom to date without commitment.

Needless to say, Lennie felt betrayed, but war had taught him to fight for what was his, and back home he continued his war on a personal scale. At first his aggression was limited to checking up on his "girlfriend" to see if she was home in the evening, and he insisted on knowing where she had been if he discovered she was not there. Soon his surveillance expanded to phone calls at odd hours and notes slid under the door.

Finally one night when Lennie's jealousy wound him up so tight he couldn't stand it any more, he went to the woman's apartment where he saw her leaving with a man who was picking her up for a date. After a loud altercation at the door Lennie left, but a little later came back and waited until the woman and her date returned. From his car, parked in the shadows, he watched them go inside.

Armed with the baseball bat he kept under the front seat of his car, just in case he needed it to defend himself, Lennie went to the porch and rang the doorbell. It took a while before the woman opened the door to tell Lennie to go away and not come back. That is when Lennie snapped. He forced his way in and took over as he had learned to do when entering houses in a village where enemy combatants were hiding. He knocked the boyfriend unconscious with the baseball bat. Then binding the woman to a chair and gagging her with a scarf he found on her coat rack, he forced her to watch him murder her unconscious friend with a kitchen knife pulled smoothly across his neck. He also forced her to watch as he mutilated his victim.

Apparently Lennie had no intention of getting away with the murder, nor did he make any effort to cover up the evidence. He left his victims there. One lying on the floor and the other tied to the chair. As a souvenir he took along the kitchen knife as well as the ears of the man, who happened to be with the wrong woman at the wrong time. Mutilating victims and collecting ears of the enemy as souvenirs was something he'd learned while fighting Viet Cong guerilas in Vietnam.

The trial was sensational in part because Lennie's defense attorney was brilliant at drawing out all the gruesome details to prove that Lennie was insane. The news services picked up and published the most lurid parts of the story because that sold papers and drew in viewers for the evening news. It was shocking. I know this because I went to the library and found the newspaper reports on microfiche. The articles gave a sketch of Lennie's family, and included a picture of his mother who faithfully appeared at the trial each day. The article also told that Lennie's two brothers were away, serving time in the military. One in the army and one in the navy. I wondered if Ross ever read the articles in the paper or saw the reports on the news. Is it possible that the only versions of his family story he heard were the censored ones sent to him overseas to explain why Lennie was in prison?

I did not go back to Ross immediately to tell him that I had uncovered his family's secret, because I didn't know how he would react. The sheer ugliness of the story, Lennie's insanity and cruelty, made me feel as if I were digging around in something off-color, almost pornographic. My greatest fear was that Ross would break up with me for prying into his family's business.

When I met Ross and began dating him regularly, one of the things that attracted me to him was that he was serious about marriage and looking for a woman who was committed to creating a family with him. He had served his time in the military and was responsible and self-disciplined. All these things were important to me because I had no family. Marriage in the future was my prospect for finding stability and having a family again. More than anything I didn't want to be alone. I had perfected the persona of a free and unencumbered young woman enjoying her student years, but deep down I was lost and homeless.

Discovering the horror story of Lennie shook me up, but it did not alter my belief that Ross was a good man. The hard times in my own life had persuaded me that "beggars can't be choosers," and I didn't think I could do better. I am not proud to admit that my thinking about myself took that turn, but I also can say in my own defense that losing my parents and becoming a lone survivor had taught me to be modest about expectations for good luck. Furthermore, I lacked the self-confidence to assert that Ross owed me an explanation; after all, I frequently deflected questions when someone asked me about my own family and my own past. When I encountered Ross's resistance to answering my questions about Lennie, I turned things upside down. Rather than seeing Lennie's story as Ross's liability, I accepted that my need to know about Lennie was my problem.

Only later, after we were married and it was clear that I had cast my lot with Ross, did I dare to tell him that I knew about Lennie. Ross's response to my revelation was simple. "Do you regret marrying me?"

I told Ross, "I have no regrets. I married you, not your brother. I don't have to make excuses for your family." It did occur to me sometimes, though, that Ross's own need to compensate for Lennie had something to do with why he worked so hard at being an honorable man. I felt hurt that he did not trust me enough to tell me about what must have been one of the worst things that ever happened to him.

Once a few years before Ross's death, when we were alone at the lake house, I brought it up to him again, asking him why he wouldn't talk to me about Lennie, about how his family had dealt with this disaster and the shame it brought down on them. It was one of the few times in all my years with Ross that I saw rage in him. He raised his voice and shouted me down, "Maggie, butt out! Leave it alone! Don't bring it up again, because I won't tolerate it. I mean it. Don't test me." That was enough to silence me, and I never brought up the matter with Ross again.

Facing Ross's death I knew it was our last chance, but I also knew it could disrupt the gentleness with which we were walking down this last stretch of road together. That is how I rationalized it. I told myself that this was Ross's death, and the choices regarding what he wanted to concern himself with in the time he had left were his to make, not mine.

There were other difficult things we did talk about because Ross chose to. After losing Steven, Ross seemed to grow old fast. He became tired and less interested in things he used to find entertaining. When we talked about Steven, Ross's eyes grew misty sometimes; it surprised me because he had never been a man who cried about anything. He could remember many of the hardest moments in his life with a dry eye, but he couldn't remember Steven that way.

Before we knew that Ross was ill, I said to him once that I thought Steven's death was aging us prematurely. We never imagined it was melanoma sneaking its way through Ross's body. After we lost Steven, Ross said repeatedly that he believed it was up to us not to let our family be defined by Steven's death. Doing that, Ross felt, was giving the last bad choice in Steven's life too much power. I can't say that I ever "got over" losing Steven. That is language that only parents who have never lost a child would use. Those of us, whose children die before we do, know how permanent grief is. What was clear to me was how differently Ross and I bore that grief.

Ross wouldn't give in to self-pity about his son. Even as Ross himself lay dying he remembered Steven again. The good things. How as a little boy he laughed from so deep down in his belly that he drooled, and that would make us laugh with him. What a keen eye Steven had for seeing things that the rest of us did not see until he translated them into his drawings. How at the table he always wanted to sit next to me and claimed that place by announcing, "I get to 'cause I'm the littlest and she's the biggest." Steven didn't understand why his older brothers would snicker about that. "You see," said Ross, "he was a treasure, and as long as we remember him that way, he is still a treasure."

We also talked about Jenna's request that Ross be at the party after his funeral. Was Jenna a dreamer? Is it possible that Ross would be there in some other form watching his family and friends having a party together? Would he try to communicate with us from somewhere else? What if he tried, and we failed to pick up the signals, to get the message? We talked about people we knew who believed they had gotten messages from the other side. Was there anyway to know for sure? We even talked about setting up a signal system, something like a private code word or a message that we would immediately know was from Ross.

Ross and I talked about these things because there didn't seem any reason not to talk about them. It was our remaining opportunity, and there is something about the awareness that death is coming closer that strips away hesitation. But it was Ross who settled the matter. "Don't waste time thinking about whether I'll reappear in some form, Maggie. Just go on living. It's not wise to waste the time you have left trying to outsmart the system. I'm sure I'll be okay, and you will be too."

One of the most remarkable exchanges between Ross and me during his last months had to do with the gun. Soon after we moved into our house on Woodward Street Ross purchased a handgun. He was sure he needed it, and I hated it. The gun was kept in the second drawer of the bedside stand on his side. He kept it in a gun case that had a combination lock on it, and he was never reckless with it. I can't recall that it was ever out of the case at all, but it felt like an intrusion to me nonetheless. First that we would have this chunk of violence in our house, and then even worse that it was in our bedroom.

Ross had grown up with guns. As a boy he hunted with his father and their family friends. They taught him to handle hunting rifles and shotguns while they trained him to be a man. The men in his family took pride in hunting correctly, which meant never shooting at an animal unless they were sure they could bring it down, and always packing the animal out and turning it into food. Ross, who hardly ever cooked, prepared this food himself as part of the hunting ritual.

But the handgun in the bedroom was different. I said mean things about the gun and ridiculed Ross for suggesting that if an intruder were breaking into our house he would have the calm to open the combination and get out the gun before the intruder could harm us. Ross ignored the nasty tone of my complaints and responded to them as if they were sincere concerns. "Of course I could get it out, that's why I have it next to where I sleep, and I've practiced the combination so many times I can open it in the dark."

"How do you know that in a face-off of two men with guns you'd be the one to win?"

"Because I know how to handle guns, and I'd be ten times more motivated to protect my family than an intruder would be to harm us. So I'd win."

A few times in the gun arguments I lost control and said things I shouldn't have. I called the gun "the damn gun." I told Ross I thought the damn gun was a macho toy and needing to have one was a feeble way to prove that he was a man. I knew that in the things I was saying Ross heard criticism of his family. I intended that. I hated the idea of using violence to solve problems; it reminded me of Lennie. That's what the gun meant to me. That damn gun reminded me that his family was always there with us, hidden away maybe, but still there in the conviction that a weapon in your hand was a way to run away from fear.

Although the things I said insulted Ross and made him angry, he wouldn't let it get to him. That was one of his rules. He often said to our children "Never let someone else become the master of your rage, because then you'll lose for sure." Ross was a man who lived by his own dictums, and how he'd learned this was obvious enough to me, even if it wasn't to the children.

His whole life Ross had been standing separate from Lennie, doing everything he could to not be like his brother. At the same time he stood up for his family to defend them against the undeserved insults of those who threw the shame of Lennie's crime into their faces. Ross stonewalled, refused to talk about things that made him uncomfortable. I went to great lengths to break open Ross's resistance by provoking his anger, but I never won using that strategy, and it definitely didn't work with the gun. In the end he kept the gun, and I gave up trying to talk him out of it, but I never gave up resenting it.

All of this is background to one of the most remarkable things that happened during the last months of Ross's life. He was still up and around. Often very tired, but not so tired that he couldn't go out to do an errand or two. After one of these ventures out of the house, he came home and said in an off-hand way, as if it didn't amount to much: "I went to the gun shop and sold the gun."

Without the gun our home felt more peaceful, at least it did to me. The second drawer of his bedside stand no longer felt like a war zone. On that first day without the gun he also seemed light-hearted. He chuckled at a few things I said. I smiled more easily. Or maybe I just imagine that. But I did actually sit with him in his den and watch part of a baseball game, and it felt sweet to be in his company.

A few days after the gun was gone, out of nowhere Ross said to me, "Maggie, I'm sorry I made you live with a gun."

And I said to him, "Honey, I'm sorry for all the mean things I said about it."

He continued then, "There are other things too. If I could do it all over again I'd try to do it better."

"I feel that way too," I admitted.

"There were things we should have talked about." He said it in a very soft voice almost as if he were talking to himself. I knew what Ross was referring to, and he knew I understood.

"I know," I said in a whisper, and I could see in the tenderness of his look that he understood I was acknowledging what he had said, but also was admitting that it was as true of me as it was of him. We had both lived with secrets thinking the other didn't need to know. We'd each tried to believe that the other couldn't see what we were hiding, and that was our worst mistake.

We were quiet for a bit. And then Ross said, "We don't have to go back to those things anymore, do we?" He didn't say it as a question or even as a way of evading anything more that would be difficult to talk about. It was a conclusion.

And I said, "No, no we don't. That's all past now, and we can let it go."

Chapter 9

# WILL COMES HOME

After Ross's death the family reorganized itself around the empty space. A planet had been removed from our constellation, and its absence altered the orbits of the rest of us. All of our children came for the funeral and almost as soon as they arrived they found tactful ways to let me know how long they'd be staying. They had lives to go back to and things to do, but they made promises to come back soon.

Laura and Robby and their children stayed at the farm with Jenna and Jak's family. There aren't many families with a son-in-law like Robby, who knows how to step up and take part as steadily as he did. Row and Andrea with their children stayed at a hotel with a swimming pool, which all the cousins appreciated because Laura had called ahead to remind them to bring swim gear. Apart from fussing about whether her husband and her children were dressed right for the occasion, Andrea added little. Every chance she had, she escaped to the pool, or to get her nails done, or for a massage because funerals are so stressful. I welcomed her absence.

Will stayed at the old house on Woodward Street with me, and I was grateful for his company. To be alone would have been hard, but I was relieved that the others didn't stay with us, because as much as I held on to the comfort of knowing they were not far away, I was tired. I needed quiet even though it was a different quiet than I'd ever known before.

In the days before the funeral the children made calls to friends and relatives, and Row met with the funeral director and the minister to review plans for the service. I had thought the visitation would be difficult, but it wasn't. The children were there, each taking a share in greeting those who came, and they were touched by the kind sentiments offered about their father. Jenna reminded everyone to stay tuned for a summer party she called The Celebration for Ross. Soon everyone was referring to it that way, and we knew it was something to which we could look forward later.

Row honored his father's request to create a meaningful service and entrusted responsibility for the eulogy to his son, Zach, who did not disappoint. As he has grown to his full height Zach looks a lot like Steven, has the poise and clear-eyed gaze of his Uncle Will, and has the creativity of Row. In preparation for the eulogy Zach had contacted each of the children and grandchildren and asked for a one-sentence statement of gratitude for what Ross had meant to them. At the service, after highlighting some of the important events in Ross's life, Zach declared "these are the things for which we are grateful." Then in a clear voice, as if he were making declarations, he recited the list. At the end he summarized: "We are thankful for the life of Ross Philip Barone. Thankful that he has left us with so much to cherish."

In the hours after the funeral the mood lightened. The boys took off their suits and put their jeans back on. The girls took off their heels and padded around barefoot. We spent the rest of the day together at Jenna's house. In the evening when I decided it was time for me to go home, the others encouraged Will to drive me and come back for a nightcap. I told him he should take the opportunity to be with his sisters and brother, but he declined, "Right now, Mom, I'm your guardian." And he was an angel. There was tenderness in him I'd never known before.

Friends who have tended the deathbed of a loved one at home have told me that the energy doesn't leave immediately when the mortician closes the door of the hearse and drives away with the body. People of a more mystical bent have names for this. The spirit. The ether. I didn't know what name to give it, but I was fully aware there was something in me that resisted letting go of Ross as a presence still living in our house. I couldn't empty his place and move forward as if he weren't there.

Will's presence grounded me as I found my way through this in-between time during Ross's departure. And then it was over. In one wave after another I said goodbye to my children and took comfort in the fact that they were going home and picking up the stream of life where they had left it a few days before.

After the others were gone Will was still there, and he hadn't mentioned his plans for returning to California. There is a feeling that lingers in a room when something needs to be said or done. I've never liked referring to it as an elephant in the room. It's subtler than that. Sometimes it's little, like a mosquito. When it is quiet and you think it has found a way out, it starts to hum again. It's searching for its right time.

Finally after dinner it appeared that Will was ready. "I want to talk with you about something, Mom."

"I guessed that. I could feel it coming."

"Do you know what it is?"

"No."

Will reminded me of the summer when he was in college and took off to California. Of course I remembered. How could I forget? Ross and I were bewildered, as any parents would be in that situation. We wondered what we had done that our son would need to get so far away from us. There was something symbolic in the place he chose to end his journey. He could not have gotten farther away unless he'd ventured out across the ocean to an entirely new continent.

Will had his memories of the time too. He speculated that we'd thought he was trying out his wings and being utterly irresponsible about it. That is what we had thought at first, but within a few years his business successes forced us to temper that impression. The only misfortune was that he'd chosen to succeed in a place so far from us. Once the roots of success were planted it seemed he had to stay where he had put them down. Though happy for him, I continued to be sad about the deliberate distance in our relationship.

As Will and I each spoke we were comparing notes. Not only were we speaking of ourselves, but also revealing the guesses we'd made about each other. Will continued, "Well that's the thing, Mom. I wasn't wandering, and I didn't go alone." He got up from his chair, walked to the cupboard, took out a glass, and got himself water. He asked me if I wanted some, and I could tell this was not about thirst. He needed a moment to review what to say next.

"I went with Oliver. Do you remember him? My roommate?"

"You weren't alone?"

"He wasn't just my roommate." The silence was big. "We were scared. Really scared. All we could think was that we had to get away . . . go somewhere else."

Will wasn't asking whether I remembered Oliver; he was asking if I understood why they had to leave. He wanted me to see that he and Oliver were intimidated by the messages from all sides that told them there was no room for men like them. They were unacceptable.

That is how Will came up with the idea of taking motorcycles and going as far away as they could, which meant to California. He thought two guys on a motorcycle road trip wouldn't attract attention, and it would give them space to decide what to do. By the time they reached California they knew they couldn't go back to the places where they were both known.

"People were vicious," Will reminded me. Both he and Oliver had heard the things guys said. Sometimes it was the humiliation of pretending they weren't offended by the parodies of limp wrists and lisps. Even men who would never think of being bullies joined in that sort of humor. More often the remarks weren't humor. "The things people said to us were hateful and menacing. It bothered me worse that they said them about Oliver than that they said them about me. I could tough my way through, but Oliver was terrorized."

Will recalled times at the hunting lodge with his uncles and cousins. He loved those trips. He loved those men. They were his heroes. But he also wondered what would happen if they uncovered the truth about him. Might there be an accident with a gun sometime, and the others would understand it had been necessary to solve a family problem? Will and boys like him did not fit into the honor code for what men should be like, and Will had no idea how far loyalty to that code would push his uncles and cousins. He didn't fear his father, but he didn't know what to expect from those other men who, although a little more distant in the family tree, would still feel shamed by him.

"Are you shocked, Mom?"

"I'm just so sad that you carried that burden, and I didn't know. That you had to run away . . . hide away in California all these years. Should I have known?"

"You probably couldn't have known. But are you angry with me for going away?"

"It was so confusing. I didn't understand the distance." I told Will how I in particular had taken his distance as rejection. If he couldn't stand to be around us, why hadn't he just said it, put it into words and told us why he thought we weren't good enough to be his parents. His family.

Later when I heard Will talking with his Dad on the phone, it seemed perfectly friendly. I wondered what had changed. It didn't seem like he rejected Ross then. I shared with Will how sad I felt because he was alone. I guessed he was pouring himself into his business and didn't have time for relationships. At other times I secretly hoped that he had girlfriends, even if he didn't want us to meet them. Will was handsome and his successful businesses provided well for him. I imagined him in a convertible with a classy woman he met in Beverly Hills, and I blamed myself for being the kind of plain mother Will would be embarrassed to introduce to his fancy girlfriend. Will found this funny. He chuckled about the pictures in my imagination.

They were sort of silly, but they were also sad. Many times over I had punished myself by imagining what he told other people about his family. Had he told them that he had a crackpot family, and then later couldn't have us show up and walk into the bad reputation he had created for us? I couldn't put the pieces together.

"But now you're putting them together."

"I think so. It feels like a lot of lost time, Will."

Somewhere in that gap of time was Will's appearance at home for Steven's funeral. His sisters and Row each had a partner at their side, but Will stood alone, straight-backed and brave in his black suit. He fulfilled all the obligations of the oldest son, because even in his absence he had eclipsed Row and taken over that position in the family. Only now could I understand that more than being alone he was standing there without the one he would have wanted there next to him.

I asked Will if any of the other children knew. Row did from the time they were in high school when the other boys began to suspect that Will was not interested in girls. Row heard the taunts. They started with bullying Will, but he was big and strong, and it was easier to bully his skinny twin. They gossiped that Row was Will's boyfriend; they wrote vulgar things on Row's locker door and left even more vulgar things inside his locker. Because Row took the brunt of the hostility, Will felt he had to protect him. The fight when Will got his face battered was his breaking point. He decided to fight back, and Row knew why.

The details about Oliver were filled in as we talked. California was too far from his family, a close and traditional family. Because it bothered Oliver so much that he was missing out on all the times his family got together, he kept thinking up schemes for how they could move back closer to their families. It would've been a secret life, but Oliver thought they could figure it out. Will didn't think they could. Finally it wore them down, and Oliver left.

"I'm sorry. For your loss. I'm sorry for all the secrets. That through all that I never knew," I told Will.

"If you had known could you have handled it?"

"I would've found a way. It's new territory, you know. Things were very different when I was growing up. Oh, my goodness, listen to me. As if you don't know that. I would've found a way . . . because you're my son."

"I know you would have."

"Why now, Will? Why have you chosen to tell me now?"

Will didn't think his father could have accepted him as he was, and because he loved his father he couldn't bear to hurt him. "You might find this hard to believe," he said, "but the person in this world I loved the most was the one I was most afraid to disappoint." Will thought his father was a good dad. What he feared was that even if his father accepted him, he would have been disappointed that he didn't have the son he wished he could have had. It was not in Will's nature to settle for good enough. He wanted to be the best.

Oliver was there sometimes when Will was on the phone with Ross. Probably just like I was there sometimes when Ross was talking. Will would think, "If only he could look through the phone and see me, see us, me and Oliver. He would see that it's okay." But he was relieved also that Ross couldn't see them. Will couldn't decide which was more important to him, to have his father know him as he truly was, or to hide from his father what would be disappointing.

Will had good talks with Ross about business. He thought of his father as a silent partner, offering his advice from a distance. Without Ross's help Will didn't believe he would have succeeded, because Ross understood how to use equity and how to take loans, and Will could trust his father's advice like he could not trust advice from other sources in a competitive business environment.

For Will those calls sometimes felt as close as he could get to the way it had been when he was a kid and Ross took him up to the hunting lodge. They went alone a few times, just the two of them. They walked through the woods, and Ross pointed out prints in the bare soil along the path. They picked up owl pellets on the ground under a tree and determined to come back when they thought they might be able to see the owl in the branches above. They looked at rubs in the bark of young trees, and Ross explained how adolescent bucks rubbed the velvet from their antlers and left their scent in these places.

As Will described his father and their precious time together his voice trembled. There in the woods Will felt important walking beside a man who, in the eyes of his admiring son, was as close to perfect as a man could be. "I can't say that I was Dad's favorite, but most of the time I was the kid of whom he was proudest. That's the reason," said Will, "I couldn't disappoint him. I was hooked on that special approval." Then Will caught himself on this nostalgic detour. "Sorry, Mom, I got carried away. What I wanted to explain to you was that not long after those trips to the hunting lodge I began to realize that I'd earned Dad's approval on false pretences. I'd stolen it. If Dad had known who I really was, would he still have enjoyed that walk in the woods?"

I wanted to say something to make it right. Was this tragic distance between a father and son an extension of the legacy of family secrets, of pretended perfection? Maybe we had all let Ross down by catering to his expectations, never letting him be uncomfortable, sparing him the hard practice of learning to love steadfastly in relationships that could take us by surprise. I couldn't think of anything to say to Will now that could change the past. I couldn't speak to him for his Dad, because he and his father had their own connection.

I said the only thing I could think to say. "I'm glad you told me now. In the time I have left I want to love you better. I want to be your mother."

"And I want to be your son," Will said.

I would like to say that by the end of the evening everything had been set straight, but it's not as easy as that. This was my son. There were lost years. I felt guilty about never having noticed his struggle. I wondered how he felt going down the highway on his motorcycle with Oliver, heading west determined to go until they could go no more because they had to hide from the families whose love they couldn't trust. Why had I never asked myself why a boy would paint his room black, seal out the light, and sleep on the floor?

## Chapter 10

# LEAVING WOODWARD STREET

From just before Jenna was born and until a year after Ross died the old Tudor house on Woodward Street was home. Even after the children were grown and had moved to places of their own, it was still our family home, furnished with memories gathered over the decades. The old Tudor house seemed oversized for just the two of us, but from time to time we could fill it up again with children and noise when everyone gathered for holidays. That was excuse enough for staying there.

After Ross died that changed. My children took charge and began working on me. They didn't put up the for sale sign immediately; they started with hints that fit deftly into conversations. When the ash tree in the side yard died off and Will talked about getting a tree service to remove it, Laura agreed with his plan and added parenthetically that removing the skeleton tree would make the house more attractive to potential buyers. When I talked about repainting my bedroom, Row suggested a neutral color out of consideration for the next owners. Sometimes it felt like my children were ganging up on me, and I felt like a child being made to do something I didn't want to do. Finally the decision was made that spring was the time to sell. "We" in this case was the children. I'm not sure I had a vote on the committee.

In preparation for listing the house minor repairs were done, and we replaced carpeting in several bedrooms where kids and pets had left their mark. Laura hired a landscaper to take out overgrown shrubbery in front of the house and replace it with plantings that would improve the curb appeal. On the advice of the realtor we removed and boxed lots of small items so that the house wouldn't look "cluttered." The effect was to create a house that looked as if no one in particular lived there.

While preparation for selling was going on, Laura worked behind the scenes searching for "just the right place" for me. She wanted it to be a place where I could live independently while able, but also a place in which I could get more support as I grew older and needed more help from day to day. I had some expectations too: a comfortable bedroom and bath for guests, space for a dining room table, a den for my desk and my books. And I wanted windows and light.

The process went smoothly with Laura at the helm; things always move quickly when she is in charge. Before I knew it the old house sold, and the new condo was contracted. One might think these two transactions would signal that the project of "moving mother" was nearly complete, but for me it was the beginning of the worst part. With the papers signed and the real estate settled, Laura shifted from being efficient to being tough. She took charge of thinning down my household in order to empty the old Tudor and furnish my new space. Her first step was to put tags on furniture that I would keep. Her second step was to email her brothers and sister to let them know if there were things from the old house they wanted, now was the time to speak up.

Laura's request was the first on the list. She wanted the piano because she had the perfect spot for it in her house, as if having the perfect place meant that there was no point in anyone else asking for it. Her children asked for small things. Nothing that would take room. Things that could be put away neatly in drawers.

Kate requested the hand mirror from my grandmother. The glass in the mirror had been replaced once after it cracked, but the back of the mirror was still a beautiful bouquet of inlay. Jeremy liked the small barometer that hung in the hallway because he remembered his grandfather predicting the weather with it. Sam was interested in Ross's fountain pens. Robby asked for Ross's cuff links with gold "R's" set in onyx. I was pleased that no one suggested taking them to the jeweler and melting them down for the value of the gold in them. It didn't seem to bother Robby that no one wears cuff links anymore.

Will asked for his father's desk and the bookcase with glass doors that had furnished Ross's den. After carefully dissembling and packing them, he shipped them to California. Row took a few books, but what he really wanted was my promise that someday when I was done with old family letters and pictures he could have them. What Jenna and Jak took was enough to fill a truck. For the time being they stored most of it in the large barn on their property. Some of the items were things from the attic that I hadn't seen in years.

It is far harder than one might think to dissemble a household that has been growing over a lifetime. It occurred to me as I watched my children choose what they would like, that they didn't need any of it. Their households were already complete. They were taking mementos. I had to chuckle when I considered that these were the things by which they would remember Ross and me. But, isn't that the way it always goes? The few things I still had that came from my parents were not practical. They were tucked away and out of sight. Taking space in the corner of a cupboard or carefully stowed in one of my desk drawers. Still I couldn't part with them. I was the guardian of a memory, and those objects were my family relics. It shocked me that now I was moving into the stage of producing relics.

Furnishing my new condo was also difficult because, while I did not want to begin with a home that was too full from the start, I also did not want it to feel empty like one of those vacation rentals that have all the basics so you can survive there with only a few personal things you bring in a suitcase. The things I ended up taking were the most familiar. They were my own mementos of a chapter of my life that had closed.

I don't want to complain about Laura; without her help I could not have made this move. Still, the difference in her style and mine created painful moments, like the day she was emptying my kitchen, sorting through the cupboards and drawers with Jenna by her side. As she unloaded the cupboards, she assigned each item to one of the large boxes labeled "condo," or "sale," or "dumpster." I understand that the chop sticks from The Great Wall Chinese takeout, though still in their wrapper after all these years, probably did need to go to the dumpster. I didn't feel that way about the old wooden soup ladle and my mother's potato masher with a cracked wooden handle, but they went to the dumpster anyway.

The vase, which I got out each spring because it was the perfect shape and height for peonies, probably was a candidate for the estate sale. It was obvious that I would have neither a garden with peonies nor a space for a large flower arrangement in my new condo. The pain of relinquishing the vase was not that it was valuable. I grieved that I would no longer greet spring with the ritual of getting it out, washing it carefully to get rid of the dust that had collected in it over winter, and then polishing the glass till it sparkled. I had to face that the number of spring times remaining in my life was growing smaller. And even during those I had left, I would not have the joy of watching peonies bloom in the same backyard where for many years I had watched my children play.

I left the room sometimes as Laura worked her way through my belongings. I knew we had to get it done because the estate sale was already scheduled, but the worst episode was when Laura sorted out the closet and dressers in our bedroom. On Ross's side of the closet his good leather shoes were still on the floor. And in his chiffonier, which is what we called his tall dresser to distinguish it from my lower horizontal one, there were still some of his monogrammed handkerchiefs. "You won't need two dressers anymore, Mom. Decide which one you want to take," Laura said. It hurt to think of getting rid of Ross's dresser. It seemed easier to let go of my own. In the end I took his chiffonier, but not because it was more suited to the space along the wall in my new condo. I took it out of loyalty.

In the closet was Ross's tie rack. It didn't take much room, and I liked sliding my fingers through the strips of silk and fine wool because it felt like a walk through time. Ross had kept the tie he wore when he was President of Rotary. The ones from Zach's christening, Steven's funeral, and the funeral at which Ross gave the eulogy for his father were there too. The bow tie Ross wore with his tuxedo at Jenna's wedding was on the rack even though the tuxedo was long gone. My favorite tie was the cashmere one we brought back from Scotland. Although Ross had never worn it, the feel of it comforted me.

There were fleeting moments during which I resented the sorting so much I thought of calling it off. The whole process felt like that episode from *Little House on the Prairie* when the plague of grasshoppers swoops in and levels everything so that nothing living remains.

I did spirit away a few things before they fell victim to the sorters. Even now tucked in the side of my own tall dresser I have a few of Ross's handkerchiefs and two ties. They are carefully wrapped in tissue along with Steven's faded t-shirt. For the rest of the sorting I could not watch. If I had stayed to see the final emptying of Ross's closet, I might have ended up standing by the dumpster weeping, with Ross's leather shoes clutched to me. It was better to walk away.

Before the house was completely empty it went through the step of seeming fuller than it had ever been before, because everything in the cupboards and drawers was pulled out for display at the estate sale. All the old things in the attic were brought down so shoppers wouldn't have to climb the worn wooden steps into the stuffy attic. Then came the dreaded day of the sale itself.

The children made it clear to me that the professionals would handle the event and the family was not to be there. I understood. It would have been too much, having me there to watch as all the things we had gathered over the years were slipping away, carted off by strangers. But here I have another confession to make. I did not stay away completely.

By the day of the sale I was already living in my new condo, but I could not get over the fact that the old house still felt like my house, my home. So I got in my car and drove over to the old neighborhood on Woodward Street and parked down the block in a spot where I could see both the side and front doors of the house. From there I watched strangers take away the things that had been mine and now were theirs.

The large framed painting of birch trees and trillium went home with one of the shoppers. It was not great art by any stretch of the imagination, but it had hung in the breakfast nook for years. At first the children's heads only reached the bottom of the frame, then later reached the flowers, and finally when the boys were teenagers they were tall enough to be almost perfectly framed against the background of the birch trees.

A woman walked out with our living room drapes in her arms and just behind her was a man with the wooden valence covered in the same fabric. He balanced it over his shoulder, and it bobbed as he walked. I never liked the drapes because they were too heavy, and I had seldom closed them. I tried to imagine them in another house somewhere. The drapes slightly faded and the valence a little too large now blocking out the light at someone else's window. It was one of the few moments when I chuckled.

A young woman in high heels took the plastic rocking horse that had been stored in the attic since Jenna's youngest had outgrown it. I wondered if she noticed that the handhold had been lost or if she had a husband who would replace it with a length of broomstick. The lamp I never liked went into the backseat of a car. That's the way it went all morning. Our family life being strewn like a tornado was passing through.

In early afternoon a police officer came to the window of my car and asked, "Is everything all right, Ma'am?" I lied. I told him I was waiting for my niece who was checking out the estate sale. I'm sure he knew I was perjuring myself. He would have known if he'd looked at my reddened eyes and the mound of tissues on the passenger seat. Police officers are trained, aren't they, to do a quick visual scan of the contents of a car?

I decided it was time to go home because I didn't want to be parked there on Woodward Street if the police officer circled back for another look. Besides I had seen enough. When I got home I felt restless until the numbers on my digital clock said 6:00. Then and only then could I say, "It's finished."

I went back to the house one more time. There was no need for me to go, but I had to gather my last impression. The day after the sale all that was left was gathered up and sent off to the Goodwill store. Finally when the house was completely empty I walked through it from room to room for the last time. It sounded different. It sounded hollow. Where pictures had been removed from the walls there were blank squares with nail holes in them. The furniture had left odd faded shadows on the carpet. And I couldn't believe how much dust was left behind.

In the den of my new condo, which is really just a fancy name for the smaller second bedroom on the main floor of my home, I have kept pictures of Ross. One is of him grilling on a patio. In another he is surrounded by sons and grandsons after a tag football game. The yard must have been muddy because their shirts are dirty. Ross is holding the football, and he has a huge smile. The picture was taken in the backyard of our house on Woodward Street.

Very soon after Tee first came to stay with me she asked about the pictures and if the den had been Ross's. I explained that Ross had never lived in the condo. All of my memories of him are in other places. This condo is the place to which I moved after he died, a part of my memory separate from him. Tee was curious about the house on Woodward Street and asked if I still drive by it. I explained that it isn't on a street I normally would take on my way anywhere. It's a side street. A quiet residential neighborhood in the old part of town. A place you would only end up if you intended to go there for some reason. I hadn't seen it since the day I turned over the keys to the new owners.

Tee and I talked about places we have each lived. Changing places changes the story. We mused about the fact that when I tell her about incidents from my children's early lives, she imagines them as if they took place in the condo where I live now, the place where Tee has gotten to know me. "We imagine people in places," Tee said. We don't just think of them in a vacuum." She looked pensive as she spoke. I guessed she was thinking of her own places, the ones that were gone now. "I think we should go back and have a look at your house on Woodward Street," said Tee. "Maggie, your family was lucky to have all those years together there. Let's ride by the old house together sometime."

So Tee and I went back to Woodward Street. We turned slowly into the block where the old Tudor house stood. I remembered with some tenderness how the old growth trees created an arch over the street. And I remembered how in the fall my children raked the leaves. Back in the day when it was still permissible to burn leaves at the curbside, we roasted marshmallows.

The houses along the block look different now than I remembered them, as if they have changed colors. Unlike the images of my memory, there are very large SUVs in the driveways. The one that looks the strangest is the old Tudor. The front door has been painted dark blue and there are large pots of geraniums with sweet potato vine on each side of the steps. Beside the front door there is a new mailbox with a name on it in letters too small for me to read from the street.

## Chapter 11

# WAS LAURA BORN THAT WAY?

If anyone were to ask me who of my children will live longest, I would say Laura, but if anyone were to ask me now who of my children seems most vulnerable, I also would say Laura. I'll never forgot what Laura said when she returned home after the hellish days during which she was missing. She must have sensed something was very wrong when the police kept her overnight, and her first reaction was to worry that I was angry.

Already then strong-willed Laura was concerned not to disappoint. She was deliberate in assuring me that she would never have considered not coming home. In her own eyes, the three-day jaunt with Jenny's dad was something she'd had a choice about. She didn't understand that she'd been abducted and was in danger, nor did she have any idea how frantic we'd been. I wonder how much those three days when Laura was eleven years old put a stamp on our relationship. How much did it lock in the kind of mother and daughter we would be together, with Laura always in charge and me trying to reassure her?

That all came back into play again twenty-five years after those days Laura went missing. She called me and in a choked voice told me she had cancer. "Mom, you know how this goes: first the bad mammogram, then the biopsy. I was still thinking it would turn out okay until the doctor called this afternoon." It was a courtesy call late in the afternoon on a Friday because the doctor knew Laura was waiting for results, and she wanted to let her know before the weekend. The doctor told Laura she would need surgery, and for Laura this meant her family had some planning to do.

As Laura told me this on the phone her voice was thin. As I listened my own mouth went dry. I didn't know what to say. I had no way to fix it. "Laura, do you want me to come?"

"Can you? Right away so you'll be here when I have surgery. Mom, I don't have time for this. I have work and kids. What am I going to do?"

I reached for everything I could think of to comfort her. Not that it did much good, but it was all I could pull together at the moment on the phone. I said, "You'll do what you have to do." I reminded her that Robby is a good husband and will be there for the kids. I promised I'd help anyway she needed me. I reminded her that these things never happen at the right time, because we don't want them to happen at all, but we find a way to deal with them. All the things I said were platitudes even though they came from the bottom of my heart. At last all I could think to say was "Oh, Laura, my precious Laura!"

Her response surprised me. It was like she was straightening her spine and trying to get control again. The moment she felt me falter, her own courage rebounded. "Mom, when you had cancer I don't remember that you got so upset. You always seem so together when stuff happens. I've got to handle this. I've got to figure it out." I could hear Laura scrambling to keep control of herself by talking tough. I could hear her false bravado.

I'd not handled my cancer any better than she was handling hers. On that terrible day when my doctor called to give me the bad news, I'd had the worst possible thoughts about what was going to happen to my children and to me. That's what the word CANCER means. From one minute to the next I felt my life spin out of control. It took a few days until I decided that even if I couldn't control cancer, I could control how I acted around my kids. It was my only defense, the only thing I felt I could do for them. So I decided to be calm, if only on the outside. I didn't say any of this to Laura on the phone. Instead I said, "I know you can handle it Laura. If I did, you can."

It seemed hard-hearted to respond that way, but it felt better than admitting how frightened I was for her. I wanted to prop Laura up, get back to talking to her as if she were my invincible first born. "Trust your instincts," I said, "they always come through for you. You don't have to do it the way I did it. Give yourself time to catch your breath, and you'll figure out how to do this your way."

When I got off the phone I cried. Harder than I had cried when the doctor called my house and used that terrorizing C-word. Harder than I cried the day I got the news that Charlene, who often sat next to me when we were both at the clinic for chemo, had lost the fight. All I could think was that this was my baby. My little Laura. The one who had been given back to me after those wretched days she was missing. The child I never again could take for granted. The one I so often told myself was, of all my children, the one blessed with flawless health. And now I was thinking about a surgeon cutting into her with a knife. Making a deep gash on her chest. Digging out a vicious tumor, and then stitching up her soft skin like it was torn fabric. I felt sick, and when I was done crying, I still felt sick.

The time I spent at Laura's house gave me a look inside her world. I saw how loyal Robby was. I'd never gotten to know him, and sometimes thought he was a little boring. The handyman. The luggage tender. Now it was his turn to step up, and he proved not boring at all. He was sweet to Laura when she was shaken, and patient when she was cranky. Laura was not used to having a household where she wasn't in charge. Her standards were high. But still I saw that she did not take Robby for granted; she thanked him for the things he did. Even though they were both stressed, they were good to each other.

The children also seemed to handle Laura's illness well. They went to school and the routines continued. They played sports. They argued about whose turn it was to clear the table. Now and then they asked hard questions.

"Is my Mom going to die?"

"Your Mom is doing everything she can to get better."

"Gramma do you still have cancer?"

"No mine has been gone for a long time."

"Do all girls get cancer in their boobies?"

This was Laura's youngest, Kate, her only daughter. And while her brothers chuckled at the naïveté of Kate's question, I couldn't help but think that this was exactly what Laura would have asked at that age. Exploring what this means for her personally and thinking ahead so she can take charge of it.

One of the hardest days was just after Laura's surgery when at the follow up appointment her doctor explained that the lab reports indicated Laura should plan on having chemotherapy and radiation. She was frank about the details. Laura would be tired and her hair would fall out. It hit

Laura hard. She was quiet in the doctor's office, but once we got in the car she erupted. "Just when you think you've done the hard part you get worse news," she shouted. "It's not fair. I have to go back to work. I have year-end reports to file. My team can't do that without me. You can't stay here helping us forever with the kids. What about my kids? What about Robby?" Her fear was pouring down like lava, demolishing everything in its path.

Then in a heartbreaking wail Laura blurted out what mothers with cancer fear most. "What if I die?" Laura sobbed and sobbed. I held her while her tears and snot soaked my blouse. She didn't even try to dry them; she gave in and let them run down her face and onto me. There was nothing I could say. I felt rage at a Cancer that could crush my precious Laura this way, but there was no way to sidestep her question.

After a while the sobbing grew quieter. It burned out. She remained still, but several times I heard the staccato inhales that usually we only hear from children after they have cried in deep distress. The short gulps for breath that I heard from her now were the same that I had first learned to distinguish when she was a small girl, and I could tell in her cries the difference between true anguish and crocodile tears.

As I held Laura in my arms, I could feel the deep exhales of someone giving in to fate. Sinking into what she knew she could not fight with her usual means of taking charge. I was hoping that the fate to which she was relinquishing herself was not the dark side of hopelessness, but just the beginning of finding her way. At that moment, however, there was no way to tell which it would be.

There were times again later when Laura's eyes teared up. There were times again when we talked together about having cancer, about treatment, and about the cloud of worry that floats over your head for a long time as you learn to call yourself a "survivor." I did share with her that after a while the worry changes. It comes back for doctor's visits and can get stirred up by the news of someone else's diagnosis, but it doesn't stay there with the same tenacity forever, because life won't let it.

Laura regained her strength and her hair grew back. She took charge of the things that she'd set down for a while. She went back to running and was more meticulous than ever about the family's diet: no meat, only fish, no additives, and local grown. She became the old Laura again, and our relationship too returned to what it had been before.

There were several times after Laura had cancer that I could feel her pulling back, ripping herself away from me. The first time was when she complained that she had to do everything herself while she was sick, and that no one had stepped up to help her. I was tempted to ask her what she meant. "You mean at work? Or in your neighborhood and with the kids?" But I didn't ask because I didn't want to hear her repeat her blanket judgment if it included me. I told myself that during illness accurate memories are too much to expect. And I understood that on the one hand Laura didn't want to be someone who needed to be helped, and on the other hand she was angry that she had been forced to go on the long march of feeling helpless and vulnerable.

There was a second time that I felt Laura pull back. She was telling me that she worried about Kate having breast cancer someday, that Kate would inherit bad genes from her and me. I told her that I'd been screened for the known gene markers linked to breast cancer and that there was no evidence my cancer was linked to a familial pattern. I also asked her if she'd been tested, and that's when she lashed back at me, "Oh, you think you can get off easier if you blame Dad? If daughters get breast cancer from mothers the least they deserve is some sympathy." I realized then that I was being blamed both for her cancer and for her fear of the future, and the two were not separable.

When first she was my darling Laura and I her fresh and naïve mother, I loved her so much I sometimes felt my heart could burst. When she was returned to me after she went missing I knew even more deeply how precious she was. The thought of a life without her was agony. One I could not imagine. Thinking about how deep the root of that love goes still brings tears to my eyes. But after Cancer I came to love her in a different way still. I knew that even if the sweetness was gone, I could love her fiercely.

On the day when I told Tee about Laura's cancer and acknowledged the strength of my feelings for this oldest daughter of mine, I also admitted that I was disappointed that the closeness did not endure. Sometimes the manner in which she pushed me away from her pain seemed unduly harsh. Of course I was overjoyed that she was well, but I had hoped that the connection we discovered by going through hell fire together would stay with us.

Tee said she understood Laura's caution. "My mother loved me that way. I was the only kid she had. But after her car accident she couldn't take care of me. Sometimes I'd catch her looking at me, and I knew she was sad. I didn't like that look."

"Do you think she was sad about you or about what had happened to her?"

"I don't know if it was her sad or my sad. It was just a big awful sad, and I wanted to get away from it. Maybe kids don't like it if their mothers love them too much. I mean, it's not that I didn't want my mom to love me, but it's a lot of responsibility if her love for me makes her sad."

"Did you feel you had to take care of her?"

"No. It was something different. I felt I had to be happy. It's one thing to be happy, but it's a whole different thing when you feel you're *supposed* to be happy because you owe it to your mother. Especially if that happens right in the middle of feeling terrible. And that made me mad. Obviously I wasn't happy, and I wasn't very nice to her sometimes. I wasn't exactly mean to her either, just cold. I acted like she wasn't there. Like she wasn't important."

"Do you think that's how you learned to be so independent?"

"Maybe. I don't know. How independent am I anyway? What choice did I have?"

I was stunned by how thought-through Tee's reaction to her mother was. When I lost my mother I struggled on like a shipwrecked sailor floundering in the waves and hoping to make it to shore somewhere. I wondered about Tee's mother. What kind of person was she? No matter how fierce or strong a mother's love is, it's still a gamble. But, is it invincible? Does a hopeless mother finally give up, give in to the terrible realization that there is nothing more she can do for her child? Tee had expressed it in words that made me shiver when she called it "a big awful sad."

The days I spent with Laura facing down cancer didn't change either of us on the inside, at least not as much as others might expect. We are who we are, and after tough times we want to get back to who we were before. That's where we feel safest. I think that's the way it was with Laura. Maybe with Tee too. And I can feel it was that way with me. When life tests us we aren't softened by it. We're toughened by it. I still love Laura fiercely, but there is always a degree of distance and formality in our affection because Laura is in charge of it. She defines the distance. It must feel safer that way. If she doesn't get too close, she won't notice how I feel. She won't have to worry about me. This is a different kind of power, the kind that surfaces from being tested. About this power, I don't think I can say she was born that way.

# Chapter 12

# SORTING NAMES

Tee was paid each Friday with a check written out for her in my handwriting. After a few weeks of picking up the checks off the counter, she commented about my name. "Your real name's not Maggie, and you kept your own last name when you got married? Your check says Mary Margaret Barnes. It's a nice name. Sort of elegant."

"You can't tell much from a name can you?" I asked.

"Maybe not. In my English course we're reading a short story about a woman named Maggie. She's not at all like you, but I think the name fits you both."

"Who wrote that story?"

"Toni Morrison."

"Do you like the story?"

Tee paused for a moment to assemble her thoughts. "It's complicated, but I like it. It leaves out details that confuse the reader. I suppose an author can do that intentionally if it's a way to make a point. Maybe some time I'll go back and check it out again. But anyway, back to your name. Do you like your name? I mean your real name?"

I explained to Tee that I'd grown up in a parochial school where there were so many Mary's we all went by our second names. And there were enough Margaret's that we had to invent nicknames. Mine was one of the easy ones. My family called me Maggie before I started school. The worst nickname was Gret's because she was one of the unlucky ones whose parents named her Mary Margaret but spelled it M-A-G-R-E-T. It's possible they didn't know how to spell it.

I remember Gret's dad and can imagine him in his muddy overalls fidgeting to get through the line where he was waiting to register her name. Fidgeting because this bureaucratic detail was making him late for work. Spelling a middle name correctly was the least of his worries. He was a man who carried the weight of the world on his shoulders. You could see it when he trudged home each evening with his empty lunch bucket barely swinging beside him as if it were filled with rocks.

I wanted to tell Tee a more upbeat story. When I was in fifth grade a new girl, Mary Rosamond, came to our school. Her name sent the girls in the class scurrying to the book of saints to determine if hers was a consecrated name. Really. A consecrated name. I don't know if that was something the church actually did. Catholics consecrate people and churches and all sorts of other things, but I don't know if they consecrate names.

Either we made up this thing about consecrated names to lend more importance to our own, or one of the adults we considered an expert on such things told us this to impress upon us that the names we had been given at our christening were serious stuff. Anyway, lucky for Mary Rosamond, both of her names were in the book. In a complete turn around from suspicion to envy, we all ended up wishing we had a name as exotic as hers.

"Did you give your children Catholic names?" Tee asked.

"No. I married a Protestant. Some Protestants become Catholics for the sake of marriage, but I was one of those Catholics who went in the other direction. After I became engaged to Ross I became a Protestant."

"Why didn't you change your name when you married? Were you being a rebel or something?"

"No it wasn't political," I tried to explain. "I liked my own last name and didn't like Ross's. And it wasn't just the name. I didn't want to become a member of his family. My surname was the last little bit I had left from my own family. They were all gone. The name was all I had. It was complicated."

"What did your parents think of you keeping your own family name?" Tee asked.

"Well, that's it. My mother died when I was eleven, so she wasn't around to weigh in on my choice. By the time I got married my dad was a weary old man, so he didn't have much to do with it either."

"Did you have brothers and sisters?"

"A younger brother and sister. Twins. After my mother died my Dad couldn't manage three children. The twins went to live with Mom's sister, and because she didn't have children of her own, she wanted to adopt them. They actually took her name. My Dad was quite a bit older than my Mom, and I think after her death he was worn out. When my aunt said she'd take care of the twins if she could adopt them, my Dad just gave in. He didn't have any fight left for the bargain."

"Do you think twins run in your family? I mean . . . it's sort of interesting that you have twins too."

"Who knows? Actually I've never given it much thought."

"Why didn't you go to live with your aunt?"

"I don't even know who made the decision. Maybe three was too many for my aunt. Or maybe my dad needed company."

"Did you cook and clean and do laundry for your dad?"

"No. The house didn't get cleaned much . . . or at all. My dad brought food into the house. Mostly the kind that didn't need to be cooked much. When I was hungry I'd help myself, and he did the same. Once in a while he'd say to me 'Maggie, it's time to wash up those dishes.' I washed my own clothes without being told because having dirty clothes was embarrassing."

"What did your dad do? Did he work?"

"When I was young we lived in Oklahoma and Dad was a country doc, but after my Mom got sick he gave that up. When I was in high school we moved to Chicago, and he was a security guard at a plant entrance. He kept freeloaders from parking in the lot. There were some big apartments across the way from the plant, and people had to pay for parking if they rented spaces along with their apartments. They tried to save a little by parking on the street or in the parking lot at the factory. My Dad's job was to keep them out. At home I mostly remember Dad sitting watching TV. Sometimes he bought a few bottles of beer with the food. Not always though. But he smoked. Watched TV and smoked. He didn't have much of a life after Mom died."

"Not very healthy for a doctor. Did he take better care of you?"

"If I needed something I walked down to the plant entrance where my Dad was tending the booth. I'd ask him for money if we were out of cereal or milk. I learned you could survive if you have cereal and milk. Once in a while I asked him for money so I could go with the neighbor kids to the movies on Saturday afternoon."

"It's sad, Maggie. You seem like such a good sport about it."

"It's long ago, and I don't think about it much. Once I married Ross I tried to leave it behind."

"What was Mr. Barone's full name?"

"Ross Philip Barone, but he only used his middle initial. He was proud of his family name. In his office he had the family crest. I used to tease him that it was a knight with three hearts who had a bird sitting on his head."

"The knight had three hearts and a bird on his head?"

"No. The knight was on the upper part of the crest, and below him was a shield with three hearts positioned in a chevron. There was something on the knight's head, but I never figured out what it was. Who knows what this family crest meant, but it meant a lot to Ross. I think for him it meant he was English and not Italian. Someone in his family dug back into records and unearthed the name in the Virginia record of the 1600's. It was a lucky find and a source of family pride."

"Did you get into that family pride thing too?" Tee asked.

"No. I didn't think it amounted to much. Well that's not exactly true. I got into it enough to needle Ross about it." I explained to Tee that I don't think this family name stuff means much to most women. We shed our names like hermit crabs shed shells. Outgrow one and find another. "You know Alice who lives around the corner, the one who brought over the little pot of daisies? She married young. One of the boys who never came back from Vietnam. She remarried, but divorced that husband. And then she married again. A really nice man. Along the way she had four last names."

On a whim I went on to tell Tee how Ross and I used to get into a snit about the name thing. We didn't fight very often. Maybe we should have fought more because we also didn't talk about hard things as much as I would have liked. But anyway, the name thing was something we could get unpleasant about. The tension about our last names began well before we were married.

Tee seemed surprised. She nodded a little as I spoke, as if she were slowly digesting what I had said, but then she asked the obvious question, "Was there really so much about names that you could bicker about?"

"Are you sure you want to hear this silly story?"

"Sure, why not?"

I laid out the basics. Ross's name was Barone. Most Barone's are Italian, but apparently some go back to England and Ireland as well. A few came from France. My name was Barnes. It's definitely English. That was my first touché during our little fencing match. It didn't matter to me that my name was English, but it galled Ross. He would mount his argument that his family never went to Italy, and he was sure they had come straight to the United States. He boosted his argument further by claiming that whether spelled with the final "e" or not, the name probably referred to being a baron. This fit in well with the knight on the family crest. He assumed the crest was proof in hand.

Ross could go into endless details explaining that there were six ways to spell the name. He'd list them off in a full out spelling recitation. When Ross was done trying to raise the honor of his family name, he would turn to running down the value of mine. He was sure that Barnes means "from the barn" and that my ancestors had probably been poverty-stricken peasant farmers. Just as his family crest proved that his ancestors were barons, the fact that my dad was from Oklahoma proved we were farmers. Ross had a hard time imagining that there was any culture west of the Appalachians, except possibly in North Chicago where his family was from. You see, it wasn't about names; it was about importance.

I had to argue back in my own defense that Barnes could have meant anything because old names were spelled phonetically. I am a university librarian and know that the phonetics of old names is a quagmire. In fact probably Barnes actually had long ago been Barens, which of course would make it the one spelling variation of Barons that Ross had not mentioned.

It's ironic that in the end we may have had the same last name just spelled differently. I was okay with that, but clearly Ross wasn't. You'd think by the end of one of these quarrels we would be laughing at ourselves. It was ridiculous. But we weren't laughing. We were annoyed with each other. I tried to sum it up for Tee. Ross was perturbed that I was not showing respect for his family name, and I was insulted because I thought he was trying to prove that my family was unimportant. In the end I put my foot down and decided to keep my own family name. I justified it by complaining that I'd given up just about everything else that came from my family, the least I could do was keep the name.

That's where I stopped. I didn't tell Tee the rest of the story, the hardest part of it. I was well practiced in steering conversations away from too much talk about my family: losing my mother before I graduated high school, my father's collapse into a depression that seemed never to brighten again, and the wretched years of learning to be alone. The feeling of not belonging to anything was miserable, and I probably never adjusted to that completely. That's why making a family with Ross was important to me. That's also why it hurt me that Ross minimized my family, and it enraged me that he thought I was lucky to be grafted onto his family, as if that could be a replacement for the family I'd lost. I didn't want to talk about any of that. The well-trained voice in my head said, "Don't go there, Maggie."

Meanwhile it seems Tee was still thinking about my claim that all couples have skirmishes. "Do all couples fight?" she asked again. I assume she was trying to appraise if sometime in the future she would be half of a fighting couple.

I tried to explain to Tee that an insignificant fight is a way to side step the real issues that dog us for a lifetime. Each couple finds its own private matters to fight about. We carve out a little arena where we can do our martial games. These quarrels have to be personal enough to hook into our pride and expose the edges of our wounds, but not so vicious that they can break the bond of the relationship. "I knew a little poem once," I said, "let's see if I can remember it."

Let's bicker 'bout it for a while,
I need to know the fighter that you'll be,
And in the end you'll win the space you need,
But kindly leave a little room for me.

The little verse brought us back to neutral territory. "Who wrote that poem?" Tee asked. It's kind of old-fashioned, but it fits right in with what you're talking about.

"I can't remember who wrote it," I admitted. "That happens to us oldsters, you know. We think we know a name or a title, but we can't get to it. It may come back to me in an hour, or tomorrow, or never." Then I admitted to Tee one of my eccentricities. "I keep a small notebook in my desk drawer. If there is a name or a word I haven't been able to bring to mind, and then if later I remember it or see it written somewhere, I put it in the notebook. That way if I forget it again, I can look it up."

Tee laughed when I told her this. I had a feeling she wanted to ask me how full the notebook is, but she didn't. Probably she didn't want to embarrass me. I added just for fun, "Even though the name of the person who wrote that little ditty is lost in my memory, I can tell you this for certain, it wasn't Gerard Manley Hopkins."

A little later Tee got ready to go out. The way she often did, gathering up her things, putting on her coat, and this time she paused a moment before leaving and said, "Maggie, I'm sorry your life was so hard. Nobody would ever guess that about you. Most of the time you seem so strong and happy."

"Sometimes I am, and the rest of the time I try to be," I told her.

As Tee moved toward the door I had a random thought, "Uh . . . Tee . . . do you remember the first day you came to visit and just before you left you asked me a question?"

"Yeah."

"I still think about that sometimes. I remember that first visit, and I remember your question. Were you testing me? Did you know before you asked the question what the answer would have to be if I was telling the truth?"

"Yup . . . more or less that's it. I hadn't planned it that way. It was one of those things that slipped out and got said before I had time to stop it.

"What would you have done if I hadn't told you the truth?"

"I don't know. Is it possible that you wouldn't have? Anyway, it would have made it hard for me to trust you. That's . . . um . . . water under the bridge now though . . . don't you think?"

She walked to the door, and just before she stepped through it she looked back and said, "See you later, Maggie."

Often after Tee leaves I sit in my chair quietly. Not reading. Just thinking. And though it is late afternoon or early evening, I don't feel tired because in our conversations I find fresh energy. I like having time to myself to think about things we've talked about and also the things we haven't talked about that have been churned up in my thoughts. Normally in conversation I'm cautious. Reserved. But in my conversations with Tee sometimes I take the risk of being more revealing.

## Chapter 13

# ANDREA'S EXIT

Row and Andrea came to visit in early spring when the University had a break. It was their alternative to visiting at the Christmas holiday because Andrea had decided they should be at home so they could celebrate with their friends and with Andrea's family. I had the feeling that Row was visiting because he wanted to spend time with me, and Andrea was visiting because she had a social duty to fulfill. They arrived while I was out at an appointment with Tee, but I had instructed Row to buzz the building sup to get in, and we left a key under the mat in front of the door to my apartment. Tee had moved her things into the den on the main floor so that Row and Andrea could have the guest room in the loft.

When Tee and I returned we could hear voices from the bedroom upstairs. Perhaps they didn't hear us come in, or they may not have realized how easily voices carry across the slanted ceiling, but we could hear their conversation. It was about their plans to go with Jak and Jenna to watch Philip play basketball. Jak and Jenna were parents who never missed a game, and by inviting others to join them they could also have a "post-game party."

I heard Row suggest that they take me along. He'd already thought through the logistics because when Row made any sort of proposal to Andrea he always first had to do an extensive feasibility study in preparation for countering all the reasons why his idea wouldn't work. This time he suggested they could pull up at the entrance to the gym and drop me off. Then while I waited there with Andrea he could park the car. To further sell his plan he added, "I'm sure with a little help she can handle the bleachers."

It was predictable that Andrea would want nothing of it. "Can't we just have a night out with your sister? Does your Mom have to be in on everything?"

Row is practiced at knowing when to give in and when to fight while making plans with Andrea. Apparently he thought he still had a fighting chance with this one, because he politely objected to the implication that he had some pathological need to include his mother in all their social activities. In a gesture of compromise Row revised his proposal and suggested, "We can take her just for the game, bring her home, and then go out with Jak and Jenna."

This was the point where Andrea decided to use weapons that do damage. She accused Row of being a "mommy's boy" and told him it was time for him to cut the leash. It was obvious now from the tone of Row's voice that he also was getting mad. "Stop, Andi. Listen to yourself! All that stuff you're saying is bullshit, and you know it."

Andrea is a fighter who gets energized by conflict, and she was just getting started. "Grow up, Row! Do you ever think of anyone but yourself? What about your sister? What about me?" She reminded him that the net effect of his plan was to deprive his wife of a fun night out. "This is my vacation not your mother's." Then she fired a shot from her biggest cannon. "This is it. I hate these mommy visits. This is my last one."

I heard Row's voice again, but now it was surprisingly calm. "Well let's agree on that. I've never enjoyed bringing you home to visit my Mom any more than you've liked coming. You're an embarrassment to me. Let's make this the last one, and I'll consider that a win. For now we'll leave Mom home."

I heard the door open and close. I heard steps on the stairs. They were slow. And I could hear Row breathing in and then breathing out in long deep breaths. He sounded like a man hauling a heavy suitcase down the steps. But when he turned and came into the living room he was only carrying a light jacket over his arm. Row came over and gave me a hug. Asked about my appointment. He complimented me on how well I looked, as if that was something I'd accomplished through working out and a fitness regimen. I asked about his children, and he gave me a little news update on each.

While it may have appeared that we were visiting, in fact Row was just filling in while he was waiting for Andrea to get ready. Idling after he was ready while Andrea finished preparing herself for a night out was something Row knew how to do very well from years of practice. He knew she'd take as much time as she needed, even if it made them late, and he also knew how to busy himself in a way that would allow him to drop whatever he was doing the moment she appeared and was ready to go. He wouldn't want to keep her waiting.

After a few minutes Andrea came down the steps, tapped my cheek with hers, blew a cold kiss into the air, and didn't acknowledge Tee who was in the kitchen, but still clearly visible from the living room. "We've got to get going," she said to Row. And to me she said, "You'll probably be sleeping by the time we get back so we won't wake you." Then to Row again, "Honey, do you have a key so we can get in?" She was all business, and he was dutiful and polite.

Tee heard this all from the kitchen. Once the door closed and Row and Andrea were gone, Tee came into the living room and sat down on the sofa across from where I was sitting. "That is so not fair. You don't deserve that, Maggie."

"We don't all get what's fair, and it's not Row's fault, you know."

"It's not his fault, and I don't want to argue with you, Maggie, but maybe he should stand up to her. Why does he let her treat him that way? And why does he let her say those things about his own mother?"

I wouldn't be telling the truth if I didn't admit that I felt insulted by Andrea's words. It wasn't the first time I had ugly feelings toward this daughter-in-law with her arrogance about what she deserves, and it felt good that Tee came to my defense. It also wasn't the first time that I'd seen Row let her get away with it. Andrea took my son for granted. I was angry that she treated him that way, and I was disappointed with him that he accepted it. Life hands out the good stuff unevenly, and sometimes gives good deals to those who deserve them least. Andrea was lucky. Row wasn't.

Over the course of the evening I thought about Andrea. I never liked her. Not long after Row and Andrea married, I told Ross that I'd learn to like her, and if I couldn't then I was determined to act as if I did. Ross had his own way of boxing off his irritation with Andrea because she was nice to Ross the way she was nice to all men except her own husband. By being slightly flirty she could get their attention, and once she had it men tended to treat Andrea well, the way they usually treat women who are especially pretty. They treat them as if they are on the same team.

Andrea was stunning, and she knew it. I recall the first time Row came home with her. Her well-cut face, her dark hair, and stylish clothes on a good build were the first things most people noticed about her. As she put on a few years her beauty hadn't waned because she is one of those women whose architecture stands up well to time. What nature gave her in beauty, it didn't give her in temperament. As much as men are inclined to admire her, women are inclined to resent her because Andrea is a queen bee.

Both Ross and I were critical of the way Andrea managed money. Her sense of style was expensive. She liked brand names, and didn't like last year's clothes. She managed their house the way she managed her wardrobe, demonstrating her expensive taste in a constant cycle of replacement. Ross always worried about whether Row could keep up financially with Andrea's demands. He had a good job, but his income was not enough to provide for Andrea because whenever he increased the revenue she increased the expenditures.

Some of the money Andrea used to fund her shopping came from her family, and this was one more reason she seemed to feel entitled to talk down to Row. He was under constant pressure to take on extras that would supplement their income. He taught course overloads and summer sessions, but each time he thought he was making enough so they could catch up, she proved to him all over again that what he provided was inadequate. Row was Andrea's workhorse.

I didn't mind being home while Row and Andrea went out. As the evening wore on I decided I should at least lie down in my bed so that if I could sleep, I'd be in the right place. I did fall asleep, and I dreamed.

My dream had a vague resemblance to a picture of the Last Supper. In this case the figure at the center wasn't a man with an Italian Renaissance face sitting in a row with his disciples; it was an old woman. All the guests had circles around their heads like those round fluorescent bulbs we used to have in the kitchen ceiling. There was only one guest who didn't have a light. It was a young woman sitting at the end of the table where she was fiddling with her mobile phone, probably reading her messages. Most striking about the picture was the companion who was leaning on the old woman as if he needed a nap.

That's what I remember of the picture of the last supper that was in our parish church. The companion leaning on Jesus was his favorite. As I think about it now it strikes me as nearly impossible that Jesus would play favorites. It must be that it's not about who's favorite but rather who's familiar that decides closeness and distance. There are some people about whom it is true that the closer they get to us the more on guard we feel. And there are others about whom it is equally true that the closer they get, the more at ease we feel. In the cluster of my children Row was the easiest for me; in the circle of my family Andrea was the most difficult.

After Row's last visit with Andrea he began to call more often. I think he called from his office at school because the room had an echo that didn't sound like home. A typical call began with a check-in about how I was doing. Then I'd ask him about his kids and his work so he could assure me they were all fine. We'd talk a little about books we were reading or movies we'd seen. Sometimes he would humor me with a little story about one of his students. Rarely did either of us mention Andrea.

I could usually tell almost immediately if Row's call was a quick one being made between two events on his schedule. After class and on his way to a meeting, for example. I could also tell if he was calling because he felt like talking. Those calls had a different tone. On one of the calls soon after the ugly visit with Andrea, Row launched right into the serious part of the conversation with a question. He wanted to know if I thought Andrea was a bad wife. I snapped into good mother mode. "It's not my job to judge if she's a good or bad wife. You picked her and it's my job to get along with her."

"Well, your reply answers my question, doesn't it?"

"That's one way to put it, but I could say your question says you may have doubts."

Row went on to explain that even if Andrea is difficult sometimes, she's a good mother and she treats her kids well. She'd do anything for them. She loves them, and they love her.

"Your kids deserve a good mother, but I don't like it when she treats you badly. Don't let her put you down, Row. You're a good son, you're a good dad, and you're a good man."

"You have to say that. You're my mother. It's your job to say that, right?"

"I'm not saying it because it's my job. I'm saying it because it's true."

He was quiet for a moment. And when he spoke again his voice was soft. "Thanks, Mom." And then after another pause, "I have to get going. We'll talk soon. I love you, Mom."

"Love you too, Row."

The issue did not go away, and later Row picked it up again. He's like a hovercraft sometimes. He can circle ideas endlessly and never settle on a conclusion. This time he told me Zachary had asked why he'd married Andrea. Apparently their children see the tension. Row admitted he didn't know how to answer Zach, so he said, "Sometimes we invite people into our lives to add texture." I had a glimpsing image of fine silk being raked by a cheese grater.

## Chapter 14

# AUNT DORIS

When Tee was a child her father was in the army, and sometimes Tee and her mother followed him to places where he was stationed. More often, after Tee was old enough to go to school, they just lived without him. Her mother didn't want Tee to be a "military brat" who was always leaving and starting over again somewhere else. Over time Tee realized, however, that there was another reason. She heard the adults talking about her father and another family, a wife and kids.

Tee and her mother did okay. Tee was a good student and made friends. Her mother had her own friends and her own work. This all changed when Tee's mother fell asleep at the wheel while driving home late one night after a double shift. While her mother was in rehabilitation Tee stayed with Aunt Doris. That wasn't a difficult transition because Aunt Doris was her landing pad after school when Tee's mother worked long hours, and Tee liked going there.

Although Tee's mother survived the accident, she did not return to consciousness for several weeks, and when she did she was moved to rehabilitation, but she made only slow progress. It became clear that she would not be able to return home, and the family decided to put her in a nursing home in Indiana where Tee's Aunt Gloria worked.

The plan was that Tee would move to Indiana with her mother, and she would live with Aunt Gloria, but Tee didn't want to move. She liked school and didn't want to start over in a strange town where she didn't know anyone. Being the new kid was miserable and living with Aunt Gloria sounded terrible. Tee didn't like Aunt Gloria, didn't like Aunt Gloria's cooking, and especially didn't like the fact that Aunt Gloria's apartment always smelled like a greasy fast food restaurant and sweat. The deeper reason was that Tee wanted to stay with Aunt Doris.

Tee gathered her complaints and told them to her Dad, but she did not tell them to Aunt Doris who would've told her to watch her mouth because it was not fitting to talk about her Aunt Gloria that way. What Tee did tell Aunt Doris is that sometimes Aunt Gloria smelled like whiskey. This complaint seemed to carry weight, so when it was time to move Tee's mother to Indiana, Tee stayed back and lived with Aunt Doris.

The first time Tee told me this part of the story I asked her if Aunt Gloria really smelled like whiskey or if this was something Tee made up because she knew it would impress the other adults. It seemed clever. It turns out there were other things that bothered Tee much more than Aunt Gloria's whiskey. She had a nagging voice and bad breath. She complained a lot about small things like the neighbor's dog that barked during the night and the price of milk at the convenience store. Aunt Gloria never ran out of things to complain about. She was a downer. All of this is not to say that Tee was not clever. Of all the things that made living with Aunt Gloria an unacceptable option for Tee, she was smart enough to know that the one that would turn the tide of adult opinion was the whiskey. Tee had learned early to watch and listen when she was around adults. She understood how to help them make up their minds.

Aunt Gloria was a sister of Tee's dad, but Aunt Doris was her dad's aunt. At first the plan was that Tee would stay with Aunt Doris until she finished high school, and Tee's mother would stay permanently in the long term care facility. But it did not turn out to be long term because Tee's mom needed surgery, and during the surgery she had a stroke. She didn't survive. That's when home with Aunt Doris became the only home Tee had.

Tee affectionately described Aunt Doris as older than Methuselah. Once when I asked Tee how old Aunt Doris really was, she said she didn't know. Maybe that was a polite dodge because in Tee's eyes I am probably older than Methuselah too. In the eyes of most twenty-two- year-olds anyone over fifty is already pretty old, and both Aunt Doris and I were way past that. Anyway, Aunt Doris had been around for a long time, and for a lot of that time she lived in the same house, a house that Tee loved.

I enjoyed listening to Tee describe Aunt Doris's house. She had a cat that now and then had kittens. There was a huge garden closed in by the neighbor's garage on the back and by tall fences along the sides. The garden was a magical world where a curious little girl could feel safe and happy. It had lots of flowers and butterflies. Tee captured caterpillars in a box and fed them leaves. On one of her explorations she discovered a nest of tiny mice, but they did not survive after she picked them up. Together Tee and Aunt Doris gathered vegetables for dinner when they were in season. Along the back of the garden were raspberry bushes, which though scratchy, were a favorite place for Tee to forage for her own snacks.

Tee helped in the garden sometimes, but it was a garden with a set of rules. Sometimes Aunt Doris would come in from the garden with sweat pouring off her face and send Tee out to gather the rest of what she wanted for dinner. She'd give Tee a rundown of the garden rules: "Don't step on the plants or squash the bugs. Just gather the food. Don't just pick the best either. Those vegetables that are crooked or knobby are perfectly good." Aunt Doris took good care of things and did not waste. She protected her garden the way she protected Tee.

There was a time when Tee was harvesting beans and noticed weeds around the plants. Wanting to impress Aunt Doris, Tee pulled some of them up, but she had barely started when Aunt Doris came storming from the house. She was watching from the window. "What are you doing ripping those things up? Leave them be."

Tee tried to explain that they were weeds, and she was trying clean up the garden. When Tee told me the story she added that she thought Aunt Doris was getting so old she couldn't see the difference between a plant and a weed. But that wasn't it. "If those little seeds pick that little spot to drop down and grow, and if the good Lord gives them rain and sun so they can grow there, who do you think you are telling them they've picked the wrong spot. You just go mind your own business and leave them be."

So Tee went back to picking the beans and didn't bother the weeds. On other days it was tomatoes or squash. Sometimes she pulled onions or gathered in the peppers. But she never pulled weeds. Over the summer the garden got fuller and fuller. There was always food, and Tee likes to say that finally their garden looked like the Garden of Eden. There was not one empty space where something wasn't growing. That is the way Aunt Doris wanted it.

Aunt Doris was not a fluffy disciplinarian. The good thing about that was that you knew what to expect. The bad side of that was when you made a mistake she did not let you off easily. Tee discovered right from the start that Aunt Doris intended to unteach some things that Tee had gotten used to. Tee knew it was coming when Aunt Doris would say, "Child, you just don't know how the world works."

One of the first things Aunt Doris changed was Tee's nickname. Aunt Doris insisted on calling people by their right and proper names, and a nickname like Tee was not suitable. That's why at Aunt Doris's house Tee got used to being called Tanesha, and sometimes if Aunt Doris wanted to make a point, she would bring out the full Tanesha Shinae. Her reasoning was beyond argument, "When the Lord wrote your name in the Book of Life he did not use some silly short name. He used your full name. And someday when you are standing before the gates of glory and ready to go in, your real name will be called. You better get used to recognizing it."

Only after Tee came to live with me did I know that on Wednesday evenings she went to choir practice. On most Sundays she went to church where she sang in the choir. That is also part of the Aunt Doris story.

When Tee was little enough to need a babysitter, or at least an adult to watch her when her mother worked the late shift, she often stayed with Aunt Doris overnight. On Wednesdays Aunt Doris went to choir practice, and that meant Tee went with her. The first time this happened Aunt Doris sat Tee down in one of the pews and told her in no uncertain terms that she should stay put there and not make a fuss because the choir was doing the Lord's work.

Tee did not make a fuss or interrupt. Minding Aunt Doris was not negotiable. But Tee also didn't interrupt because she loved watching the choir sing, even when they were practicing certain parts over and over. What she liked especially was when the choir was ready to sing one of the "offerings" all the way through, sing it the way they were going to at the Sunday morning worship. That's when they would sway. They would catch the beat and move back and forth, all of them together in a perfect smooth motion with a little bounce at the end. Sometimes Tee couldn't resist. She'd stand in the pew and sway with them.

Aunt Doris did not look at Tee when she was standing in the pew swaying, because Aunt Doris was busy. But as Tee came to know, Aunt Doris could see everything. Tee actually believed Aunt Doris could see around corners. The way she knew that Aunt Doris had seen her moving with the choir was that later Aunt Doris explained to Tee that it was the spirit moving her.

One night when they went to practice, instead of parking Tee in the pew Aunt Doris steered her up to the choir. She put her five from the end in the third row between Aunt Doris and Sister Maddi. Of course Aunt Doris never called her Sister Maddi. She called her by her proper name, Sister Madeleine, and if anyone thought to use the short name, Aunt Doris would huff and remind them that especially in the church, nicknames had no place.

So it happened that when Tee went to choir practice with Doris Williams Greene, she stood with the choir. She could hear each of the voices and all of them together. She could feel the spirit when they began to sway, and she swayed with them. "It was the most beautiful thing," she told me once. "If someone asked me what heaven is like, I would say that's it. Standing with the choir tucked in there between Aunt Doris and Sister Madeleine."

Over time Tee learned the music. She learned the words and sometimes when she was riding the school bus or sitting waiting for the bell to ring at the end of the school day those songs would be streaming through her mind. At home she and Aunt Doris would hum together as they worked on something in the kitchen or in the garden. Once Tee got to know the songs well enough so that she could hum a good strong melody line, Aunt Doris would harmonize. It made Tee eager for Wednesday night. She was even more eager for Sunday when the choir would don robes, the Pastor would walk the pulpit, and all the families with children in their Sunday best would be there to hear her choir.

That's how Tee came to think of the choir. It was her choir. So it is not surprising that the day came when standing there between Aunt Doris and Sister Madeleine, Tee felt a nudge on her arm and heard Aunt Doris whisper, "Sing it, Tanesha!" And that is how Tee became a member of the choir at Mount Carmel AME Church.

Leading up to Easter Tee was gone more. She had extra choir rehearsals and told me the church was gearing up for a big event. A few days before Easter she asked me if I'd like to come to hear her choir on Easter morning. That's why on a Sunday in April, I was a visitor at Mt. Carmel AME Church. Tee led me in, and parked me in the pew. Toward the back. She explained that if the service began to feel long and I needed to excuse myself, I would be able to walk up the aisle and out without causing an interruption. But I didn't leave, even though the service was long. It wasn't the kind of event that you can walk away from like a concert in the park.

The service was not like Easter masses I attended as a child. They were impressive too. Often there were lots of celebrants, and the vestments were white. The procession was long, and incense filled the church. Some families filled whole pews with children in new Easter clothes, grandmothers with Easter corsages, and aunts and uncles visiting for the holiday. On one of those Easters I had a new pair of lacey white gloves. That was exciting in its own way.

The service at Mt. Carmel AME Church also was not at all like the Protestant services I attended over the years with Ross and the children. The women's new spring hats made the congregation look like a garden in full bloom. It was a good service because the choir anthems were grand, the congregation was full, and the hymns for the day were familiar so that the singing nearly raised the roof. The organ postlude was so good most of the congregation stayed seated to listen, and the big sounds rang in our ears all the way home. We have photos of the family taken over the years because Easter was the perfect time to catch us all in our Sunday best.

This service at Mount Carmel AME Church was different. It throbbed with energy as if at any moment the earth was going to break open and the dead were going to be raised and at the same time chains would be broken and captives set free. It wasn't just a celebration of something that happened long ago. It was happening all over again, and we were in the middle of it. A few times I felt the urge to tap my foot, or clap my hands, or sway a little from side to side. This was all new to me.

When we went home and had our Easter lunch at the dining room table I asked Tee which one in the choir was Aunt Doris. I think I asked if it was still Aunt Doris she stood next to, because I had looked at the women on either side of Tee and tried to decide which one could be Aunt Doris. Neither of them seemed old enough, so I gathered that now Aunt Doris stood somewhere else in the choir. Tee just looked away as if she had not heard my question. It was awkward for a moment, and then she said, "She isn't in the choir. She has passed."

I was stunned. I had no idea when or how Aunt Doris had passed away. And I didn't want to ask questions as if I deserved a report, so instead I said,

"I'm so sorry Tee. She sounds like a remarkable person. I wish I could've met her." I know it was an awkward thing to say, but I wanted to say something.

Tee's eyes shifted toward me and in place of the light that usually was there, her eyes were dark. She pushed her chair back and left the table. I heard her go up the stairs to the loft, and then a few minutes later I heard her steps coming down. As she headed out the door she said, "I'm going out."

I was gob-smacked. I didn't know what had happened. I had the whole afternoon to think about it, and the evening too. It was Easter, and I was alone thinking about this woman who'd passed away and her niece who'd just walked out of my house. The problem was I couldn't get a purchase on what had transpired. What was the reason? What had upset her?

Did Tee think my wish to meet Aunt Doris was nosey? Or did she think that saintly Aunt Doris wouldn't have approved of me? Or would it simply have been a terribly awkward instance of two paths crossing, the meeting of two old women who wouldn't have known how to start a conversation with each other? Of one thing I was sure, Tee had never told me that her Aunt Doris had passed away. I would have remembered something as important as that.

The more I thought the clearer it became to me that though I didn't know exactly what was so offensive about what I'd said, something had landed wrong. I'd blundered. I wanted to know about what I'd done so I'd know how to be guilty. I thought about it for so long and from so many angles that I started to feel guilty about not knowing. Am I really that dense?

When I heard the key in the lock I got up from my chair and walked toward Tee so that she wouldn't disappear up the stairs before I could speak to her. I said, "Tee, I'm sorry. I know I said something stupid, but I didn't intend to offend you."

"You did."

"Well, can we talk about it?"

"No, just leave it alone."

She brushed past me and went upstairs.

I heard her shuffling around for while. I assumed that in the morning she would come down with her backpack and the boxes with which she'd moved in. Not only had I offended her, but now I had offended her twice. I began to imagine what I'd say as she left. Would I wish her well? Or would I tell her that I was still open to hearing what she had to say? Or would I say one more stupid thing like, "I'm sorry, Tee, and Good Luck!"

It occurred to me to reprimand Tee and tell her it's not fair to take offense from someone who didn't mean ill. But it was clear that wasn't how she felt, and it was clear that she'd decided I was the guilty one. It was plenty to think about. I slept poorly.

Toward morning I woke up and rehearsed it all once again. Then I heard water running upstairs. Foot steps in the loft. And finally I heard Tee come down the stairs, walk to the kitchen, and start the coffee.

It felt as if during the night a huge storm had passed through, breaking branches, tearing off leaves, and unearthing big trees. Then there was a miracle. By morning the debris was cleaned up, so that with first light everything was ordinary again. It was the Monday after Easter, but it was like so many other Mondays. Just an ordinary day.

Chapter 15

# FIGHTING ROW

I have had the strangest confrontation ever with Row. He came two weekends ago for one of his fly-over visits on his way home from a conference. It worked out well because it was a weekend that Tee was away staying with Jenna's kids. From the moment Row walked through the door of my condo his presence felt like a shoe that didn't fit. Within an hour of arriving he went to the cabinet and poured himself scotch. Not a lot, just a "nip," as he called it.

I always find scotch so cagey. Just a little in the bottom of a glass. Nothing big and colorful like beer or wine that catches the light and shows off. These others are more honest in exposing that the point of drinking them is something other than quenching thirst. Scotch looks like nothing, and is taken in little sips with lots of air as if it is being smelled rather than guzzled, and that's the deception.

"Give me my Macallan," said Row, raising the bottle and the glass as if he were proposing a toast. "Spare me that heavy smelling perfume my father and my brother drink. They pick spirits distilled on an island with names impossible to spell and the heavy odor of an old tweed coat stored in mothballs. I, ladies and gentlemen, prefer the fresh air of the north and the company of Lady Mary Margaret."

I had no idea what he was talking about, except for the odd reference to me using my full name in a sarcastic way. His behavior was bizarre. If I hadn't known Row's penchant for words and his love of drama I might have thought he was . . . well, you know . . . a little off. Row had assumed the posture of a Shakespearean actor delivering a soliloquy. He was standing with one foot a little ahead of the other, his shoulders squared, chest out, and he was holding his glass in a toast raised to no one in particular. I assumed it was his first drink of the day, but he was already talking like a drunk.

Row's behavior was reminiscent of Ross's brother Charlie. We'd always referred to him as an affable drunk because the more he drank the louder he laughed. We also knew, however, that the more he drank, the more likely it was that when we least expected it, he would blurt out something cruel that a sober man would regret the next day. Loud boisterous laughter with which he delivered the insult didn't do much to ease the embarrassment of his victim. I wanted to see Row's behavior as humor, or at least a try at it, but his mood made me uneasy.

We went out for dinner to a lovely little place called Lunette. A young couple that is the new breed of gourmet chef runs it. Everything fresh and local, nothing too complex. I like it because the space is small and the ceilings aren't too high, which means, it isn't noisy. At my age that's a factor in comfort. If the seats are comfortable and the ceilings low, the rest will probably be satisfactory.

Once we were seated Row ordered another scotch. I cautioned him discreetly by saying, very quietly, "Are you sure that's a good idea on an empty stomach?" His reply was snotty and loud. "Who do you think you are, my mother?" It had an edge I'm not used to with Row. Normally he is a son I can count on to have good manners. He is often clever with words and somewhat complicated, but these outbursts lacked good humor and were snarky. To cover up, Row asked the waiter for bread sticks and instructed me to have some because this wasn't a fast food restaurant, and it might be a little while before our food came to the table.

When I think back now on that miserable evening beginning at the Lunette, I see us sitting in that little booth next to the alcove window with a broad ledge and an arched ceiling. I also remember noticing that the window was not glass but rather a faux painting of a scene from Italy. And I noticed that along the bottom of the painted window the artist had added a hint of a window box to suggest something hanging outside on the side of the building. I noticed all that because I was trying to distract myself. I wished I were outside the window . . . or in Italy. My son was embarrassing me.

Over the course of our meal Row continued with wine and became more and more like his Uncle Charlie. He tried to tell jokes, and all of them were either off color or awkward. He laughed at his own jokes and his laughter was annoyingly loud. Some comments he made to the waiter were about me, and they were insulting. When my meal came to the table he told the waiter he would cut up the meat on my plate for me; "I have a lot of practice doing it for my kids," he said. Neither the waiter nor I found it funny, but he forced a smile and raised an eyebrow in sympathy with me.

I knew I had reached my limit when Row launched into what he thought was a hilarious story about his son Zachary's research assignment. The students had been asked by their English teacher to find an idiom and research its origin. Zachary had discovered that the expression "blow smoke up his arse" referred to a folk medicine method for reviving an unconscious person or even a drowning victim. It involved using bellows filled with tobacco smoke, which introduced as a smoky enema stimulated the victim to breathe.

Under normal circumstances this might be a tidbit of information that could hook the curiosity of a retired university librarian, but shared with the entire restaurant in the loud drunken voice of my son, it was more than I could handle. I gestured to the waiter, and when he came to our table in a very definite voice I said, "Please bring our check, and would you also please ask the maître d' to call us a taxi."

Row interrupted in a condescending voice as if he were helping an old woman who was having trouble with her memory. "We drove over, Mom, remember?" And then to the waiter, "We don't need a taxi. We came over in our car." But I was having no more of it, so I caught the eye of the waiter and countered in a very slow and definite voice, "We do need a taxi. Thank you very much." And then after the waiter had walked away, and as an aside to Row, I said, "I assume you'll object to me driving us home because you're incapacitated, and I'm not sure I'd feel comfortable driving with you in the passenger seat, given the mood you're in. We'll pick up the car tomorrow. I'll ask Tee to help me out."

When we got home Row poured himself another scotch and brought me a glass of water. As soon as he was seated I said to him that I was worried about how much he'd already had to drink. He was agitated. He held his glass in his hand even while it was resting on the side table, and as he spoke he placed his hand across the top of the glass and slowly turned it in circles as if he were screwing it into the tabletop.

"Ever heard of liquid courage, Mom? Are you proud of being someone I don't dare to talk to until I've had enough to drink?" There was no use responding. He was way past that. So instead I tried to feel my back against the chair and my feet on the floor. Then I waited for what he had to say next. It was what he had been revving up to talk about all evening.

"I'm divorcing Andi. I've lived with that bitch long enough and I'm done." He eyed me with the bleary look of a drunk checking to see if I was listening. "She's a ball-buster. Like one of those women in a gray uniform who are prison guards in bad movies. Everyday by the end of the day I feel like an emasculated toad. A little fool hopping around trying to avoid her so she won't step on me."

I could feel my annoyance mounting because I could barely stifle the impulse to remind him that he was mixing metaphors and not making any sense. There were points in Row's tirade at which he said things about Andrea and his injured ego that were particularly vulgar and excessively revealing. I interrupted him to say, "I'm your mother, Row. I don't need to hear this." But he wouldn't be silenced.

"Oh, now look who has chaste ears," he said and continued in much the same vein. "The only women who take me seriously are the ones I take home from the bar, but I don't have to talk to them. We keep busy with other things. So what do you think of that, Mom?" Finally Row paused, looked at me and said, "Well, do you have anything to say?"

"No, I don't. But I'm listening" I replied.

Row could not resist another punch. "That's such a friggin Maggie Barnes thing to say. You're a coward. You're withholding. Always trying to do it right. Not wanting to be judgmental. You think we don't know the real Mary Margaret Barnes Barone, university librarian, mother of five . . . oops four, respected widow in her nice little neighborhood, proper old lady who goes to church? You make me sick."

Then something shifted as if Mr. Hyde disappeared and the real Rowland Barone took charge again. I suspect he wanted to prove to me that he wasn't as drunk as I judged him to be. He took his glass, still with a just visible amount of scotch in the bottom, and walked slowly to the kitchen in falsely steady and measured steps. In the kitchen Row poured the scotch out into the sink, rinsed out the glass, carefully, thoroughly, and dried it with the tea towel before returning it to the cupboard. Then he walked back to the living room in the same false steady gait and came toward me, reaching for my water glass.

I stopped him. "Row just leave it. I'm going to sit here a little to read." I had no intention of reading, but neither did I have any intention of getting up to go to my own bed, and certainly did not want to suggest that I was waiting for the conversation to continue.

Row turned and said "Night," then disappeared into the den where he was sleeping on the pullout. The next morning was awkward. He took long in the shower and ate his breakfast at the kitchen counter. By noon he made his way to the airport and was gone. When I asked Tee to retrieve the car for me, I did not explain why we had left it at the restaurant, and she didn't ask, although she probably guessed when she saw the empty scotch bottle in the trash.

Any mother who has had a confrontation like this with a child knows what follows. The rage, the numb feelings, the blank worry of where this will all end up. Tee asked me several times if I was feeling well. She stopped asking after I told her "my visit with Row was very difficult."

Then Row called. He wanted to talk about what had happened. But first he wanted to tell me more about what was going on with him. He was still adamant about divorcing Andrea. In the process he'd been seeing a therapist, and he'd also processed his visit with me during one of his appointments.

Apparently his therapist has tried to help him see that when facing a life changing decision the apprehension builds up over time because there are continuous reminders of what the change will mean. The habit of believing that you're always in the one down position and your opponent is always entitled to the last word creates anxiety. Add to that the unknowns of a major life decision and "it starts to feel crazy." Those were the words Row said his therapist used, and he agreed. "I feel sort of crazy quite a lot of the time."

Empowered by this insight Row was able to admit to his therapist that in his own thoughts he has been divorcing Andrea emotionally for years, but in reality he couldn't make it happen. The therapist gave Row a way of seeing why that was different now. He was doing something to mount his courage. He was provoking skirmishes elsewhere that served as dress rehearsals for what he would have to face when finally dealing with Andrea.

Row admitted that he'd been disagreeable with numerous people, including me. At work he was impatient about minor things. He had been less understanding than usual with his children. One of his interactions with his good friend Roger was uncharacteristically aggressive, and to his credit Roger had laughed it off. Row's tirade with me was another rehearsal for his interactions with Andrea. He had to prove to himself that even in the presence of a strong woman he did not have to back down.

As I listened to him I did not stop worrying about him. I only worried more. He was speaking with two voices. My son Row had called to apologize, but mixed in with his voice was a new voice, the alien voice of his therapist. This foreign voice was thanking me for giving Row the opportunity to test his might by having a skirmish with me? I found that offensive. Did he and his therapist think the ugly evening at the Lunette and in my living room was a rehearsal for a pas de seul in Row's ballet, and I was nothing more than the floor on which he practiced his most difficult leaps and turns? I was furious.

If my phone conversation with Row had ended there it might have been possible to dismiss it as an awkward case of family theater. At least I would have found some comfort in the fact that we were back in touch. He would have said what was on his mind, and I could have found a way to set it aside without fighting back. But family drama is not like the theater when the curtains close, the lights come on, we go out for dinner after the show, and life goes on as usual. Family drama is not so simple.

I decided to defend myself against Row and his therapist. "Your therapist may be getting to know you, Row, but she doesn't know me. All she knows about me is what you tell her. So apparently you wish I would be more forthcoming about what I think. Unfortunately with you sometimes that doesn't feel safe. Feel free to tell your therapist that."

Row was not finished telling me about his therapy. I should have known. He went on to tell me that his therapist believes some of his fear of strong women originates with me. Thankfully he did not report that his therapist thought he'd married a woman just like his mother. It was more nuanced than that. She suggested that Row had learned from me how to stop the expression of his feelings at the point where it would've been healthier to soldier on through. My refusal to tell Row what I thought of his decision to divorce Andrea and his relationships with other women were examples his therapist appealed to in helping Row see this dynamic.

"You know what she said, Mom? She asked me what it is about my Mom that she holds her cards so close. I give you the perfect opportunity to tell me what you think, and you don't. You just leave me standing there. The moment my therapist said that the pieces fell in place. She's right. You have been doing that to me my whole life."

So what should I have done? Powered on through this phone conversation and told Row that his therapist missed the mark? Sometimes digging deep does bring to light what needs to be seen. Just as often digging deep only leaves deep holes.

Row's words brought to the surface what I do not like about him, despite all the things I appreciate. Sometimes when Row is getting too close to the real issue, he is evasive. That is when I can't trust him. He is a master of intellectual legerdemain. What's really Row's own struggle suddenly gets handed off to me. He sets me up to solve the problem, and then he comes along as a spectator. That way he can have it both ways. He can have the answer, but doesn't have to do the dirty work. The more serious the matter, the more slyly he does this.

I remember after Steven's death that Row and I were talking about grief, walking along the shore and sharing our agony, and then as if a wave had grabbed Row he was gone, and instead walking next to me was a stranger telling me about how the death of youth is handled in Greek tragedies. Their view of afterlife and what happens to the soul in it. It was like a classroom lecture, but a bad one.

There at the water's edge I shouted, "Row, this is not a Greek tragedy. You have no right to calmly interpret Steven's death the way you might discuss it with half-bored students in a classroom. This is our Steven, and he has been turned to dust. What's wrong with you?"

Row's response to me was cruel. "Calm down, Mom. I know this is still a raw issue for you." And then he quoted Maugham: "the sharp edge of the razor is difficult to pass over . . . the path to Salvation is hard."

I couldn't let Row get away with that, so I shouted again. Into the wind, over the sound of the waves. "How can you say that to me about Steven? He was a baby I gave birth to. He was your little brother. And now he's gone. Forever."

Row gave me that look men give to women when they think a female is being hysterical. "Gee, Mom. Ease up. Get yourself together. Maugham didn't say it about you. He was quoting from the wisdom of the ancients. It's just a good quote in general."

How could he do that? How could a man who sometimes is so sensitive, so fine tuned, be so blind to my agony? How could he use his intellect to distance himself so far from life, from his own real pain? I had a flash of insight about why he married Andrea, but I could not hold on to it for more than an instant. Instead the struggle brought me back to what I have experienced about Row so many times. He is an exquisite soul with a limited capacity. He is a fearful man. Not fearful of snakes or intruders. He is fearful of feelings so big they could drive him crazy. And he is fearful of truth. But he is my son, and I love him.

## Chapter 16

# STEVEN REDIVIVUS

I thought it odd that Laura was coming for a visit and hadn't told Jenna about it. The moment I saw Laura I knew something was wrong because she looked gloomy and nervous. She said she needed to get away for a rest, and my condo seemed like a quiet place. Tee offered to move into the den so Laura could have the loft upstairs, but Laura didn't want that. She insisted that she'd be fine on the pullout couch.

When Laura was ready she began to talk, and the problem was Jeremy. Every grandmother thinks her grandchildren are smart and handsome, but Jeremy really is. And for a child given a considerable supply of potential at birth, Laura and Robby were ideal parents, the kind who did everything possible to assure that Jeremy's potential wouldn't go to waste.

The purpose of Laura's visit was to tell me that Jeremy was in trouble. He'd been arrested. It was the kind of arrest that would make most parents want to take a kid by the scruff of his neck, bend him over a knee and give him a spanking, even though we don't do that anymore.

Jeremy had been arrested for shoplifting, not just ordinary shoplifting but organized shoplifting, if you can imagine such a thing. He and his friends had devised a game that involved creating a shopping list of items at various stores: Target, Walmart, Best Buy, Macy's and others. They weren't small items. They were big, expensive ones like a computer screen, high priced brand name clothes, play stations, and other expensive gadgets. These boys weren't just sticking candy bars in their pockets. They were plotting their thefts and devising major trickery to get out the door with the items they were stealing.

At a party at which Jeremy and his friends first shared liquor they'd lifted from their parents' cabinets, they dealt the cards on which they'd written the stores and the items. The contest was to see who could show up first with the stolen items on the cards in the hand he'd been dealt. To make a long story short, Jeremy got caught. It briefly occurred to me to take some minor comfort from the fact that my grandson was not a good thief.

Laura and Robby were devastated, and they were especially angry because Jeremy was glib about the trouble he was in. They thought he had put his entire future at risk while he thought they were being petty because "a couple hundred bucks for a lawyer is no big deal." There was another element to Laura's distress. What if Jeremy turned out like Steven? What if this was just the beginning of his downward spiral? That is what she wanted to talk to me about.

I was clumsy in my efforts to follow Laura's questions. She wanted to review with me all the ways in which Jeremy might be like Steven, creating an index for her own fears. Any way in which Jeremy resembled Steven was a nail in Jeremy's coffin. But it wasn't easy to make the comparisons because some things that sixteen year olds do indicate nothing about their future character. For example, what adolescent doesn't stay up half the night and then sleep until noon at least once in a while? What sixteen-year-old boy doesn't look at pornography if given the chance, or sometimes go out with his friends to somewhere he's not allowed to be, and lie to his parents about where he's going? Of course this upsets parents, but it doesn't predict future disaster.

Each time I tried to reassure Laura she ignored me. I only realized well into the conversation that she was ignoring me because she wanted me to say more, add more reassurances to the ones I'd already offered her. A few were not enough. She needed me to keep trying. She wanted me to add layer upon layer to the case I was making to convince her that Jeremy would be okay.

Somewhere in the conversation it felt as if we switched teams. I recognized some of the concerns she expressed, such as the fact that Jeremy's grades had dropped off and he was skipping school often. When I admitted alarm about this pattern, Laura immediately argued back against me as if I were misrepresenting Jeremy. She needed to talk me out of the things I was saying, and she did so as if she were Jeremy's only defender and I his accuser.

Finally I caught on. Laura didn't need me to explore with her, she needed me to decide for her. So I took charge of the conversation and ended the back and forth. Without allowing her to interrupt me again, I told her that anything she could do to help Jeremy was worth doing, but that comparing him to Steven wouldn't be helpful at all. The two boys weren't at all alike. That was as direct as I could be. And this seemed to ease Laura's panic.

Laura had more questions. She wanted to know if she should tell the younger children in her family circle about their Uncle Steven. Again I took charge of the conversation, not leaving room for her to argue back. I told her that the greater risk was that someday they would find out anyway about Steven, and then would be angry because no one had trusted them with the truth about their family. I wanted to break the pattern of family silence; I didn't want the tragedy of Steven to become a source of fear or shame for another generation, the way Lennie's disaster had been in Ross's family.

The moment I mentioned truth and trust, I knew I'd stepped on a landmine. Laura's voice changed. "You didn't always tell me the truth. Remember the time I went away with Jenny and her dad? You never told me that the police said it was kidnapping, and you never told me that Jenny's dad killed himself. I found that out from the kids at school." Laura looked at me with the tough look of a prosecutor. "Well, do you have anything to say? That was pretty rotten of you, Mom."

"I should have handled it better," I said. "I'm sorry. I hope you can learn from my mistakes."

"Mom, I've never understood how you can just breeze through things like that . . . Steven dying, me being kidnapped . . . as if they're no big deal. Where was your head when all of that stuff was going on? Did you ever think about us and what it was doing to us? Your own Mom died and you had to raise yourself . . . I'm sorry, I know that was tough . . . but did it ever occur to you that we didn't need to grow up like a bunch of orphans?"

"You'll never know how hard those days were when I didn't know if I would ever see you again," I told her. "I didn't know if you were dead or alive. I was sick with worry. It was torture. And then when you did come home, I only wanted to protect you. Not make it worse than it was by going over it all again."

"But here's the part you didn't get," said Laura. "The police acted so weird and suspicious when we came back. Like they thought Jenny and I had done something wrong. They actually made the doctor check us out. That was awful. Why didn't you insist on being there with us?"

"I remember that too. They had a manner that made everyone feel guilty. That's hard to defend against when really what you're feeling is scared to death. They wouldn't allow me to be there with you." I stifled my impulse to add that Ross had been no support to me at all, but I knew it was no use throwing a dead man under the bus. How fair would it be to tell the truth about how Ross had behaved during those dreadful days while hiding the truth about myself?

There are episodes in my life that are marked by a shadow. I cannot help but think of that shadow from time to time because newer events over which I have so little control bring me back to it. This time it was Laura accusing me of indifference to my children during those days when she was missing. To this my own memory adds in the shadow, the memory of Thomas that I cannot share.

My reverie was broken by Laura's next question. It was a brutal question in which I found an escape because it called me back out of those shadowy memories and into the presence of my nervous daughter, who still wanted to know what had happened. Her girlish memories were not sufficient. The mother in her demanded the truth.

"Do you think Jenny's dad was planning to hurt us? Molest us? Abduct us for good? Kill us? The police asked so many questions, like they thought Jenny's dad did something really awful to us. I don't think he did, but maybe I just block that out. Why did he kill himself?"

I'd had the same worry as the police. What had gone on in that motel room? Only Laura and Jenny really knew, and now Laura was asking me. So I said, "Jenny's dad was a desperate man who made a terrible mistake, but he didn't intend to hurt you girls." As I spoke I tried to recall as accurately as I could what Jenny's dad had written on his suicide note, and I recounted it for Laura. He couldn't live without his daughter, and he wanted her to remember the good time Jenny had with her friend on their adventure. He wanted that to be her last memory of him.

"That's weird isn't it? Like he didn't get it that the last thing she would remember about him was that he killed himself?"

I understand how frantic a parent can be when losing a child. I understand about not wanting a child to have bad memories. But I also understood there was no use going into this with Laura, especially not right then. Laura might always seem to be put together and in charge, and Laura might appear to be convinced that she is completely right when she levels a criticism, but the truth is that often Laura is not strong enough to deal with uncertainty. When she is most uncertain she searches for someone to blame. This time I knew it was me who was close at hand. I decided to take a stand. "We'll never know for sure what Jenny's Dad was thinking, but at least we know for sure that during the three days you were with him he didn't harm you or Jenny."

Laura looked at me with a mixture of surprise and relief. It seemed we had reached a place to put the conversation on pause, and soon after we both went to our beds. However, after only a few minutes I heard soft footsteps outside my room. Then Laura's voice saying, "Mom, are you still awake?" And when I answered she came into my room and sat down on the edge of my bed farthest from me and closest to the door. "I have some other things I want to ask you," she said.

She'd been meeting with a therapist who was helping her process her anxiety about Jeremy, but in the course of their work they'd also explored Laura's family and her own role in it. They concluded she had a lot of responsibility in the family, and that the uneven burden she carried had left her feeling anxious.

Laura felt she couldn't fulfill all the expectations. To illustrate what she meant she brought up the things that Ross had asked each of the children to do for him as he was preparing for his own death. What Laura saw in the requests was a pattern of manageable requests for the others, requests that could be fulfilled, could be finished. But in her case she saw complex expectations that could never be completed. Row prepared the funeral. Jenna planned a party. When the events were over their responsibilities were complete, and they got loads of praise for doing them well. Laura's responsibility for keeping the family together was ongoing. "You see," said Laura, "the things that are expected of me are never done. I never get to say they're finished and ask how well I did, because one year is barely past and I have to start on the next. You know what that means? It means I never get any credit."

I wanted to argue back that what Ross had asked of her allowed Laura to collect accolades every November all over again. The family always lavishes her with praise for the first rate job she does arranging our annual Thanksgiving. But I didn't say that. Instead I asked her, "Is this something that your therapist has helped you see?" The question made Laura furious. She immediately shot back, "What difference would that make if it's true?"

While Laura was listing out the unfair family chores, I was thinking of Will who has shouldered many responsibilities since Ross died. So I asked Laura, "What about Will? His responsibilities are ongoing." Bringing Will into the picture made Laura's anger more intense. She reminded me, with full-blown disdain, how Will had walked out on the family. Left us all worrying for years. Turned his back on us. Then came waltzing back in as if nothing had happened. Not only did we receive him back, but also we made a fuss over him. Her last comment was a perfect summary of her anger. "Why does Will deserve to be the crown prince anyway?"

Laura added fuel to her fire by reminding me how Ross had always adored the things that Jenna did. And then, as if to place fair blame on everyone, Laura reminded me that Row has always had a free pass because he is my favorite and can do no wrong. It seems Laura was trying to get clear in her own mind how all of the family roles fit together. She was rolling facts around like pieces on a Rubik's Cube, and she couldn't get the colors to line up. Each of her siblings seemed to enjoy benefits withheld from Laura, and the role left to her didn't give her what she wanted.

As Laura spoke I had an inspiration, a gift straight from the angels. From out of nowhere I remembered a bit of advice from a counselor when we were seeking help with Steven. He had said, "don't *analyze* Steven, *look* at Steven." And so I looked at Laura, and I noticed how uncomfortable she was sitting there on the side of my bed, twisted around forty-five degrees so she could see me, peering at me through the semi-dark. "Laura, honey, you look cold and uncomfortable," I said. "Crawl in here where it's warm. Here use this pillow so you can sit up." And she did. She crawled in under the blankets and propped two pillows against the headboard next to me.

When Laura looked comfortable I acknowledged that she carries a heavy load in the family. It isn't easy being the first-born daughter. Just because she is competent, it doesn't mean it's fair to expect her to do more than her share. I admitted to her that sometimes the efficiency with which she worked made really hard things look easy.

The hardest thing about being so good at things, I complained with Laura, is that while doing for others we set aside doing things we need for ourselves. She interrupted me. "No kidding. I wanted to join Community Theater, just for a small part, just for the fun of it. It would be a way to meet some interesting people and do something creative for once. But I can't take time away from the family. Robby is one of the best dads I know, but he gets to play golf in the summer and basketball in the winter. It's just not fair."

Laura seldom says anything to make Robby look bad, but this time she complained about him. All winter he'd played basketball on Tuesday nights. On Thursday nights he worked late and rolled in from the office as late as 10:00. Laura noticed there were two sets of basketball clothes in the laundry, and she asked Robby about it. He confessed he hadn't been working late on Thursdays and lied to her about it because he didn't think she would approve of two nights of basketball each week.

We chatted on and on. About work. About children. About to-do lists and laundry. She admitted she hates to fold laundry. "There is no reason Robby couldn't learn to do it; it's not rocket science. You know the problem," said Laura, "You and me, Mom, are just a couple of worker bees."

I was telling Laura that the household task I hate most is vacuuming because of the noise. She was quiet, and I noticed that she was drifting off to sleep. So I stopped talking. After a few minutes I looked at her. Her hair against the pillow. Her eyelids still and relaxed. Her breathing untroubled. I remembered the plump little baby who used to sleep against me on the balcony in Geneva, soaking in the sunshine and oblivious to the noise of the traffic below.

Sleep is a gift to the young and doesn't come easily to me, so once I was sure Laura's sleep was sound, I tiptoed to the den and crawled into the pullout bed on the side next to where Laura had left her phone. I put my head into the hollow she'd left in her pillow. I couldn't help noticing it smelled herbal and clean, probably from the all-natural verbena shampoo she uses. It was comforting to have the scent of her there.

## Chapter 17

# TEMPTING DOUBT

On one of Row's visits a while after our miserable evening at the Lunette, we were sitting at the kitchen table having a breakfast that he had prepared for us. Scones with whipped butter, a small bowl of fresh fruit carefully cut up into even pieces, and coffee. Row knows how to charm with food. Or maybe it is that he is loving with food. In any case he can make a table with the simplest food very inviting by setting a tone that makes it easy to linger.

Out of nowhere he broke the silence with a question. "Mom, do you pray?"

I was surprised by the question, but I answered, "Uh . . . Yes . . . I do."

There was more silence. "That's all?" he asked.

"Apparently you want me to say more?"

"Of course, why do you think I asked?"

I tried to gather my thoughts to tell him something honest. It isn't comfortable laying out my own habits of prayer for examination, but there was no use giving him an abstract theory about prayer either. There are books to read about that, and I could show him where to find them in the library.

When I was a little girl I learned the prayers we said in church, and we always said the same prayer at the beginning of our meals. It was the one said in every Catholic family. I liked that prayer because it has an adjective clause that is slightly clumsy. If you don't know the prayer well, the rhythm changes and you get tripped up, but after you've said it hundreds of times, the fact that you've caught the rhythm and can rattle it off effortlessly makes you feel like you know the code that opens the door to a special club.

After I was no longer living with my family, the habit of that mealtime prayer fell away. It would have been awkward to cross myself and recite the prayer in the dorm cafeteria. I didn't think there was much point in telling Row about my college years, so I jumped ahead in the story and told Row that when I first had children I prayed alone by myself each day. I lit a candle and recited the names of all the members of my family, my friends, people I love or was concerned about, and sometimes added a note about something going on in the world. I didn't tell Row that I also recited the names of my parents who were no longer living, and I didn't tell him that sometimes I cried. I did tell him that after I had set out all my worries and sadness, I would think of God's love coming out of heaven like beams of light, and spreading over everything. It was a little simplistic, but I meant well, and it was fitting for who I was then.

"It sounds a little like going to therapy," Row commented. He wasn't kidding. "I don't remember ever seeing you do that. I hope you aren't lighting candles anymore cause I'd have to get you one of those candles with a battery so you wouldn't forget to put out the flame and end up burning down this building."

That was so like Row. He could shift from being serious to cracking a joke from one word to the next. I suspect he does it to lighten the conversation, even though he's the one who wants the serious part of it. He wants to know personal things, and then he pretends that he is trying not to get too personal.

"Did you keep praying?" he asked.

"I did."

"I remember you used to say bedtime prayers with us."

"Sometimes I envied people who found comfort in prayer that came forth spontaneously like a conversation with the divine. It seemed more natural for them than for me. I wasn't very good at just chatting with God. So I took a course on Ignatian prayer offered by a Jesuit who taught at the college. He wasn't a fire-eyed Jesuit. He looked a little like Berrigan, not Daniel but the other brother."

Row was listening intently. "What was that like?"

"I put it on my schedule and just did it. Like working out. The instructor wasn't bossy. He was kind about it, but the point was to be consistent. To pray everyday. Not to skip. Meanwhile I was thinking how busy our household was, and I wondered if I could find time everyday. I didn't think I could pray at bedtime because by then I was so tired I would have fallen asleep. So I thought, well if it's the best I can do I'll pray in the shower. At least there I'll stay awake."

"Did it work?"

"I prayed daily partly because I said I would. The method appealed to me because it focused on one day at a time, not the whole world and not a whole lifetime. One day at a time was as much as I could handle. Sometimes when I missed praying in my morning shower, I prayed at lunch instead. It was the quietest part of my day, especially when I was at work."

"How did you manage that? Were you obviously praying in the lunch room? By then you weren't a Catholic anymore so I suppose you could be subtler about it. Not crossing yourself. Maybe you just looked like you were catching a quick nap."

"Sure, Row. You know me. How much I like making a public spectacle of myself. So I stood up in the lunch room and told everyone to be quiet while I said my prayers."

"No . . . seriously, how did that work?"

"Well, the first step was a review of the day. I'd think about my morning. Walking the dog and then getting Laura off to kindergarten and you twins off to daycare. It took patience to walk Wagner, because if he felt hurried he wouldn't pee, and if he didn't pee he would go on the kitchen floor where we kept him penned up while we were out. If I could get Laura on the bus, you guys on the van that picked you up, and Wagner in the kitchen, then I would get in the car and race off to work."

"That's it? That's all?"

"No. At first I didn't see much to pray about. Just did the review. I wondered sometimes if there were angels watching out for us. On the bus ride. Through traffic. So I added some gratitude for that to my prayer. I even was thankful some mornings when Wagner peed. That worked pretty well until one morning Wagner would not go, and decided to pee in the entry just as I walked back into the house with him. I completely lost it. In front of you kids. Like a mad woman. And later when I prayed I reflected on that. Stupid and guilty for showing my kids that a dog could determine my day."

"I vaguely remember that Wagner was your nemesis."

"He was. Why along with a house full of kids we also had a dog makes no sense to me now. I can't remember that anyone really liked Wagner. And I can't remember that anyone else ever fed him or walked him or even petted him on the head when he came rushing to the door as soon as he heard it open."

"He ate shoes sometimes, didn't he? And once he chewed up Laura's brand new mittens that were under the Christmas tree. So did Wagner mess up your prayers?"

"That day when Wagner tripped me up, once I paused to think about it I saw we had all gotten where we were going that morning. You kids were still the same happy kids. I was grateful that I alone on my own did not have power to ruin my children even if sometimes I was a witch. And a puddle in the back entry seemed pretty small in proportion to all of that. Apparently God didn't give up on me because of my meltdown. That's sort of how the prayer worked for me. I felt observed. Not in a cruel way, but in a way that felt like someone was there. That I was not alone. That I wasn't invisible. And that meant everything to me."

"Did you keep it up?"

"I tried. It helped me look at things a little more important than whether Wagner peed. Like not resenting your dad because he left me with too much to do. It helped me see small things I could do for other people such as visit Mrs. Leonard. Do you remember her, the old woman who lived next door to us? One time I figured out while praying that if I couldn't find time to go over and visit with her, I could send you. Now and then I'd send you over with a plate of food for her supper. When I was cooking for the whole crew anyway, it wasn't that hard to spoon out a plate for her. And she thought you were a delight. You were good at talking with adults."

"I remember that vaguely, but I had no idea it was Ignatius who sent me."

"It wasn't Ignatius, Row. It was God."

We looked at each other strangely. We laughed a little. I'm not sure why we chuckled. Maybe it was like Sarah snickering behind the curtain when God told her she would have a baby at age ninety. I wanted to believe that God has something to do with the protection of my children, with acts of kindness, with my own ability to navigate the obstacles in a busy family morning. But I was so used to thinking about my life in mundane terms that it seemed a stretch to speak of the power of the sacred in these ordinary things. I didn't trust Row would take me seriously, and it put me on the defensive. I shouldn't blame Row. I don't think Row could figure out if I was being apologetic, or trying to lighten up the conversation with humor, or if I really meant it. I probably didn't know myself.

"Is the priest the guy who had a green VW bug convertible? I liked that car. I remember a few other things about when we lived in that house too. Like I remember that Laura used to cry because she missed Daddy. And I remember that Mrs. Leonard used to give us candies that had wrappers, but they were so sticky we couldn't get the wrappers off. You told us to be sure to thank her for the candies and then throw them away when we got home."

"It's long ago," I said. I looked across the room at the bookcase, and focused there for a moment in order to get steady. I told myself not to be distracted, and not to go down the rabbit hole following the momentary reminder about Thomas.

"Do you still do your noontime prayers?"

"No."

"You mean you don't pray anymore?"

"I do, but there are lots of ways to pray."

"And . . . ?" Row waved his hand like he was directing traffic, signaling me to proceed through the intersection. "Come on, Mom, stop making this so hard."

"Okay. What do you want to know?"

"How do you pray now?"

"Hm . . . these days I say the Our Father."

"You mean The Lord's Prayer? You never did give up being a Catholic in order to become a true Presbyterian, did you? Anyway, why that prayer?"

"I learned it as a girl when we said it in school and at mass. I learned it first in Latin." I described for Row how we kids used to have contests on the playground to see who could say it fastest. Two kids would line up and a third one would say, "Go." The winner was the one who got to "amen" first. I was fast. I'm sure the nuns wouldn't have approved.

"Why did you go back to that prayer after all those detours?" I could tell he was serious. He genuinely wanted to know.

"It seemed like a good thing to do. Maybe it appealed to me because it was something I had believed before I began to doubt. When I was very little, even before I started school, I'd say it with my mother in English. She'd hold my hands folded inside hers, and I knew we were doing something important. Long after my mother died and I married your father and became a Presbyterian, we recited the same prayer in church. It didn't bother me that it was a prayer by a different name. It still comforted me. In church it was a moment in which I felt at home. When I would say, "Our Father who art in heaven," instantly in my own mind I would think "where my mother is too."

Telling Row something so sentimental, so vulnerable, was easier than I would have predicted. "I know the Our Father effortlessly the way I know the alphabet. Once I start with the first few words, it moves as naturally as my breath moves in and out. It's imprinted in me."

I noticed Row was no longer diluting the conversation with humor. "Mom, I never knew this about you. I never knew that you take this stuff so seriously."

"It's strange, isn't it, that something important to me wouldn't be obvious to my own son."

"Does the prayer help? Other than reciting it, does it really make any difference?"

"Different parts of it catch my attention at different times."

"How does that work? Don't you say the whole thing?"

"Of course I say the whole thing, but sometimes one part or another speaks back to me."

"How?"

"Well . . . for example . . . it's frightening to grow old and not know what I can count on, but when I ask for daily bread, for just what I need today, it shifts my focus."

Row didn't say anything. He nodded a "yes."

"The forgiveness part is hard for me. It's embarrassing to admit this to my own son, but . . . why not? I feel sometimes like my mistakes keep washing up out of the past like driftwood out of the ocean. That's the one side. The other is that forgiving is hard because . . . well how can I describe it . . . maybe my heart's just not big enough . . . it's a work in progress."

Row was still nodding as I spoke. I could tell Row wanted me to keep talking, but I also could tell he was uncomfortable being so personal with me about God. Row is a thoroughly modern intellectual; talking with his own mother about God is more difficult than talking with her about sex. I actually said this to him.

"True enough," Row replied. "They're both personal, but sex isn't quite so mystical. You don't have to guess if it's real or imagined."

I would have stopped there, but Row was the one who pushed the conversation forward again. "Well at least at your age the third one about not being led into temptation must be getting easier." He gave a kind of naughty chuckle. The kind we use when we're thinking of sins we're proud of. "I assume you're not collecting too many demerits for falling into temptation these days."

I felt uneasy with the way Row looked at me. As if he were watching me to see how I would react when he said that. Maybe he wondered if I'd caught the innuendo, or maybe he wondered if his aging mother had ever felt uneasy about falling into temptation. Knowing Row he could have been thinking both of these at once.

"I've revised that one a little," I replied. "I don't say 'lead me not into temptation.' I say 'lead me not into doubt' because . . . that's the big temptation . . . I mean really . . . isn't that the evil from which we all want to be delivered?"

"Mom, do you have doubts?"

"Less and less."

"Well, keep saying that prayer then."

There was sweetness in his voice, but I couldn't tell if he was being serious or if he was patronizing me. In any case, I sensed that we had reached the point at which a conversation like this has to close. Not because it isn't important. Or because it isn't dealing with something true. It's not even because there isn't more to say. It had to pause because it was enough for one day.

Chapter 18

# YOU NEVER KNOW

During our visits Will tried to set the record straight about the years he lived disconnected from me. He didn't want to dramatize that time as if it were a great emancipation, nor did he want me to feel sorry for him as if it were all trauma. He wanted me to understand that he was an ordinary son, just like any other son, who had all the usual things in life to figure out, along with a few that were unexpected. Little by little he told the story.

The first years in California with Oliver were difficult. Moving the problem two thousand miles didn't changed it. Oliver was homesick, which meant he was only half there. And Will was impatient with Oliver for not adapting, not starting over, even though now he blames himself for not understanding Oliver.

Will tried to persuade Oliver by giving him all the reasons he should adjust his expectations, but it takes more than reasons to persuade someone to stop suffering. Furthermore, it takes more than reasons to convince someone to do what you want him to do instead of doing what he wants to do himself. Will shifted his strategy. He stopped arguing with Oliver and tried to convince him that California was the place for them by giving Oliver things like a new house, a new car, and nice vacations. This still wasn't what Oliver needed to relocate his happiness. He needed people, and in particular he needed the people who made the circle he called "home."

When Oliver left to go back east, Will was stunned. "I did everything I could to make him happy. I don't know what more I could have done," he lamented. Will is the kind of man who doesn't like to fail. Instead of accepting the single life as a hurt, he acted as if he were proud of it, had chosen it as the better arrangement after all. He'd say, "Relationships are too complicated. I don't need those problems in my life. It's not worth it."

Will's medicine for loneliness was work. It didn't bother him if there weren't enough hours in the day. What he dreaded were idle hours, and he made sure there were few of those. The time was right for success in California, and Will found satisfaction in wielding power. He was running his own company, which meant he was the boss. He'd go onto a job site and tell his workers he was giving them promotions and a raise so he could feel superior to those men with calloused hands who got enthused about a dollar an hour more on their paycheck. He noticed that even more important than the money, these guys liked being given a new name for the same old work. The titles mattered to them, and Will had the power to confer them. He was the man who went around handing out names: project manager, supply clerk, employee of the year, shift supervisor, quality control auditor.

Looking back now Will understands why his workers treated him as if he were important; they knew better than to treat him as if he weren't. The people with whom he did business flattered him too because they knew that was the way to get the best deal. In the hours he did take away from work, Will socialized with other men like himself, and he went to places where they gathered. He describes it now as a club for show-offs. They drove expensive cars, dressed well, groomed well, and had personal trainers.

Finally Will was driven to admit that he didn't like the man he had become. He could order people to keep him company, but he still felt empty. He could buy his way into any gathering he liked, but he was lonely living as if he owed no one anything and needed no one to share his life. He had become vain and arrogant, so that beneath a thin layer of outer confidence that fooled others, there was uneasiness that didn't let him fool himself. When he looked in the mirror, the truth was staring him in the face: *it is not good for a man to be alone.* Eventually he met John and with him created a life they could share.

"What happened to Oliver?" I asked.

"He's dead."

"What do you mean he's dead?"

"It's not a mystery question, Mom. A gay man in his thirties dies. How? I'll give you three choices. AIDs, AIDs, or AIDs. He chose a high-risk lifestyle. That was his decision. Living cozy with his nice traditional family, and then sneaking off and living his secret in hazardous places. If we had stayed together he would probably still be alive. Too bad. His choice."

"That's harsh, Will. My gosh, have a little mercy." I took a very deep breath. "Stop pulling your shoulders back, sticking your chin forward and acting like nothing can hurt you!" Something had gotten to me. Maybe it was my need to push back against Will's persona, his effort to appear that he always has everything under control. I wanted him to know that I could see through it. Sometimes Will reminded me of Ross. Or maybe I'd reached my own limit for being nice even when Will wasn't.

"Raargh. What's this, the new Maggie or something?" he shot back.

I'd started this confrontation and couldn't stop now. "Does it ever occur to you that my clock is ticking, and if I don't start telling you what I think, I may time out?"

Will was ready. "I thought most people mellowed with age."

"Will, don't be smug. I'm done censoring what I say so I won't upset you. Beside, if you don't know by now that I . . . ." I didn't feel like finishing the sentence just then, so I dropped it.

"Go Mom! This is a new side of the family matriarch I've never seen before."

"You're a smart-ass, Will. This jousting doesn't prove anything. Do you think if you get the last word it'll prove you won? "

He didn't answer. Instead he got up, walked to the counter where I had set out two truffles for our dessert, put them on a small plate, and brought them back to the table. The silence was obvious. As he set the plate between us, he looked up and smiled. Only after he sat down did he say, "Well, has it been long enough? Do I get to speak again without being accused of having the last word?"

"Yes. You have my permission." I said with a grin.

"Okay. Which one would you like, the sea salt or the cacao?"

"The sea salt."

"Aw, that's the one I wanted."

"I'm fine with the cacao. Go ahead, have the sea salt.

"Gotcha. You see, Mom, you're not really tough. Strong? Yes, probably. But tough? Not at all. You want everybody to be happy, and that makes you an easy mark." He paused then for a moment as if he were shifting gears in his own thoughts. "I'm sorry about Oliver, what I said. I still feel guilty, and

I still feel angry about it." He'd been looking down at the truffles as he spoke, but then he looked up at me. "I like you better when you're not so predictably nice. At least then I know where I stand with you."

I must have looked at him as if I didn't believe him. "Seriously. I mean it," he said.

"Okay, I'm going to try to believe you."

"Mom, are you afraid I'll go away again if you piss me off?"

"Maybe. But it'll be different this time."

"What do you mean?"

"If you try that again with me, be careful when you open your front door cause you'll find an old woman sitting on the stoop, and you won't be able to get rid of her." He could tell I meant it. Of course I wouldn't be sitting on the stoop, but there was no way I would let him get away with closing me out again.

Will picked up the remaining dishes from the table and loaded them into the dishwasher. He cleaned up the rest of what was still on the stove and stacked in the sink. As I watched him move around the kitchen it occurred to me that I had never seen Will do dishes before. He put the soap in the door of the dishwasher and pushed the start button. Then he looked at his phone to check the time. "I need to call John before it gets too late."

"It's not late in California. It's three hours difference."

"He'll be going out to choir, and afterward he goes out for coffee. I want to catch him before he goes."

Will's conversation with John on the phone was long, and when he came back to where I was sitting in the living room he had a serious look on his face. "I want to talk with you about something." Whatever it was, I guessed he'd just been talking with John about it.

Not long after John and Will moved in together a woman named Carolyn had come to their door looking for Will, but he wasn't home, so John took a message. She said that her mother used to know Ross. Since her mother passed away Carolyn had been trying to get information about the years before they moved to California. John didn't ask for details. He agreed to ask Will to call her.

"I didn't get back to Carolyn right away," Will explained, "but John kept reminding me. Finally I called her, and she seemed nice enough." The first time they met Carolyn apologized for showing up at his door. When

Will told her that his Dad had passed away, she was sympathetic. She's an only child, and her Mom was a single parent. They moved to California just before she was born so they could be near her grandparents. Since her mother's death she had been going through old papers and found receipts for money orders sent to her mother by Ross. She googled Ross's name and found his obituary, then googled the names of his children for contact information. Will lived closest. He was quick to add that Carolyn didn't seem like a "bunny boiler." I had to ask him to explain the term.

"What did the notes from Ross say?" I asked Will.

"She showed the notes to me when she came back for another visit. It was Dad's handwriting. There's no mistake about that." One note said, 'I hope this will cover the deposit and first month's rent for your new apartment.' Another said, 'This should cover costs for camp. Use the extra to get clothes for Carolyn before she goes.' Stapled together there was a stack of receipts from the orthodontist for Carolyn's braces. There was no note attached, but it was in the same envelop with the other receipts and notes.

Will looked at me, waiting for me to add to the story, but I shook my head. "I don't know anything about it. I don't know why your Dad was sending her money."

"Really? You've never heard of Carolyn or her mother? Her name was Sandra. Did you ever hear Dad talk about someone named Sandra?"

"Never."

"Think of anyone you ever knew named Sandra."

I thought back over the years. "Your Uncle Charlie and Aunt Rita had a babysitter named Sandra. She was someone Charlie knew from AA, and he got her to watch their kids and our kids once on New Year's Eve. When we came home we found her passed out on the couch. From the empty bottle it seems she'd had her own little party at their house. Rita was furious, and she blamed Charlie. Rita and Charlie are both gone now, and I have no idea what happened to the sitter."

"What do you make of this stuff with Carolyn?" Will persisted.

"Well, it could be someone your Dad helped. It sounds like she was in a tough spot. That's the kind of thing he might have done. He was a rescuer, and usually practical about it."

"But, Mom, there's another possibility. You get it, don't you? I hope you're not being evasive because this is painful history and it hurts to talk about it."

Will was waiting for me to respond. Of course I knew what he was implying, but if I didn't know anything about it, what could I say? Besides, I was stunned. Who wouldn't be? This came at me out of nowhere. "I'd like to think your Dad is innocent, and I could try to say something in his defense, but I'd be guessing. On the other hand, I could jump to the conclusion that you've unearthed a buried secret of his. Maybe you have. You never know about these things. What did Carolyn say? Why did she think your Dad sent money?"

"When she was little and asked where her daddy was, her mother said he was dead, and she didn't like to talk about it because it made her sad. That doesn't make sense, of course. Why wouldn't you tell a kid the name of her dead dad, even if you didn't want to talk about him very much?"

"You're right. That wouldn't make sense now. In the past people heaped a lot of shame on mothers who weren't married. The burden of raising the baby was left to the woman while the man got a free pass. The father's identity was kept secret if he was married. Carolyn's story doesn't sound that strange to me, but it probably does sound odd to you. I'm not saying this points to your dad. There's just no way of knowing, is there?"

"There are ways of knowing. We could do DNA testing. I don't think Carolyn was suggesting anything like that, though. I didn't pick up hints that she wants to make trouble for anyone else. She's trying to get answers for herself.

"What are you going to do, Will?"

"I don't know. Do I really care if years ago Dad was trying to help some woman who was down on her luck? And then there's this other thing. Do I really want to know if Carolyn's a half-sister of mine? How much do I want to get Row and my sisters mixed up with this? Jenna could handle it. But Row would turn it into a drama, and Laura would turn it into a project. Do I need that?"

"What does John think you should do?"

"He thinks I should ask you. That's what we were talking about on the phone."

"I wouldn't rush into it. Once you go forward, you can't go back. Give yourself time."

"But, Mom, I'm not asking you what *I* should do. I am asking what *you* want to do about this. Do *you* want me to pursue it?"

"It's a lot to digest. I feel shaken. Can you give me time to think about it? Is that okay?"

"I'm here for you, Mom, whatever you decide. You can count on me. Remember, I'm your man." Will came over to where I was sitting and hugged me warmly.

# Chapter 19

# JENNA'S DIVORCE

I had a phone call from Will to ask if I had spoken with Jenna that morning, and it wasn't even noon. I could tell he was worried. Life at the farm during summer vacations was often moving and shifting, but this summer was way beyond the usual vacation chaos. It got worse, step by step. The beginning of the end occurred when Jenna came home earlier than expected one afternoon and found Jak with one of his fellow teachers skinny-dipping in the pool instead of preparing their lesson plans.

Jak made excuses about needing to cool off in the pool because it was hot weather. He insisted they were just friends, but that didn't persuade Jenna. As she got increasingly furious, Jak's excuses got more absurd. He attributed the skinny-dipping to the fact that Sabrina didn't want to get her clothes wet and had no swimsuit with her. He tried to argue that cooling off in the pool was more energy efficient than running the air conditioning.

Jenna wasn't persuaded by flimsy excuses. "Where are the materials you're working on? Why weren't you working at school? There are swim suits of all sizes in the house; why didn't Sabrina borrow one?" The angrier Jenna got the more desperately dramatic Jak became until finally he was whining that Jenna was heartless and it isn't fair that "a guy makes one little mistake and all hell breaks loose."

I have never thought of Jenna as a woman who wouldn't forgive a free spirit who makes one little mistake. She'd been living with Jak for years, and there had been plenty of mistakes to try her patience. Jak was the kind of husband who'd forget to pay bills or toss the envelop with the payment under the seat of his truck instead of into the mailbox. It wasn't mindless; it was intentional. He wanted to use the money in the checking account for something else. He'd put the household bills out of mind until they got shut-off notices from the utilities. On one impulse he bought a new truck they couldn't afford, and for her birthday he gave Jenna gifts he wanted for himself, like a new sound system for the barn. At Christmas he gave Jenna a table saw along with the promise to build bookcases. He got some use out of the table saw, but the bookcases never materialized before he traded the saw for a new electric guitar. It was a deal too good to pass up. Jak was inventive about his mistakes. He had a strategic plan all his own.

Jenna had always shown remarkable grace in taking Jak's behavior in stride, but this time Jak himself knew he'd pushed Jenna too far. He was offering his defenses between loud sobs while wiping his nose on the back of his hand and then onto his shorts. His behavior was partly theater, but it was also desperate.

While all this was going on Sabrina had disappeared around the corner of the house, but her car was still in the driveway. Jak suggested that he should go and tell her good-bye, but Jenna knew that Jak wanted to get Sabrina over to the quieter side of the house so he could apologize for his crazy wife while also making an arrangement to see Sabrina later when things calmed down. Jenna was having none of it. She said she'd tell Sabrina good-bye herself. As she went Jak was begging, "Jenna, don't be rude. Have a little mercy. Sabrina didn't have bad intentions."

Apparently Sabrina also had no intention to shoulder any more than her small part of the blame, because while Jenna was standing there in her own driveway, Sabrina let her know that she wasn't the first visitor to the farm on afternoons when everyone else was gone. Jak had a long list of admirers. Women with whom he worked or with whom he partied at places around town where he was known as "Jak, the guy with the open marriage." A few of the names Sabrina listed with special emphasis, like rubbing salt in a wound, were women who Jenna counted as friends. In short, Jak had a reputation, and it had just blown up in his face.

Despite Jak's tears and apologies, along with promises that it would never happen again, Jenna calmly told Jak to get out. "Find somewhere else to stay. This is it. We're done. I've had it with you, and there's nothing more to talk about."

"Can I stay in the barn in the loft," Jak begged. "I'll give you your space. I know you're upset with me, but I don't want to walk out on the kids."

Jenna didn't compromise. This was really about moving out; it wasn't just sleeping on the couch until the crisis passed. The loft in the barn wasn't far enough away for a guy who was seriously being shown the exit, because Jenna knew that Jak would find some excuse to come to the house. He'd need something from the kitchen. He'd want to get his favorite shirt from the closet or his soccer cleats from the back hall.

"Too little too late about the kids, Jak. Where was your concern about them two hours ago when you were soaking in the pool? You're out. I'm going to take the kids and camp out overnight at a hotel with a pool. You'd better start packing because when I come back tomorrow morning you're out for good. I'm getting the locks changed."

Apparently Jak knew there was nothing more for him to argue. By the time Jenna returned to the house the next morning most traces of him were gone. He had loaded his truck and left. In the weeks that followed he checked in regularly with Jenna and made a point to talk with the kids by phone. And then there was one more thing.

That's the way it always went with Jak. He had an accident while speeding down the county line road where he missed the curve and rolled his truck. Fortunately he had a seatbelt on, and it looked as if he would pull through despite an open leg fracture. Unfortunately the woman in the passenger seat was not belted in and was in very bad shape. Unconscious and hanging on by a thread.

The first responders to the scene thought the woman in the truck was Jak's wife because, while Jak's ID was in his money clip, there was no ID for his passenger. Once Jak and his passenger were loaded into ambulances, the police went to the house. There they found Jenna. It quickly became obvious that the woman in the truck was someone else. Of course Jenna was shocked, but she also had the good sense to call Laura before rushing off to the hospital to be at Jak's side. Laura's advice was solid. She told Jenna to stay home and comfort her children; it was time for Jak's family to take a turn. One of them could go to the hospital to support him.

The events rolled out like a bad movie. Drama upon drama. There were friends who came to Jenna's assistance, some of whom were a little too eager to share with her what they'd picked up about Jak via the grapevine. After it was clear that Jak wasn't going to be as much fun anymore, the number of people who counted themselves among Jak's friends began to shrink.

In the middle of the chaos were Jak and Jenna's kids, and standing strong for them was Jenna. I had no idea this younger daughter of mine was so steady. She didn't track back to patch things up with Jak just because he was in the hospital with fractured bones and a broken spirit. What she did do with amazing grace was create a comfort zone for her children. For them she was like a mother hen with chicks under her wings.

While Jak was still in the hospital, Will came for a visit because he wanted to deal with a matter that had been arranged by Ross before he died. In our family Jak was Peter Pan, the boy who would never grow up, and Ross hadn't trusted that the family set-up with Jak would remain solid. He worried that Jak might not stick around long enough to grow up with the children or grow old with Jenna. Despite this Ross had never been unpleasant with Jak because that's not the way Ross operated. When he was convinced there was a problem, he didn't dawdle over complaints. He took action to fix it.

Not long after Jenna and Jak had children, Ross took out a life insurance policy for himself and made Jenna the beneficiary. He figured that as long as he was alive he could watch out for his daughter and grandchildren himself, but he wanted to be sure that if anything happened to him there would be an umbrella of protection over them that would continue. He set it up so that upon his death the proceeds of the life insurance would be held in a trust for Jenna and her children, and Will was appointed the trustee to manage it. When it came to being provident Ross left nothing to chance.

Will helped Jenna sell the farm. Jak was done with it, and Jenna didn't think she could manage it as a single parent. Until Jenna found a small house in a quiet neighborhood near a good school, Will stayed with her, and before long Jenna's life seemed stable again. We had always thought Jenna was dependent, and needed someone strong like Jak to lean on, but she surprised us. She was a rock.

Jak was not done being a child; Ross had guessed right about that. Within a year after their divorce Jak lost his job as a teacher and coach. Late one night police pulled over Jak's truck for a routine traffic stop. He was uncooperative when the officer suggested the vehicle smelled of marijuana, and they found it in the ashtray. Jak told them it belonged to the guy to whom he'd given a ride home from the bar, but the drug test suggested that

Jak had also been using. Jak's employer was not willing to look the other way, and Jak was dismissed from his job as a teacher and coach.

To fill in for lost income and to save money on transportation Jak sold his truck and replaced it with a motorcycle and a rusty little car he used only on days when he had visitation with his children. The rest of the time Jak was not embarrassed to be seen around town with various women on the back of his bike. Just because Jenna had kicked him out of his house didn't mean that he had to go around acting like a dejected man. This was one more thing Jenna handled with grace. She didn't make it her business to pass judgment on the women who lined up to help Jak repair his reputation as a charmer.

And then the next thing happened. That was the reason Will was calling me early in the morning to check if I had been in contact with Jenna. Jak had an accident on his bike. Alone at the time and not wearing a helmet, he was thrown from his bike. He had closed head injuries and damage to his spine. Jenna took up the slack with the children while Jak was in rehab, and after he moved back into a wheel-chair accessible apartment, Jenna made sure the children visited him. They were not able to stay with him, but she didn't let that be a reason for them not to spend time with their dad.

I feel I never got to know the adult Jenna until she stood alone, until after her divorce. One afternoon I stopped by her house to drop off produce I'd picked up for her at the farmer's market, and she invited me to stay for tea. She was baking cupcakes for the booster club bake sale, and while she puttered in the kitchen we visited.

We talked about kids, and I shared news about her sister and brothers. She surprised me when she said she was the member of our family least like the others. "I'm definitely not like Laura who always has everything under control and is good at making decisions." She said this with a voice full of little sister admiration. "I'm not like Will either," she continued, "he's a fighter when he is sure something is unfair." That was obvious because Will had been defending her. "Row is a brainiac and that's not me."

"Don't compare yourself to them," I said. "You are your own person. Look at all you've been through and how strong you are. Look how well your kids are doing. You've been such a good mother for them."

Jenna was taking a different tack. As she mused about her place in the family she was looking for the differences. That's what she wanted to see. The similarities didn't interest her at the moment. She grew sober. "The person I always thought I was similar to is Jak. When it dawned on me that he and I aren't alike at all, it broke my heart." Jenna described the struggle to separate herself from Jak. "No matter what, I'll always love him, but I can't live with him anymore."

I could recall that before their break-up Jenna seemed quieter. Maybe depressed. Or exhausted. I had no idea what it was at the time. Jenna explained how every time she said "no" to Jak she felt she was reclaiming a lost part of herself. Jenna discovered she didn't want drama; she wanted a calmer life. She didn't need to throw big parties so Jak could be a star; she was content to spend quiet days at home with their family. "I couldn't have made it without my kids. The way I am with them now is the way I want to be. This is the life I want." She was very definite about it, and said it with a smile.

It seemed like a good time to share my memory of Jenna in the cherub choir singing about being a sunbeam, but I resisted, This was her moment, not mine, so I put that memory away for another time. Instead I said, "You're one of the kindest and most loving people I know, Jenn. You deserve a life that fits you."

"Thanks, Mom. Do you think my life would fit me better if I weighed twenty pounds less?"

I was startled by her comment. I had no idea she felt insecure about her weight. Was she being cautious about taking my view of her too seriously? Or, was she joking?

"What? Why do you look so surprised?" she said.

"Oh I'm caught off guard by the twenty pound thing."

"I know what you're thinking, Mom."

She turned toward me with a hand on her hip, a grin, and a few of her curls tucked behind her ear. Her kitchen apron had smudges of chocolate on it, and her phone was in the pocket of her jeans. I thought, "What a beauty! What a flourishing beauty." But I said, "Oh so you can read my thoughts, can you? Well, I'll tell you what I'm thinking if you promise to tell me if you guessed right."

"Okay. Go ahead. Tell me what you're thinking."

"Well, first I'm thinking that once you let the scale be your judge, you'll never be satisfied with your weight. You're beautiful just the way you are. And second I've been thinking the whole while we've been sitting here that we should share one of those volcano fudge cupcakes you have on the counter. The booster club won't miss one cupcake will they?"

"Oh, Mom. Okay, you win. If that's really what you were thinking then maybe you're the one in the family I'm most similar to. Neither of us ever wants anyone to feel bad. You don't, do you? And, I should have known about the cupcake, because we both like chocolate."

After a cupcake I headed home. Jenna walked out to my car with me. Before I reached for the door, she reached for me and surrounded me with a hug. It was a sweet hug, just like her voice. So natural and easy. It's a little embarrassing to admit this, but sometimes when Jenna hugs me I feel like a little girl. She's taller than I am, her body is soft and warm, and she hugs like a mother. As I pulled out of the driveway she stood waving and smiling. That image of her is one that stays in my mind. Sometimes it makes me smile, and other times when I recollect it I can feel all over again the tenderness of her love, and it brings tears to my eyes.

On that day as I drove home, I was thinking about Jenna, but after a bit my thoughts shifted to Jak. He puzzles me. I have seldom met anyone with less malice, although I would have to say I have seldom met anyone more impulsive either. He's a human magnet. There is so much about him that we all desire to be. People are drawn to Jak because they like what they become when they are around him. Light-hearted, playful, generous, never dull.

Jak's life became messy, but how could it possibly be as payback for bad intentions? He didn't have any. Jak always meant well. In that respect he and Jenna were alike. They wanted everyone to be happy. Although this similarity is still obvious to me, it definitely is not a similarity I would point out to Jenna now.

As I think back to the time when my young daughter joined her life to Jak's, I understand why she was drawn to him. On the cusp of becoming an adult, Jak's days were full of joy, and his curiosity made everything around him sparkle. If we had doubts about Jenna marrying Jak it was because it was too soon and they were too young, not because we thought Jak was a bad man. I understand better now, though, why Ross worried that Jak would eclipse Jenna.

Jak loved Jenna. I'm sure of it. He probably still loves her. He adored his children and was interested in other people too. Was Jak's flaw that he loved too much and couldn't keep it contained? I remember the time he handed me a Leonard Cohen CD and said, "Mom, I bought this for you.

Listen to the one about a crack in everything that lets the light in." You see, Jak wasn't shallow. He was thoughtful, and forgiving, and kind. All these are good qualities, and his list is long. Doesn't that count for something? Can this all be undone by the fact that fear didn't block his impulse to love? That worry didn't slow him down until his better instincts could take over? So what was it about Jak? How did he end up a broken man in a wheelchair? That puzzles me about Jak, and it worries me for the rest of us.

# Chapter 20

# SECRETS

Jenna and her children spent two weeks in a vacation house at the lake, and Laura, Robby and their children shared it with them for the last week. I was there too. From my comfortable spot in a beach chair under an umbrella I watched the children throwing Frisbees and burying each other in sand. I watched with envy as they played tirelessly in the water.

The cousins seemed happy together, and my daughters hit their stride as sisters. Jenna seemed grown up in Laura's company, and Laura seemed at ease when Jenna was around. Robby was the loyal guardian at the beachfront, and without complaint he made multiple trips per day to the store. I felt surrounded by happiness.

I called Tee the last afternoon I was there to ask if she would pick me up so I wouldn't have to be packed in with kids, dogs, and laundry for the ride home. I also suggested that if she came early she could swim and stay for dinner. She politely declined the dinner invitation and asked me exactly what time I wanted her to be there to pick me up.

On our ride home I mentioned to Tee that I'd noticed she wasn't spending much time anymore with my children. I wanted to assure her that if it had anything to do with Anthony, whom she'd been dating for a while, he was welcome too. "There's always a place at the table for the people we bring with us," I told her.

"I think it's time for me to step back from your family," she said.

"Is there something I'm missing here? Is anything wrong?"

Tee said she found it awkward to spend time with Jenna and the children since Jak and Jenna had split up. "It feels like choosing sides. I can't spend time with Jak, but I feel sorry for him. I'm sure he knows what gets said behind his back now that he's been thrown out." The accusation in Tee's voice caught my attention, because I wasn't aware there had been much negative talk about Jak in our family. We were very careful about what we said in front of his children and their cousins. We went to great lengths to be polite about Jak and Jenna's divorce, and the way we did that is by avoiding much mention of Jak altogether. But Tee had a heart for victims, and Jak had been through the wringer.

It's hard when two people who both are likeable decide to divorce. Those of us who enjoy them together would prefer they stay together. Maybe our family silence was guilt. Should we have seen Jak and Jenna's breakup coming? Had we chosen to ignore risks? Could the family have circled the wagons round and helped them more? Sometimes after the parties were over and everyone left there would be no one at the pool or on the patio, but there would be a light in the barn loft and one car left in the drive. Should I have played the parent and asked questions about who was lingering for the after-party?

Was my mistake a sin of omission? I tried to reconstruct the scene. As Jenna closed down the house for the night she would say to leave the backdoor unlocked because Jak was still outside "tending the embers." How odd was that? Was she asking for help? Should that have been a warning signal? In the context of the relaxed life at the farm, however, many unusual things didn't seem remarkable.

Tee listened to my reflections and then added her own. She knew more about the story than I did, and she wanted me to know that Jak was not the only one stepping-out. When Jak was gone with his soccer team, Jenna sometimes asked Tee to come and stay with the kids so she could go out to the bar with Luke, the drummer from Jak's band. Jenna made no effort to hide the evidence from Tee. Once as she walked out the door she called back over her shoulder that it might be very late because "what's good for the gander is good for the goose."

As Tee explained, I began to see why being caught in the middle of this could be uncomfortable. What I didn't understand after hearing this story is why Jenna was so furious when she came home and found Jak in the swimming pool with Sabrina. If what Tee was saying about Jenna was true, then Jenna was in no position to point a finger at Jak.

The story was more complicated than that. Apparently Jak and Jenna had known they were on thin ice. After counseling and at Jenna's insistence they made an agreement to stop the fooling around. That Jak cheated again after that agreement was the last straw for Jenna. It wasn't that Jak had made mistakes. It was that Jak wouldn't change; he didn't understand that he couldn't keep making those mistakes.

As Tee spoke I was wrestling with my own view of my daughter; I wasn't used to seeing her as a wife who would go out with other men. It was easier to frame their divorce by making Jak the villain and Jenna the victim. When marriages break, families ally with their own member. Even after fifteen years Jak did not have a claim on our loyalty that was equal to Jenna's. I wonder now how fair that is. Not that we should have been less loyal to Jenna, but shouldn't we have been more loyal to Jak?

We drove on, and after a bit Tee started up again. "There's something else. I'm sick of secrets. Not just everybody else's. My own. They feel like a reflex. A bug flits near your eye and you close it. It's something like that. But I'm done with that. I was one of Jak's girls. Not the only one, but that doesn't really make any difference." It was all I could do not to gasp audibly.

Tee sketched the scene. It was one I remembered too. Around the fire at those parties it looked like everyone was happy, like there were no cares in the world. Jak was sweet and easy. He was a man always looking for more attention and approval because what he had already was not enough. Jak was the star of the show. Jak had completely stolen Jenna's heart when they were kids because he seemed so confident, so full of ideas about what he wanted, and so happy in pursuit of it. He was still stealing hearts. Jak loved drama and adventure, especially when it involved women.

In describing Jak, Tee was not making excuses for herself; she was not trying to shift blame onto him. Instead she described them as two people drawn to each other mindlessly. It was a force. Not love. Not good sense. Nothing really except a pull that drew them together because they recognized in each other that they each were searching for something. She longed to be carefree, and so did he. It didn't seem to matter that the cares from which he wanted to be free and the cares that she longed to escape were entirely different.

Tee knew immediately that what she found made her more miserable than what she lacked. She walked around with butterflies in her stomach. Then Jak just happened to drop in at the coffee shop where Tee studied in the afternoon. She tried to tell him that their relationship was a betrayal of Jenna, and it couldn't happen again. That's what lovers do when they huddle for confession. They wallow in the intimacy of their secret guilt. In hushed tones Jak and Tee reviewed all the complications, and by the end of the conversation they knew their secret would repeat itself, because if it were truly over they would not have been comparing notes with each other. They would have avoided each other. That's the way it played out round after round until Tee decided she could not to go out to the farm anymore, and she started going to a different coffee shop.

I remember that time. Tee was distracted, rarely home for dinner, and often out until very late. It was a little after this time that she stopped accepting invitations to the farm and made excuses about having other things to do. She seemed uninterested in plans for parties, and she didn't ask about Jenna's kids who always asked about her. I thought she'd had tension with Jenna. Tee was reserved, and Jenna had soft boundaries. Maybe Tee was uncomfortable because Jenna asked too many questions or talked too much.

By the time we got home Tee had finished telling her story. She didn't hold back. She added into her judgments of herself that she should've known better because she remembers how bitter she was when her father left her mother for another woman. How that bitterness grew more intense after her mother's accident, and it was her father's family and not her father himself who took Tee in and cared for her. Tee felt her father had walked out of her life and forgotten about her long ago, and he had done that for another woman. She hated that other woman. And now Tee had become the other woman herself.

Anger toward her father made Tee think men can't be trusted. Her Aunt Doris and her Aunt Gloria were loyal people. Her father wasn't. But that assumption about female loyalty proved false. Tee watched her friend Cicely break men's hearts. Like a siren she could draw men in and convince them they'd finally found the one and only, and as soon as they believed it, she found their competition and doubled down on the power of a lover's triangle. Cicely reveled in the drama she could stir up when not one man but two men were in pursuit of her.

And now this. Tee was questioning everything. "How different is Jenna from Jak, and how different am I from either of them?" she asked. "Why should I believe I deserve a better life than they have as if I'm loyal and they aren't? I'm no different than my Dad, no different than Cicely. No different than Jenna or Jak. When I look around at married people I don't see any whose life I'd want. They're all messy. Well, actually Laura and Robby seem to have it figured out, but why would I think I'd ever find what they have?"

I felt guilty listening to Tee as if I could hear her story from the safe perch of virtue. After we got home I could not stop the thoughts that were racing through my mind. I thought about the six months when Ross was working in Geneva, and I was at home alone in our little house on Whitney Avenue with three small children. I was lonely. I was tired. I was angry with Ross. I'd convinced myself that he worked days and had leisure dinners in restaurants at night, and that he had nothing to worry about. Who knows who kept him company?

Meanwhile at home a day never passed without something going wrong. Will cut his lip and needed stitches. Laura whined and was uncooperative because she missed her daddy. Row had a nasty flu and for several days was throwing up at night when I needed to sleep. I felt put-upon, as if I was not being given my due while everyone was using me up.

I thought about the party when I first met Thomas at Charlie's house. Thomas was one of Charlie's AA friends. When the other men drew off into the corner to talk sports or politics, Thomas conversed with the women. He was at ease and had a good sense of humor. The women liked talking with him. Rita speculated that Thomas thought he was allowed to be friendly with women because he was a priest; at other times she guessed that he did this because he was gay. She approved of neither, and it was clear that she didn't like Thomas. I was drawn to Thomas because around him I felt attractive and interesting.

Soon after Ross left to go for his long stay in Geneva I happened to see Thomas on campus near the library. We stopped to chat. He was surprised that I was still working. I explained to him that work was my leisure. It was the few hours of my week in adult company with no noses to wipe, no shoes to tie, and no quarrels to break up.

I reached out to Thomas because I was lonely. I dropped in at his office on days that I worked. He didn't ask much of me, just listened and was kind. The feeling of ease with him had been there from the first time I met him, but it was different away from the parties at Charlie's house and with Ross an ocean away. Thomas was my comfort. He never interfered with my children, and he never interfered with my work, but I could tell he cared for me.

I knew from the beginning that I was taking comfort from a man who was as unavailable as Ross was. We both knew how unworkable our relationship was. I don't know how Thomas justified his choice to be with me, but I justified my choice with my anger at Ross for deserting me. Thomas and I were two lonely people clinging to each other because, each in our own way, something we needed was withheld from us.

When Ross returned it had to end, and Thomas and I had to accept the loss that was built into our arrangement from the very beginning. Ross came back from Geneva full of enthusiasm about being home. He wanted to buy a house, and he took on the project of finding just the right one in exactly the way Ross always did things. He studied neighborhoods for crimes and schools, he made himself an expert on local real estate markets, and he determined exactly what a good home budget would require. That was the first step. Once he had narrowed down what he wanted he began going through properties with an agent. He took inspectors with him for second visits to make sure that the homes were solid inside, outside, and between the walls. And finally came the day when he announced he'd found the perfect one. "This is one we can stay in permanently. It's good for a lifetime," he announced proudly. It was our house on Woodward.

I welcomed the move because it felt like a fresh start in a home with rooms that had no memories. Ross blossomed into a family man. He was delighted to be back again with his children; he had missed them so much. It was then that we decided to have another, and then another after that. That is when Jenna and Steven were born.

It was not easy to disconnect from someone by whom I'd felt cherished and return to someone by whom I'd been disappointed. Thomas and I intended to go our separate ways, and eventually we accomplished that, but not quite as neatly as my conscience would have dictated. Before Jenna's birth I worked the calendar to assure myself that it was Ross and I who had made this child together. Sometimes I wished it were so, and sometimes I wished it were not.

Mostly my uneasiness lay dormant, but then for the oddest reasons it would surface again, and I would reach for bits of evidence to fortify my conviction that in the end it all turned out right. I found comfort in the fact that like Ross, Jenna has long toes and narrow heels. It pleased me that the color of her eyes is exactly that of Ross's sister. And most of all I took comfort in my belief that Jenna was Ross's favorite child. Not his preferred one or even the one he loved more than the others, but a child who brought a special measure of joy into his life.

There was more to my tangled feelings about Thomas. He was my comforter. That is what Thomas had meant to me those days in hell when Laura was missing. I wove together a fantasy that he was someone I could call on for strength in the worst of times, and then I flattered myself that I was strong enough not to abuse his kindness by calling on it when it wasn't really necessary.

When Steven died my friends kept me from sinking beneath the waves, and they were more available than Thomas ever had been. Not a day passed without them checking in on me, and they didn't disappear again after the crisis passed. Still, even through that time and even though Thomas was not around, I clung to the fantasy of Thomas. I hung onto thoughts of Thomas like a child hangs onto a stuffed toy for security. Thomas was moved to a new assignment; our paths no longer crossed, but I kept him like a pin on my emotional map. Long after I knew that the trust I'd placed in Thomas wasn't real anymore, I still hung on to the secret of our time together. I don't think it was even Thomas anymore to which I clung. It was a fading fairy tale that allowed me to believe that once upon a time I had been a cherished woman.

A few days after my conversation with Tee in the car she asked me again if I was upset with her. Actually she didn't ask me, but she said, "Maggie I know you must be furious that I'm still taking advantage of your hospitality even after what I've done. I know it's time for me to go."

"You haven't done anything I've never done," I told her, and then went on to tell her about Thomas, but this time determined not to tell half stories. It was obvious that this part of my story fit alongside other parts of it that I had told her earlier. She knew about the intruder on Whitney Avenue, but I hadn't told her that Thomas was there. She knew about Laura's disappearance, but she didn't know that Thomas was the one to whom I'd turned for comfort during those wretched days. "I'm sorry, Tee," I said. "I've been dishonest with you, and I'm so ashamed."

"You don't owe it to anybody to tell everything about yourself. I get why you didn't tell me. Don't be so tough on yourself, Maggie." Tee bit her lip. The soft eyes that so many times had said to me that she understood, now turned away, and she focused on a shadow on the carpet, a spot where there was nothing. "Maggie, I didn't tell you everything about the Cat Man either. It was too hard to tell. He came to my apartment once, and when I opened the door to see who was there, he pushed through. I couldn't get the door closed. I tried, but he was bigger than me. He forced me, and I couldn't defend myself. I told you afterward how scared I was all the time, but I've never told anyone how mad I am about what happened. I hate being weak." Her chin quivered. "When I was with Jak I felt invincible. He knew how to fill the moment. He didn't think forward or back, and he was fearless. I wanted to be that way too, even though I'm not. But for the little while that I was with him, I got swept up in his courage, and it was relief. With him it was so easy to forget everything. The problem is, the moment he was gone again all the fear came back."

We were quiet, each tangled in our own thoughts. I understood what Tee was saying. I have never again felt protected the way I did when Thomas ran into danger to defend me and my children from an intruder. I can still see in my imagination how he leaped up the stairs without a moment's hesitation even though he had no idea if he would face a gun or an intruder twice his size. His devotion seemed so pure, so uncompromised. Sometimes I have also had a sour fantasy that if it had been Ross there with me, he might have suggested we hide in the furnace room and wait for the intruder to take what he wanted and leave. Later when Ross bought that gun to protect us, it didn't feel quite the same as being protected by a lover made fearless by passion. For that little while with Thomas I had felt safe, and I hadn't felt alone. Later when Thomas thanked me for the tenderness I showed when I bandaged his wounds, his words took root in my sense of value as a woman. I wanted to hold on to those memories. I didn't want that feeling of connection to fade, but it wasn't real.

Tee broke the reverie. "Maggie?"

"Yes?"

"I think there's something wrong with me. I hate it when people ask me questions, even questions about good stuff. Like when someone asks about Aunt Doris, I don't want to answer. When I was little I had good times with my Mom, but I don't tell anybody about that. It's like I don't want to admit it.

I get scared. Maybe I'm scared that if I admit that it matters to me, it could get taken away. There's something really messed up about that, isn't there?"

"It's complicated. That's for sure."

"Remember when you told me about visiting your mother in the hospital? Was that still hard . . . I mean, was it still hard to talk about it even though it was a long time ago?"

"I wanted you to know you're not alone, but I still felt fragile talking about it even after all the time that had passed." I told Tee about the summer before college when I boarded with a family that had small children. In the evening from my room I'd hear them talking and laughing, and I'd think, "they have a family and I don't. I'm not like everybody else." Then I'd come out of my room, and smile, acting as if nothing was wrong.

"When you got married and had children did that feeling go away?" Tee asked.

"In a house with seven people I still felt alone sometimes. I tried to hide my fear . . . or anger . . . or whatever it was. It was a mixture of feelings that told me I could never be sure something wouldn't break up my family and take it all away again."

"Did Mr. Barone understand that?"

"No. He had his own ghosts. There were feelings he was ashamed of too and couldn't admit. He hated dealing with feelings. Whenever he sensed I was upset he went as far away as he could."

"Now that your kids are grown do you worry less?"

"I don't worry about protecting them from danger or that I have to be there to make sure nothing bad happens to them. They are as fit for life as I am. Now I worry more about disappointing them. I still want them to believe I tried my best to be a good mother, but they're hard judges."

"C'mon Maggie. What right do they have to judge you? It's not like they're perfect. Don't you get angry with them too sometimes?"

"I do get angry with them, but it isn't about their mistakes or things they do. I understand well enough that each of them has to navigate through all kinds of obstacles that life throws up in their way."

"Why do you get angry with them? Don't you dare say it?"

"I get angry about how unfair they are toward me. They are confused about themselves. They are like everyone else. Memories collect all through childhood. A clutter of things, some of this and some of that gathered up and stored away. Then they reach the 'what is all of this about anyway' point.

I don't know why it has to be that parents are the funnel through which it all passes. Parents get stuck with the responsibility for everything real or imagined that makes life hard."

"Do you think your children do that?"

"Sometimes they do."

"Do you take it personally?"

"I try to tough it out, but sometimes the hurt's very deep. How is it that being tested on the rack of parenthood themselves these fully grown children of mine are so merciless? Does this happen to every parent? Is it only the ruthless progression of nature, the same push forward that requires the acorn to fall from the oak tree and roll down the hill some distance away before it can grow on its own? Or is it like the pollywogs who first must hazard becoming food for the fish before they can grow into the frogs that call out their commands over the pond on a summer's evening? Is it just brute nature playing itself out one generation after the other? I refuse to accept that."

How could I explain to a young woman who has never been a mother that, when it comes to parents, children are unforgiving? They accuse their parents of the same things for which they forgive themselves. "I'm the hook on which my children hang their blame," I told Tee. "That's just the way it is. There is nothing I can do about it. Life is messy, and we hand off the blame for that to our parents. I did it, and my children do it too, but the relentless succession of this doesn't make it fair."

"Why are you willing to take responsibility for all the things they blame you for?" It felt good that Tee was coming to my defense, but then I wondered if she really understood, if she meant me or my kids when she said, "It sounds like a lot of blaming that never stops."

I felt defensive and wanted to qualify what I'd said. "I can trust Will. He's made his own mistakes, and he's learned about forgiveness. I trust Jenna because it's not her nature to be unkind. Sometimes she doesn't keep things private, but I don't worry about her judgment of me."

"And the others? Why don't you trust them?"

"I love them, but I'm wary of them. Laura assumes she's responsible for everything, and Row is terrified of taking responsibility for anything. I have to be careful with them, because I never know when something will provoke them, and they'll turn on me. They're unpredictable. There. Now I've said it."

"Maggie?"

"Yeah?"

"As long as we're putting it all out there, am I like your kids?"

"Why would you ask that? Are you serious?"

"Of course I'm serious. C'mon Maggie. Remember Easter?"

"I do remember Easter. What happened? What was that about?"

"I figured you wouldn't forget. I was having a bad Easter."

"A *mad* Easter?"

"No...a *bad* one. Am I mumbling?"

"No, I have old ears. Okay. So it was a bad Easter. Why?"

Tee continued, "In church I was thinking about how my Mom's white family abandoned her when she married my Dad. When she really needed help, her family didn't help her and my Dad didn't help her. They left her for my Aunt Doris and Aunt Gloria to tend. That's messed up."

"What did that have to do with Easter?"

"Whatever. Let it go. The stuff I was thinking about in church doesn't have anything to do with you."

"So . . . what happened at lunch on Easter?" I asked.

Tee continued, "I was thinking I'm sitting here with this old white lady in this nice white-folks condo, and if my Aunt Doris hadn't died, I'd be having Easter lunch with her at her house. I'd walk out to the garden, and when I'd turn back toward the house I'd smell the fragrance of the right food coming from the kitchen. It felt bad . . . really bad."

"And that's when I said I wish I could have met her?"

"Yeah. That country club thing to say. I wouldn't have wanted you to come to my Aunt Doris's house for lunch on Easter. No way! It would have been awkward, and you would have been trying so hard it would've made it worse. My Aunt Doris wouldn't deserve that. But that's where I wanted to be, though. And that's when I felt really mad. I didn't feel like celebrating Easter, and I didn't feel like being with you."

"I'm sorry."

"See that's what I mean. You always have the right thing you're supposed to say. But I feel mad that it's been over two thousand years, and it's still so messed up. Life's still so unfair. Why hasn't it gotten straightened out?" Tee shifted nervously. "Like all this stuff with your kids. The secrets you still have to keep from them. Some of that's messed up too. Why don't you stand up tall and say it's enough, and you're not going to put up with it anymore. Instead you just accept it. Sweep it under the rug. Wouldn't it be better if it just got said out loud? Everything out in the open?"

I must have gulped or looked surprised because Tee raised her eyebrow. "I just meant that as an example. I'm not going to be the one to say it. Bad choice of an example, huh? But don't worry, Maggie, my lips are sealed. You know what my Aunt Doris used to say? You can count on me, I'll take it to my grave."

We ate lunch together, Tee and I. It was quiet. The kind of quiet that follows after a lot has been said. Each of us drifting off into our own thoughts. I felt unsettled, thinking about my children, wondering about Tee's anger. It must have been twenty minutes before either of us said anything. "You look like you're deep in thought," I said to Tee.

"I've been thinking about Aunt Doris." Tee told about a time she was out in the garden picking lavender when it was in full bloom, and she got stung by a bee. Before she knew it another bee came and stung her too. All together she got four stings before she ran into the house screaming for Aunt Doris. It seemed Aunt Doris was ready for her because she took a tweezers that she kept on the windowsill in the kitchen and pulled out the stingers. Then she reached into the cupboard and took down a small jar of honey, and put some on the bites. Honey was Aunt Doris's all purpose balm.

"You always keep that tweezers right there on the window sill?" Tee asked Aunt Doris.

"I do," she said. "It's my 'just in case.' I always keep a little honey on hand too 'just in case.' It's good for scrapes, and burns, and stings. You never know when you'll need it." Aunt Doris went on to tell Tee about lots of other "just in cases" that she had around the house. The little tub she kept under the sink drain, although nothing ever seemed to drip in it. The folded up plastic bonnet she kept in her purse in case it started to rain while she was out and about. And, of course, the extra house key she left with the neighbor.

"Why do you call them "just in cases?" Where did you learn that?" Tee asked Aunt Doris.

"I learned it from my Granny," Aunt Doris told her. "Once when I was a little girl I left my shoes right inside the door, and she told me to move them. I told her I'd left them there just in case I needed them, and my Granny said shoes in front of the door are not a 'just in case,' they're a bad excuse pretending to be a 'just in case' because after your Granny falls over them it'll be too late to move them."

As Tee listened to Aunt Doris telling those stories it dawned on her that Aunt Doris was keeping her busy thinking about all sorts of other things so that the bee stings wouldn't hurt. "That's what Aunt Doris was like. I don't remember even once that Aunt Doris ever said 'I love you' because Aunt Doris didn't say things like that. She just did it. She wasn't like other people who talk about love all the time and don't do it." Tee paused as if she needed to go far away in her thoughts to check something out for a moment. "I don't remember that I ever said 'I love you' to Aunt Doris either. But she must have known. She knew that her house was the only place in the whole world that I felt perfectly safe."

I didn't say anything. I was feeling skittish about saying anything at all about Aunt Doris whom I'd never met. The Aunt Doris territory in Tee's life was a part of it in which I was a misfit. So instead I looked at Tee and smiled just a little to let her know I was listening.

"I think you would have liked Aunt Doris," Tee said. "She probably would've gotten on okay with you too, at least after the two of you got past being awkward. Or maybe not. Who knows? Anyway that's beside the point now." Tee got up from her chair. "I'm going to go out for a while." The way she said it wasn't abrupt or unfriendly. I could tell that this big conversation needed time to settle. It was enough for now.

# PART III

To love that well that thou must leave ere long.
—William Shakespeare, *Sonnet 73*

Chapter 21

# LEAVING

The arrangement with Tee couldn't be permanent. She was young, and I was old. She needed to move on because she had other important things to do. Sooner or later I would also be moving on. I always thought it would be easier for both of us if she left before I did. She was spending more time with Anthony. I would see her texting and then a little later would hear the buzzer from the entrance on the street, and she would say, "Oh, that's Anthony. I'm going out. See you in the morning."

At first when Tee met Anthony she was giddy, talking about him in a way that invited me to say nice things about him. It was easy because he made a good impression. She'd say, "He's good-looking, don't you think?" And I'd say, "He certainly is," and Tee would smile. She told me that her friends thought Anthony was a catch because he'd make a good living once he finished school. "Do you think that's important?" she'd ask, and I'd say, "Well it certainly helps," and Tee would grin. She was proud that Anthony invited her to nice restaurants that required reservations.

Although Tee was happy with Anthony, she didn't look forward to graduation. She'd chosen nursing because she knew there would be jobs, and she could make a living, but she didn't enjoy it. Unlike my grandchildren who took seriously the advice of Dr. Seuss that if you have a brain and shoes you can do anything you choose. Tee never considered she could follow dreams. She was a survivor, and experience had taught her that her choices had to be practical.

As graduation drew closer Tee questioned me about how I'd decided to become a librarian. I went to college on a work-study program, and my work assignment was in the library where I tended the front desk and reshelved books. By graduation I thought I knew something about libraries, so I applied to programs in library science and went to the graduate school where I received the best financial aid. My career choice was practical. It had nothing to do with dreams.

I met Ross in graduate school. Student life was good for both of us, and when I accepted his marriage proposal, I insisted that I needed to continue in school until I finished my degree. I wanted the security of that diploma. Today that would seem an obvious thing to do, but at the time Ross and I married many of the wives dropped out of school and went to work to support their student husbands. The man's education was an investment in the financial future of the family; the woman's work was a stopgap measure until he graduated. I admitted to Tee that I became a librarian because some doors were half open when others were closed. When I had an opportunity I didn't waste it.

Tee listened attentively. "That's the way it goes, isn't it Maggie. You take what you can get." She was wistful. "Seriously, though, I wish I could go to graduate school to become a writer or teach literature in a college. But what's the likelihood I could ever do that? I have to be practical. I don't have a choice."

As Tee's relationship with Anthony got serious she began to complain more seriously about him. While at first she admired him for being a gentleman, she began to complain that he was uptight and formal. One evening on their way out he said to her, "You aren't wearing those shoes are you?" When she snapped back that she would be happy to wear other ones if she had them, Anthony self-assuredly advised her, "We'll have to do something about that."

"He's so arrogant," Tee complained. His comment was paternalistic, but he probably didn't intend it as an insult. Nonetheless, to Tee it was an affront that Anthony would think her shoes were his business. She criticized him for buying a cashmere v-neck sweater more expensive than he could afford. "It looks great on him, but that isn't the point," said Tee. "He's too concerned with appearances. That's a weakness in his character. What would he do if the only sweater he had to wear was pilled and had a hole in the elbow? There's a guy in my class who wears a sweater like that. It takes confidence to show up in a ratty sweater. I admire him for his bad sweater."

I didn't say anything. It didn't feel right to weigh in on her grievances with Anthony. But silently I did think how proud her Aunt Doris would be of her. She had raised a young woman with a mind of her own. Aunt Doris also would admire a man who could wear a ratty sweater if that's all he had, and especially if he did it with his head held high. Tee'd had a good teacher in the school of character.

From the start Anthony was frank with Tee that he was not looking for a woman to date; he was looking for a woman to marry. He was going to settle down and build his career. At some point he wanted to have children. Unless it was necessary for her to work, he preferred that his wife would set her career aside while the children were young. Anthony was a man who designed his life intentionally. Once he decided that Tee was a quality woman, he started planning her into that life.

When Tee spoke of Anthony I often found myself thinking of Ross. We made a trip to the Grand Canyon before we had children. It was the two of us, young and strong, hiking along the ribbons of trail that threaded down the mountains, and cooling ourselves in the Colorado River. Ross was practical. I admired how efficiently he could set up a tent and get the water we needed. I don't know how experienced he actually was, but he always acted like he knew what he was doing.

Sometimes, though, Ross's expertise about everything annoyed me, especially when it was something about which I knew more. We got into a quarrel about that on our trip. I complained that he felt it was his right to be the expert until proven wrong. There was a different standard for me. I had no right to be confident until I had proven myself right. Ross listened and didn't disagree with me, but he also didn't suggest that we switch to a single standard. He knew instinctively that when you are in a one-up position you shouldn't agree to change the rules. Ross and Anthony were alike in that respect. They were alpha gentlemen.

During winter break Tee went with Anthony to South Carolina to visit his family. She liked his family, but soon after they returned they had a huge fight. It started with Anthony's job search. He had decided to move back to South Carolina, and he went ahead to set up job interviews. While there for the interviews he intended to look for a place they could live. It would be something they could rent for a while until they settled in and found a place they could buy. "If you work for a few years before we have children," he proposed, "it will give us time to save money for a house."

Tee was furious with Anthony for "running ahead" of her, and he was critical of her for "throwing up roadblocks for no reason at all." He insulted her by suggesting she had never learned to cooperate with others because she was an only child who always got her way. It hurt Tee deeply, and she complained to me about it. She needed to vent, but in the end she went back to being practical. "I'm not going to find a better man than Anthony, do you think? I'll have to put up with some of this stuff."

Tee was not the only person thinking about the future. My children were thinking about what I might need after Tee moved on. Will suggested I move to California to live near him. Laura wanted to explore a retirement home. She liked the idea of staged levels of care so that with one move we could be sure that anything else I ever would need in the future was already built into the plan.

Over dinner one night Tee said "Maggie, I'm going to miss you a lot, and I'm a little worried about whether you'll be okay all alone."

"I'll miss you too, Tee. I'll take comfort from knowing that you're with Anthony. That you won't be alone. And I'll be fine. You don't have to worry about me."

"Maggie . . . will you *really* miss *me*?"

"Very much."

"Umm . . . are you satisfied with your life? I mean not just how it is right now, but are you satisfied with your whole life?"

"Yes. I wouldn't have wanted to miss it."

Tee looked at me puzzled, "Even if parts of it were miserable?"

"Yes. Definitely. Even then. Of course it wasn't perfect. There were terrible things. And there were wonderful things. And there was a lot in between. Overall, I'm so glad I've lived."

"When did you start feeling that way? How did you convince yourself of that?"

"I don't know *when* exactly. A bit at a time. It was gradual. I think that's a fair way to describe it. But I'm more sure of it now than I ever was."

I felt the knot in my throat, like the little girl standing in front of the TB unit looking through the glass at my sick mother. I was so separated from her as I stood there behind that wall of glass, I may as well have been on the other side of the world. But the sick feeling of death that was swallowing up my mother came through that cruel wall of glass, and it grabbed me by the throat. It was warning me that sooner or later it would be back for me and for anyone I loved, and I would never know for sure when that would happen. Tee was waiting because she knew I was thinking, but I didn't try to explain my thoughts about my mother and death to her. I was wondering if my resignation in accepting life for better or worse was too cruel a thing to share with a young person just starting out in life.

I wanted to explain to Tee that I didn't figure out all by myself that I could go forward, that I could live on despite misery. I remember standing next to my dear friend, Alethea, after Steven died. We were at the funeral home. Alethea looked at me with pain on her face and tears in her eyes. She knew my pain because she too had lost a child. I could feel we were at the same spot and in the same moment. Together we were holding on to the extremes: the one that could drive us to doubt and the far point of despair, and the other that could keep us from being swallowed up by it. My living children were precious, and Steven was precious too, but he was dead. I could see the stark truth in front of me, but at the same time I could feel comfort coming to me through the warmth of Alethea's arm next to mine.

I looked at Tee, and she looked back at me. I continued, "Standing with Alethea at Steven's visitation was the moment I first consciously realized that I could face how terribly, terribly fragile life is, and I could also hold on to the conviction that it is just as terribly precious. It is a gift. Alethea was believing it with me. I couldn't have survived the gravity of that all alone. I don't think the living energy passing between us, from her warm presence to my broken heart, started with us. It was bigger than us. It was coming from somewhere else and passing through us."

"Like what Aunt Doris called the spirit?" Tee asked.

"Something like that. I suspect it has many names and shows up in many forms, but for sure it's something like that."

"Do you think you know it for sure when you see it?"

"I think so." I knew I couldn't wrap any more words around a mystery that I didn't fully understand. I didn't try. Both Tee and I were silent. Neither of us left the table to bring dishes to the counter. Neither of us changed the topic or began talking about something easier. We both stayed put.

Over the course of the summer Tee was saying farewell to her friends. After going out with them she would talk about them as if she would never see them again. She didn't dream of them coming to South Carolina to visit her, and she didn't imagine coming back to visit them. Her vision of a new life seemed to be a different life altogether.

On a Friday night Tee went out with Cicely. I didn't ask where they were going and when she would come in. I'd never gotten into the habit of asking any more about her plans than she voluntarily told me. She was an adult.

A knock on the door jolted me out of my sleep. It took me a minute to sort out that it was not the buzzer on the street level, but a knock on my apartment door, and I couldn't imagine who it could be. I glanced at the clock beside my bed. Tee would have let herself in with the pass code and key. My children and friends wouldn't call or visit at this late hour.

I was disoriented, so I turned on the small lamp on my dresser and sat back down on the edge of my bed. While gathering my thoughts, I pulled on my robe and tied the belt into a careful knot. Although it's impossible to ignore someone knocking on the door in the middle of the night, for the life of me I didn't want to answer it. Then it occurred to me that whoever was at the door might think I wasn't answering because I'd died in my sleep, so I shuffled to the door, and when I looked through the peephole I saw the strange fish-eye image of the building superintendant. Only after I opened the door, did I see a man in a uniform standing next to him. Was this a nightmare? A nightmare I'd had before?

You can't call it déjà vu if it's actually happened before, can you? A door is a door, and a knock on the door in the night is just that. It doesn't matter that one was on a door on Woodward Street and the other on a door on the fourth floor of a condo complex. It felt the same. The shiver. The numb feeling. The ringing in my ears.

What follows is a blur. Something about Tee meeting Cicely at the bar. The police investigating who else was there and getting names off of credit cards. They gathered the grainy black and white videos off security cameras, of which there were many, because the bar was near the campus. In the end they found no evidence of crime.

Cameras showed that Tee left the bar at 11:30 and walked west. A man left the bar shortly after and walked in the same direction. About a block away from the bar one of the images caught Tee looking back over her shoulder. Then breaking into a run. And that is all that seemed to be happening, until she got to Broadway. There she ignored the light for the pedestrian crossing, looked back one more time, and darted into the street. Just then a pick-up truck swung around the corner. It hit her.

Of that night what remains clearest in my mind is the officer saying "I'm sorry Ma'am." I know he said more, but I can't remember the rest. I knew immediately that "I'm sorry" coming from the mouth of a police officer in the middle of the night meant someone was dead.

For my high school graduation I received a Kodak Brownie camera. When I picked up an envelop of pictures that I'd had developed at the drug store, I would quickly sort through them to see what I'd captured. Some clear shots, always some blurry ones, and only a few that seized a moment. I still have some of them. I remember when they were taken. Mostly the memory of a feeling is what is captured in the picture. That's the way it was at Tee's funeral.

Although her funeral is not long ago, it feels far away, and already my memories are like snapshots. Some sharp, some blurry. When I go through them now it is the feeling that I recollect. The hearse outside in front of the church in the no parking zone. The choir. Flowers in the front and a white pall over the casket. Jenna beside me. Anthony and next to him a dignified, well-dressed couple. A man and a woman with children. Young people around Tee's age. A middle-aged woman. The word that comes to mind to describe her is "grizzled." And the rest of my memories are not pictures but feelings. The bench was hard. My back hurt. My throat was tight.

The only living thing I remember clearly from Tee's funeral, the only thing that didn't feel like I was seeing it in black and white or down a long tunnel from a distance, was something the minister said. His voice had the same calm I'd felt coming from Alethea's arm that time in the funeral home when Steven died, "Receive her into the arms of your mercy, into the blessed rest of everlasting peace, and into the glorious company of the saints in light." Even now when I recall the words, I hear them as if spoken by him. I hear his voice, and something stirs in me.

It was hard to go home. My condo was still and hollow. Life had gone out of it. All day long felt like dusk. Anthony came to gather up Tee's things. He looked ashen and had gotten thinner. He didn't look me in the eye, and I didn't look him in the eye either. We were not familiar enough with each other to expose our misery to each other that way. The boxes disappeared out through the door of my apartment. The same door at which I had first met Tee, the day she came for coffee, and we talked of poetry that rhymes.

## Chapter 22

# IN THE DARK

In the days after Tee's funeral I went to the dark. I did not call my children. When they called me, and I felt I had to answer, I kept it brief. I ate a little, but not much. When my mouth felt dry I went to the kitchen to fill my water glass so I could keep it next to my chair on the little table that held my books and a box of tissues. I was in retreat.

Days muddled by. Sometimes I didn't bother to get out of bed. I only took the few steps from my bed to the kitchen where I nibbled like a desperate mouse on bread or crackers. When I felt I couldn't keep my eyes open, I toddled back to my bed. And some days I didn't bother to go to bed, but rather stayed in my chair all night, gazing out the window, watching nothing. Occasionally I saw a light flicker on or another flicker off in the apartment building across the park. I was reminded that there were people out there. Living people. But they seemed far away.

In the past, while sitting in the same chair I was collapsed into now, I had imagined scenes in the dark park across the way. I tried to imagine them again. Lovers there in the cool of the evening wrapped in each other's arms and whispering sweet words to each other, or a bird sitting on a nest offering the warmth of her body to pale blue eggs. Now my imagination refused to comfort me, and I pictured squirrels lying stunned on the ground where they fell when they took the leap between two branches, this time dropping to the earth even though they had always landed safely before. I imagined pale blue eggs torn from a nest and broken open by a prowling raccoon.

My children were aware that I was in pain. They called one after the other. As they had those times before when distress intruded in our family, they pulled together like a squad of protectors. In each call I could hear echoes of the calls and conversations they were having with each other.

At the end of October, Fed Ex made a delivery. It was sent from Anthony. Inside the shipping carton was another box with a note on it. It was on a note card that had been printed for professional use with a name in good script across the top. It said Dr. Anthony Tyrone Les Cheneaux, M.D. Then in a handwriting tidy and small it said, "This is delivered to you as requested." Anthony had taped neatly below his signature a second note that I immediately recognized as Tee's handwriting. Hers is the wide-open and round script of a young person, the kind that is never standard, which makes it easy to recognize. On a yellow sticky note she had written, "If anything happens to me please give this to Maggie Barnes." It was neither addressed to anyone nor was it signed. It had the character of a "to whom it may concern note" that one might leave on the windshield of a car parked in the wrong spot.

I felt as if I were opening Matryoshka nesting dolls, not knowing what I would find inside. I recalled long ago reading a story about a naughty child who opened the dolls left by Grandfather Frost at the New Year's celebration only to find a dead mouse inside the last one. I couldn't imagine what Tee would send me. I decided to look into the box only enough to have a first impression of its contents, and then I would know if I was ready to look further.

In the box was a set of spiral notebooks. Worn on the edges. Student notebooks. Each of the notebooks had a different color, and they were stacked one on top of the other, seven altogether. Across the top notebook was another sticky note in Tee's handwriting. "Maggie, these are my stories. You'll understand. Love, Tee."

The thought of reading Tee's notebooks was too much. I wasn't ready. I didn't feel strong enough. But I did take them out one at a time and hold them in my hands, remembering that they had passed through Tee's hands too. That these were her words. Her stories. I held one of the notebooks against my cheek. It was the pale blue one that had the round stain of a coffee cup on the cover.

I wondered if Anthony had opened the box and read the content of the notebooks. He could have. In fact, if he had never sent them to me at all, neither I nor anyone else would have known. I found comfort in this thought. It was proof to me that Anthony was a man with good intentions, and Tee had been right in her willingness to trust him.

Tucked in along the side of the box was an envelope. Tee had written my name on it, and Anthony had attached a note that said, "This was with Tanesha's things." The envelope was sealed, and I had to tear it to open it. Inside was a greeting card for Thanksgiving, one that had not been sent even though it had been addressed. In greeting card print that is big and friendly, it said:

LIFE IS GOOD<br>HAPPY THANKSGIVING

Below in Tee's writing the card said, "I will be thinking of you with your family and hope you have a great gathering. Give my love to everyone. I am grateful for you. Love, Tee"

I had never talked with Tee the way I had talked with Ross before he died, about whether it was possible to send a message back from beyond. When I talked with Ross we knew that he would be going soon, but there had been no reason to plan that way with Tee. Still here it was, a message from her about a day that wasn't here yet. Maybe the message was from Tee. Maybe Anthony, reliable Anthony, was the channel.

In my heart I knew that teasing it all apart into the how, where, and why of it would destroy it. I had to resist the temptation, and for the love of it, take her at her word. The notebooks I put on the bookshelf where I could see them. I did not read them through immediately, although a few times I did open them to see Tee's handwriting and to brush my hands across the words so that I could remember that it was her thoughts that resided there, her words left in trust to me. Sometimes I read a page or two to hear her voice. On one of those pages there was a poem. On another was a letter to Aunt Doris. Farther back in one notebook it appeared she had begun a story that was incomplete.

The card from Tee I put on the table next to my chair. I read and re-read it often. I would think then of the farmer's market; it would remind me of stew on Mondays and Tee singing in the choir tucked between Aunt Doris and Sister Madeleine on Sundays. Sometimes after reading it I would imagine hearing the key turn in the door, and what it would be like if just one more time Tee could return from school and make a salad for us for supper. If just one more time we could sit at the little table in the kitchen and talk about the day. But what I also thought about each time without fail was that Thanksgiving was coming, and I would be with my family. I would tell them that Tee sends her love.

With each successive day I was more aware that I needed to prepare for Thanksgiving. Unlike the years long in the past when I had to get out extra china or check to see that the tablecloth was ironed, this year I had other preparations to make. I needed to wake myself up and be ready for Thanksgiving. I had to prepare for gathering in what is precious. I wanted to do this for my family, and I wanted to do this in memory of Tee. I determined that I wouldn't hold back or wish I were somewhere else. With all my heart I wanted to be with those I love, as fully as I possibly could, gathering in the bliss of that circle, even if it were the last time, because who ever really knows.

# Chapter 23

# THANKSGIVING

Laura has lived up to the promise she made to Ross to create occasions for bringing the family together. Thanksgiving is the holiday on which she does this, and because she does it so faithfully everyone counts on it. And Jenna, ever the team player, offers her house as the place where we all gather. Even the older grandchildren have marked it on their calendars so that they do not let other invitations pre-empt the Barone family holiday. I like the way they say it, "We are having Aunt Laura's holiday party at Aunt Jenna's house."

I wanted Thanksgiving with them. And I wanted Thanksgiving for me one more time. I want to pick up every detail and savor every morsel. I want to let nothing go to waste. I went over to Jenna's house early. It was a crisp November day. The sky was clear. I tucked the card from Tee in my purse.

Beginning already at noon the first cars arrive. Laura has promised to arrive early to help Jenna get everything set up, although most of the preparation has already been done, and Jenna has already been up early to get the turkey in the oven. They still have the table to set, and there are extra things they have thought to add to the holiday meal at the last minute.

One of my delights each year has been to listen in as each successive wave of family makes its appearance. The predictable comments from one parent to the other's children, "My Goodness, look at you. Have you ever gotten tall" Or, "Honey, your hair is just gorgeous. Oh my goodness do I wish I could still grow it that color." The comments may be predictable, but they also are adoring. Full of the kind of love that aunts and uncles have to offer because they do not have to carry the responsibility of parents.

Cousins are dear too. The girls tend to squeal when they see each other. The boys lower their voices a few notes for the, "Hey, man, how ya doin" as they give side hugs with slaps on the back and fist bumps. And then they sort out into the groups that feel most comfortable from years of having played together on this holiday or stayed together when they were at each other's houses.

Because they are nice kids and their parents have taught them manners, they come to where I am sitting and give me my holiday greeting, even if it is only yesterday that they have seen me last. They have their own names for me. Quite a variety really, but it delights me to hear each one of them addressing me with a name by which they feel connected to me. Row's children call me Gramma Maggie because Zach and Meredith have another grandmother whom they call Grandma.

Laura's children, maybe because they are a little older, have been more experimental. Jeremy tried calling me Maggie once and was immediately set straight by his dad, who insisted that he find a more respectful way to address me. Now he calls me Grams. Kate calls me Grandma and leaves it at that. Sam calls me Gram. I ask him why he calls me that, and he tells me he likes short names. The shorter the better. He also gets annoyed if people call him Samuel, because they have no right to address him with the full form of his name without his express permission. It's a respect thing.

Jenna's four call me Grand Mother with the emphasis on the second word, and they put the little pause between the two words. It sounds oddly foreign out of context, but it's a leftover from the days when there were large bashes at the farm and I was introduced to new guests and strangers as "This is the Grand Mother." I think it was Jak's invention. Melanie and Philip started calling me Grand Mother at that time, and Jocelyn and Drew have simply followed suit.

By the appointed hour there is a little steam on the windows. The table is set, and the house is perfumed with turkey. Everyone has settled in, but not too much because they have come hungry, knowing what is in store for them. Then the word goes out that dinner will be served shortly and everyone gathers at the table.

Each year when we gather it is the same circle, but each year as we gather the event is a little different because so much can happen in a year.

Thanksgiving is our family mile-marker. At the beginning of the meal we pause to reflect. Sometimes the causes for celebration are obvious, but other times it requires effort to see the good in what has happened.

My children work hard at that. Doing their best to be discreet and ending with something that comes close to encouragement or at least a brave resolve. For example, the year Sam broke his arm that was mentioned along with a word of thanks that it seemed to be healing well. And now and then when finding the bright in the dark seems like too much of a stretch, they simply offer a memory to the circle and leave it to the others to figure in the thanks.

A few times now John, who comes from California with Will, has taken charge of the holiday ritual. We are all glad that he does this, because he has an easy sense of ceremony and always finds fresh ways to make it meaningful. His years of being the liturgist in his church has trained him well. Even though he has not been part of our family for as many years as the others, he remembers to weave into our event what now has become tradition. He knows the family stories.

This year John consulted the children and asked them to think of ways in which they could participate. He wants to groom the next generation to take part in what has meant so much to their parents and to me. In the center of the table John has put out a large tray. I recognize it as one from the old house on Woodward Street. It must be one of the items that went to Jenna when she lived on the farm. It is dinged and dented from many parties. Next to the tray are tea candles and in the center of the tray is the Memorial Candle that first was lit at Steven's funeral and later at Ross's. The Memorial Candle is already lit. John suggests that those who wish may light tea candles from it and indicate that for which they are thankful.

One by one the candles are added to the tray in the center of the table. And one by one new moments of honesty are added to our family story. Normally no one is shy to speak out at our table. Our family has a history of ready performers beginning in the years with Jak at the farm. In those days the children sang and danced. They loved to dress up in outlandish costumes. Today the ceremony is more staid, but the sense of its importance is evident nonetheless.

Jeremy goes first. In his husky voice he says, "I'm thankful that I have a family that doesn't kick kids out when they mess up." Under the edge of the table beneath the cloth Row gives me a reassuring squeeze of the hand.

And Laura looks away as Jeremy speaks. I try not to think about what his comment means or wonder how it reflects the work he has done with his counselor. John just says, "Thank you Jeremy," and watches him light the small candle from the flame of the larger one and put the little candle on the tray.

Not all of the comments are as sobering. Melanie is thankful that she now has a bedroom of her own instead of sharing with her little sister. But Melanie is a tender heart, and so immediately thinking of how this must sound to Jocelyn, she adds that she is thankful also for Jocelyn that she does not have to share a bedroom anymore with her big sister. And while Melanie lights her candle she hands one to Jocie for their shared expression of thanks. Again, John says, "Thank you Melanie, and thank you too, Jocelyn."

Meredith is thankful for all her family at Thanksgiving, and her slight blush and her eyes going around the table mean she is telling us that she likes getting together with all of us on this holiday. Sam is glad that vacation means no school. Kate is glad that her choir is going to Europe. And Zach, with a glance at Row, gives thanks for all the people who keep working very hard at jobs that are no fun and for which they do not get fair pay.

There are two who have not yet spoken. In a gracious way that gives them an escape John asks if there is anyone else who wants to add something. Drew stands up and says that he would like to light a candle but does not have anything to say. His hand trembles a little as he takes the small candle and lights it from the larger one. Drew is a child who notices detail. He knows the larger candle is a Memorial Candle for his grandfather.

And that leaves Philip who stands up, takes his candle, lights it slowly with a sincere sense of ceremony and says, "This isn't exactly a thanks, but I want to light the candle for my Dad because holidays are really hard for him and I miss him." As he reaches to the center of the table to put the candle on the tray it is obvious to all that his eyes are shiny and he is blinking back tears. John reaches an arm around Philip and says, "You're so right Philip. Holidays are not happy for everyone, and we want to remember Jak too. Thanks for reminding us."

During this ceremony the children have been watching each other as if they are witnessing sacred rites. With each candle someone has gained new stature in the eyes of the small tribe of cousins. The adults have been watching too with pride and tenderness. Also with a little apprehension that parents necessarily feel when their children perform. They hope it goes well.

None of the adults light a candle or voice their Thanksgiving, not because they are not thankful, but because they do not want to detract from the beauty of what their children have just offered the family.

With the Thanksgiving ceremony complete, John asks a blessing and we have dinner. During the meal itself with dishes being passed and conversations criss-crossing the table I feel a little distant. Not uncomfortable about anything going on there, just a feeling that I am watching as a spectator and don't have the energy to keep up.

Even in the conversations that catch my attention, I initially think that I have something to add, but by the time it is clear in my mind what I want to say, the conversation has moved on to something entirely different. And so mostly I am quiet. I am absorbing as much as I can of the bliss of being with my family, but also finding that sometimes my mind wanders off to other things. Other things present, but also other times past.

After dinner is over, the children bring me to the quiet end of the house for a rest, as families do with the old folks on holidays. Some of the children have gone off to play ping-pong and others are playing cards at the table that has now been cleared. Two of my granddaughters are off in a corner on the porch talking about things that they want no one to hear, either their brothers who would tease them or their parents who might use the information later to restrict them. From the distance I can hear the sounds of the kitchen like a soft percussion section in the background.

With a firm pillow and a soft quilt I drift off in the middle of this. My dreams these days seem less the work of sleep and more the floating back and forth from the present to other places. Soon I am in that other space. At a table in a glade. It is an image I've absorbed from stories or lovely scenes in movies.

It is a perfect afternoon gathering around a heavy wooden table under fruit trees and next to an old stone farmhouse with weathered doors and crooked steps. There are no flies bothering the food or tics on the dog that lies under the table. No one here is disturbed if one of the children bumps over a glass. The conversation has no harsh tones and the laughter no hard edges. In my dream it is a peaceful place. A place filled with soft light that does not cast shadows.

In this gathering I see Row standing near the head of the table and reading out of a worn leather-bound book with a satin ribbon for marking the page. I cannot make out the words he is reading, but I see the calm and grace with which he speaks. Andrea is seated near him, and it is not obvious that she is listening to what he has to say, but at least she is there. On the other side of the table I see Will, leaning back just a little with his arm around the back of the chair, where I see John, who has filled the vacuum of Will's losses and opened up the dead spaces of his heart.

Laura is there with Robby. She is eyeing the plates around the table, trying to decide whether to wait a little longer before gathering the plates and serving the dessert, in case anyone wants another helping of the main course. Jenna is at the table too, looking serene surrounded by her children. The light of Ross's memorial candle is the same color as her hair, except for the few streaks of gray that are visible in the afternoon sun.

At the end of the table is Jak in his wheelchair looking well fed and content. He is wearing a t-shirt with a smiley face, and tucked under his arm is his harmonica, ready in case he has an opportunity to use it. It is the same silver harmonica that he played around the fire at the farm, and sometimes when he stood at the right angle the light would dance on the metal as if it were part of the music. He is smiling. Next to him I see Thomas, untouched by age. His guitar is propped up behind him, and he is not wearing the collar.

Also at the table I see my mother and father. She must have gone to the beauty parlor in anticipation of Thanksgiving dinner, but she is not wearing her dress with a high collar or the silk scarf that she often wore around her neck. When I look more closely I cannot see the scar of her surgery. And next to her is my father. He sits calmly with his hands folded as if he is waiting for something, perhaps for the chance to go back to reading the faded rose-colored book with an embossed leather bookmark. For now he has placed it on the table.

At this table too I see Ross's brother Charlie in his suit, white shirt, and tie. As usual he has propped his cane over the back of his chair on the left side so he can reach it with his right hand. After all the years of advising his AA friends that they must not be afraid to ask for help, he still prefers to keep his cane handy rather than ask someone to reach it for him.

I am surprised to see Rita seated on the other side of Charlie in the circle. She still has a stern mouth. The one about which we used to say it had been installed with a level. But her eyes are not as hard anymore. I would say they twinkle, but that might be an exaggeration. Let it suffice to say she has softened.

There among them I see Steven. He is wearing his baseball cap at the table, though no one seems to mind. And he is unbroken. He is sitting across from Alethea and Mark. Just as I glance at Steven, I notice Alethea glancing at him too, and she nods her head just a little and has a knowing look. Next to Alethea is her husband Mark on whose shoulder is a dozing infant.

Near them too is Tee. On the one side is Anthony, neatly dressed in a cashmere v-neck. He has his dinner napkin on his lap and his fork and knife neatly balanced across the plate to indicate that he is finished with his meal. On the other side of Tee is Aunt Doris, who I recognize immediately although we have never met. Tee is tucked between them in that warm space so like the one that used to welcome her when she stood between Aunt Doris and Sister Maddi in the choir.

My grandchildren are at the table with some of their friends. And other dear friends are there including the women I always refer to as "my sisters." Some I have seen recently and others are already enjoying the company of the saints in light. The table seems large enough to welcome whoever comes to join it.

I do not see myself at the table, although I see my place there and next to mine a place for Ross. I am drifting just a little above the table. The way one does sometimes in dreams where at first the floating takes effort, but then it becomes easy to navigate with just a small stroke of the hand or a small push of the foot.

Beside me, I can feel Ross. He is not where I can see him directly because he is floating just a little behind me, escorting me as he always did, by gently cupping my elbow in his hand. I know if I turn to look at him, I will see his smile. A smile that was so natural to Ross that even when he was not smiling, he appeared ready to at any moment.

As my gaze moves slowly around the table, resting on those gathered there, one after the other, I see in each one a simple beauty. I feel for each one a simple love. It is not love waiting to be discovered or love still needing to be repaired. It is complete love. My heart is full, and I am grateful.

And that is where I rest until I hear Will's voice saying, "Well, what do you think, Mom, is it time to get you home?" He nods then to Laura who goes to get my coat, and as she walks across the room says, "Jeremy, bring the car around for Gramma, will you please. The keys are in my purse." And then to me she says, "Jenna is packing up some leftovers for you for tomorrow." And then, "Row, would you like to drive Mom home?"

# Chapter 24

# THE SILENCE

This morning Laura called first. I did not answer, but she left a message. With her steady voice she said, "Mom, I hope you're sleeping in a little. Let me know if there is anything you need. We're here for you."

It was only a little later that Row called. I could have answered his call. The phone was right beside me. But I could not bear to hear his voice this morning. This is the soft son who more than any of my other children would want to know how I am, really. He would sense if I am drifting off and would try to pull me back. Back to where he is. I know he doesn't want me to go. So I let the rings echo. I can hear them one after the other. Four of them. And then I hear Row's voice leaving a message. "Mom, I'm thinking of you. I'm going to walk down to St. Elizabeth's and light a candle and say a prayer for you. If you're still saying your daily prayers, say one for me. I love you so much, Mom. You know that, don't you?"

When the phone rang the third time I could see that it was Will. My first impulse was to let it ring, but I know that would not be fair because absence has such a heavy meaning for both him and me. So I answer. I can tell Will has been talking to Laura already since she called me. And I can tell also that he has been talking to Row.

Will starts out gently. His love stands right beside a lot of muscle. He has learned to be gentle, but he still is not timid. "Mom, we need to do something for you. We're going to figure this out. I'm going to keep the promise I made to Dad."

With a half breath I say, "I'm fine the way I am, Son. I don't need you to worry." It takes a lot of effort to speak. I want to say "Slow down, Will." But he goes right on.

"You know we love you, right? All us kids do." Even though I can hear the tenderness in his voice, resistance wells up in me. I want to be motionless and undisturbed. Here in my chair.

My voice comes out as a whimper. To Will it must sound like a weary complaint. "No…Will, nothing now. I have to stay here. With my memories."

There is a long silence. My eyes float around the room. To the view out of the window. I can feel my favorite wingback chair, shaped to me like an old shoe. This room where I know how shadows cross the ceiling when cars turn the corner in the evening and how the color of the ceiling looks like it is being painted as the sunlight creeps in early in the morning. I see my books in the bookcase and the box from Tee. It looks far away now. My coffee cup is miles away on the edge of the kitchen counter. The doorknob in the bedroom over which I hang my purse is barely visible. There is nothing to explain. I am tired. So tired. Finally all I can say is "Will, I need to rest. I love you, Son."

I am floating above it all again. As if everything else has disappeared and all that is left is a small space that is a familiar extension of me, and I am cradled in this small space, enveloped in light, and away from everything else.

From very far away Will's voice is saying, "Mom, are you there? Good night for now, okay? Just sleep tight. I'll call you later. Love you too, Mom."

There is another pause, and the phone is still. The way a phone is when rather than just being silent, the person on the other end is gone. And then the beat of her heart is still too. She is somewhere else now in a place where there are no shadows.

That is where they found her reclining in her favorite wingback chair. Her glasses still on. A worn leather bound book open in her lap and her right hand resting motionless on it between the pages where the ribbon is. The light on the little table beside her is still on even though sunshine is streaming in through the window. The card from Tee is on the table. Her left hand is draped over the arm of the chair where it had been reaching for the water glass and then went still instead. The glass lies broken on the floor. They all concluded, though, that despite the broken glass, in the end it was a peaceful death.

Made in the USA
Monee, IL
02 March 2020